Crossroad of Shadows

Books by Michael S. Turnlund:

The Raggedy Edge
Crossroad of Shadows (sequel to *The Raggedy Edge*)

Coming in 2012:
Eldo's Gambit, a science-fantasy adventure

Crossroad of Shadows

Sequel to *The Raggedy Edge*

Michael S. Turnlund

This is a work of fiction. All characters and events portrayed in this novel are fictitious or are used fictitiously.

Crossroad of Shadows

Copyright © 2011 by Michael S. Turnlund

All rights reserved, including the right to reproduce this book, or portions thereof, in any form, except for literary reviews.

ISBN 978-1466274433

Printed in the United States of America

For Shirley Bullock

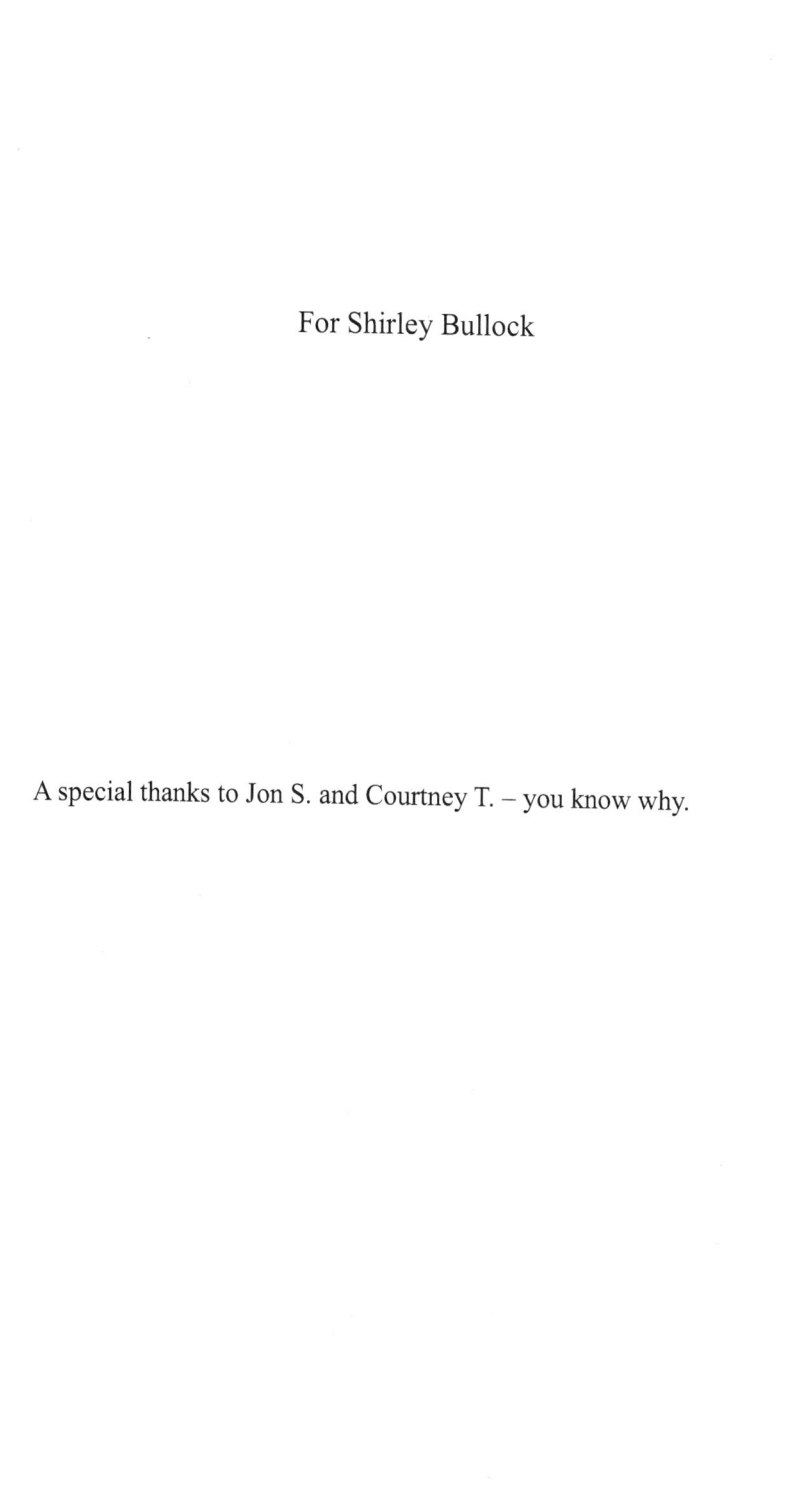

A special thanks to Jon S. and Courtney T. – you know why.

Crossroad of Shadows

Sequel to *The Raggedy Edge*

After being forced to flee to the mysterious Dome house to escape a horde of armed raiders, Jarad and Myla are again reunited with their friends in Junction. There they discover the fate of their nation and the cause of the nationwide electrical blackout, and help share in the community's grim struggle for survival against seemingly hopeless odds. But Myla has a secret: using a wind-up radio found by her son, Myla discovers a land with electricity and civilized life. Thus Myla, Jarad, their children, accompanied by the inscrutable Peter Rafferty, set out on a desperate cross-country trek to find a final refuge in a world gone mad.

Remember now thy Creator in the days of thy youth, while the evil days come not, nor the years draw nigh, when thou shalt say, I have no pleasure in them; While the sun, or the light, or the moon, or the stars, be not darkened, nor the clouds return after the rain: In the day when the keepers of the house shall tremble, and the strong men shall bow themselves, and the grinders cease because they are few, and those that look out of the windows be darkened.

Ecclesiastes 12:1-3

Prologue

One might suspect that the end was near when the local big-box retailer began selling survival foods with a thirty-five year shelf life. And it did not take a Wall Street insider to know that firearm and ammunition manufacturing was one of the few growth industries left in the American economy. Perhaps we really do create our own future.

How can you prepare for an apocalypse? Store food? Sure, but are you willing to defend that food with violence? Violence against those who only desire to feed their hungry children? A prepared person can look with contempt upon those who were less wise, but that does not alter the facts. You might have food, but there is someone out there who will one day come to take it from you – someone who is prepared to kill you for it.

The Mormon folk of Purcell discovered this shortly after that strange burglary of their local stake house. It seemed that nothing of value had been taken, not even what food stocks were left in the church pantry. The only thing that was found missing – and this much later – was a folder from a filing cabinet. Of course, everyone knows that Mormons store emergency rations in their homes, thus the wave of break-ins of Mormon properties by raiders. Alphabetically.

Solar power also proved to be a liability. What good are electric lights at night when they only serve to advertize a person's forward thinking? Such lights at night draw the desperate like moths to the flame. And many of these homes ended up that very way, in flames.

So what can people do? Arm themselves to the teeth so as to defend their property against those who did not wisely prepare, against those who did not read the writing on the wall, against those who did not pay heed to the tea leaves? Of course guns can be fearful things in the hands of the *I-told-you-so* self-righteous. But the hungry are relentless and even great empires have been humbled by the efforts of the determined few. No, there are not sufficient defenses to be had that will protect one man from another; from the one who is willing to face death to take what you would not give him. No – in the end individual people could not defend their homes and their emergency rations; they could only die trying.

***

Chapter 1

Myla again lifted the pistol with both hands, carefully cradling it as Jarad had instructed her, and then took aim. She lined up the markers on the top of the barrel and superimposed them over the target – a hand-drawn black oval with two less than concentric circles surrounding it. She pulled the trigger, trying to ignore the blast and master the recoil, before quickly bringing the gun sights back in line and firing again. She hated it.

"Squeeze the trigger," Jarad said again, this time impatiently. "You don't pull it, you squeeze it," he said, drawing out the vowel sound. "You're wasting rounds. Slow down and try again."

She tried to hand him the gun. "No, I'm done. I can load it and I can shoot it. That's all I need to know." She was angry, but Jarad was unsure if it was frustration caused by his coaching or by the fact that he was leaving. Either way he was in the center of it.

"Come on, a couple more tries. You need to at least hit the target," he insisted, refusing to take the firearm from her.

"No, I'm done. And if I have to shoot the bloody gun, I'll shoot the bloody gun. But I'm done!" He reluctantly took it from her and removed the chambered round, returning the pistol to its holster. He knew when to back down with Myla and this was one of those times.

He followed her into the Dome house, a huge cement structure that they had been living in for all of one week. He pulled shut the large metal door behind them and carefully locking it tight with a sliding bolt. They both silently climbed the staircase, neither speaking to the other. Then they headed to the bedroom and he began to remove his shirt. Myla was going to change his bandage and inspect his wound one last time. He sat down on the bed.

He suppressed a grunt as Myla tugged at the bandage which compressed his ribs. He patiently held his breath until the pain eased in his side, trying to keep his movements smooth as he slowly rotated his left arm and twisted the trunk of his body while his wife unwound the dressing from his chest.

"Feels surprisingly good," he lied to his wife. He glanced up at her from his sitting position. "It must be the good care I am getting." She was not fooled.

"You're lying to me," she scoffed. "It hurts, I can tell."

He shook his head no and continued to slowly flex his body, as if warming up for a bit of exercise. "No, I'm fine. I'm surprised at how good it feels," he lied again, this time not looking at his wife. "Maybe I wasn't hurt as bad as we both first thought."

She snorted at his words. "Jared, look at yourself in the mirror. The entire left side of your rib cage is one big bruise. Like hell you weren't hurt. You were shot, Jarad, remember?"

He stood up to put on his shirt, resisting his wife's effort to rewrap his chest. "I'm fine," he said, patiently. He turned to face her, cupping his hands upon her shoulders. "I can do this, Myla. I need to do this." He looked again into her eyes. She was listening, but she didn't want to hear what he was telling her. "*We* need to do this," he said softly.

She looked away, but did not try to leave his embrace. "I know," she grudgingly whispered. "I've known it for as long as we've been here." She slipped under his arms and carefully wrapped herself around him. He winced, but did not even so much as sigh. He gingerly placed his own arms around her, too. "I just worry,

Jarad. I just worry," she said.

He laughed softly, "the curse of women around the world." He let her go and he finished buttoning up his shirt. He needed to get a few things packed and then he would be set to go. Myla looked at the wrap in her hands and then tossed it on the bed. She then helped her husband gather up what he needed.

It had been a week, a long week, since their escape from the raiders at Blue River. This Dome in which they had found refuge was a glorious sanctuary. Its food stores would last them a year, even more if they were careful. And the electricity was a luxury; an indulgence that he had almost forgotten. Jarad found the unlimited hot water to be an addiction, so much so that he took a shower twice a day.

He also found himself frequently thinking about the previous tenants. They appeared to have had committed suicide rather than face the uncertainties of the future. At least that is what Jarad assumed to be the reason. Maybe they were lonely. It was evident by the number of pictures on the wall and tucked away on various shelves that they had children and grandchildren. Perhaps they had built this sanctuary for their family, but the "end of the world" that they had anticipated snuck up on them and before their family could join them. Thus, they had not found the peace they had sought. Their sanctuary was found wanting. Jarad felt a sort of kinship with them; he too knew what they had been feeling. Though he and his family were safe right now, he worried about his parents who lived on the coast in distant northern California. And his friends at Junction, he worried about them. Did they survive the raiders? Are they safe? Were they still waiting for him and Myla to come? He had to know.

The family all assembled in the downstairs garage for Jarad's departure. The garage was actually quite formidable: more like an oversized vault and built to resist forceful entry – like everything else in the Dome. All eyes were not centered on the huge Mercedes sedan collecting dust in the center of the large room, but on an old electric snowmobile pulling a long tracked trailer. In fact the snowmobile was one of the first all-electric models as evidenced by its use of batteries instead of capacitors. Though it was old, it was still up to the task.

Jarad stepped into his ski pants and then pulled on his boots. The sweater under his jacket should be enough, he thought to himself. The snowmobile was ready. His twin children, Cameron and Annie, were watching him. Jarad could feel their concern for him and he pulled them both close to himself.

"It's gonna be fine," he said to them with a cheerful tone to his voice. "I'll be back sooner than you know it." He gave each of them a kiss on the head and then picked up his bag, tossing it into the trailer. He was ready to go.

He gave Myla a final long hug and then kissed her tenderly on her lips. She wasn't crying, but he knew she would as soon as he was out of sight. "Lock this place up tight," he reminded all of them. "This place is a fortress when it's all battened down. And keep that gun handy." He smiled at her, though she saw right through it. She knew that he was as worried as she was. He held up this hand and made a peace sign. "Two days," he mouthed silently.

He sat himself on the black saddle of the snowmobile and double-checked the homemade scabbard that held his government-issue assault rifle. It was in easy reach and he sure did not want to lose it en route to Junction. He had almost twenty miles to go and hoped to get there before mid-afternoon. He was excited but also pensive. These past four months had given him a lifetime's worth of testing and he was tired of it. One part of him could easily have stayed in the Dome and forgotten the world, but his conscience – the dominant side, it seemed – would not allow it. He knew he had to go.

He gave his family a final smile and then headed off through the heavy metal door and across the snow, the cool breeze immediately causing his eyes to water up. He blinked hard to clear his vision. His tears surprised him. Perhaps it was not the wind causing them.

The day was actually warmer than he had anticipated but overcast, which suited Jarad just fine as he did not want to contend with sun glaring off of the snow. The machine moved easily over the surface, though the ride was rough. The snow was losing its crust and the machine sunk down into the softening surface. Not a lot, but enough to make the electric motors work a bit harder. But he was not going very quickly and the open road before him allowed him to consider what lay before him in Junction.

He wondered what he would discover there. He was almost manic with anticipation about how his friends had faired against the incursion of the raiders, the same ones that had shot him and forced him and his family to seek refuge in the Dome. Twinges of guilt again began to rise in his chest as he dwelt with this regrets for not being able to help defend the town. After all, he and Myla had resisted the move to Junction. They were happy in Blue River. They didn't want to leave and join everyone else that had moved there from Blue River, when the two communities merged to better share their resources and common defense. He now dreaded what he might discover was a consequence of his obstinacy.

It was a good seven miles from the Dome down to Blue River and then another ten miles after that to Junction. If he was in a hurry, he could probably cover the entire distance in a couple hours or so. But he wasn't. He was content to not speed, to get there safely, and not make undo demands on the machine. He also wanted to spend a little bit of time checking out Blue River and to see if his home had suffered any damage from the raiders.

He found himself following the very same tracks in the snow that this same machine had made the previous week, though going in the opposite direction. He didn't remember much from that escape, as he was lying incapacitated from the gunshot wound and only half conscious in the trailer that he was currently pulling behind himself. In that week's time he was able to get himself a bit healed, or at least in a state of health where he could maneuver around a bit. The wound itself was still tender and his ribs still ached, but he was in good enough shape to do what he had to do.

But what made that past week even more memorable, if not surreal, was the fact that Myla had discovered she was pregnant. "Pregnant," he said the words aloud to himself. "Pregnant!" He didn't know what to think. Having a child now, in this wilderness, without access to a hospital, and without any medical assistance was too much to ask. Myla laughed at that. "Women have been having babies forever without such things," she reminded him. But behind her bravado he could tell she was worried. After all, her first two children were twins born of caesarian section – it was considered risky to have subsequent children born the normal way. The uterus could burst, causing a quick death for both mother and child, though she did not share this last bit of information with her husband. Nonetheless, he was not pleased with the thought of his next child being brought into the current world, which he called a new stone age. He didn't want to even think about it any longer so he focused his attention on the landscape ahead of him. He still had to keep vigilance for the unexpected, such as people. People were dangerous.

The time passed quickly and he soon found himself almost to Blue River. As he moved eastward he descended in altitude and the road began to lose some of its snow covering, revealing the gravel road surface below it. Jarad maneuvered around the dark patches of rock and mud and tried to keep the machine on the white. He hoped that the snow covering on the rail bed would still be intact.

He paused by an open area that overlooked the ridge to his right. He had hoped to see Purcell, which lay in the lowlands to the south, but the late-morning mist interfered with the view. But it did not really matter; there was nothing to see even if he were able to glimpse his old community. He had lived another complete lifetime in the months since he had left it. That old life was now only a relic that belonged in the museum of his memories.

Moving on he quickly arrived at the bottom of the long slope that led from the Dome house and to the community of Blue River. He slowed down to a crawl. He wanted to scope out the town – really only a collection of a handful of old houses and cabins – before entering it with the snowmobile. He had learned to be cautious and never make assumptions that might involve your life or well-being. Thus he did not assume that Blue River was abandoned. He stopped near a stand of cedars and turned off the key, slipping it into his pocket. He wanted the machine to be there when he got back.

Jarad pulled the rifle from the scabbard and chambered a round. He pushed the safety off and held the gun ready, as if hunting. He paused for a long moment, just to listen to the ambient sounds before heading toward the community. Instinctively he shielded himself within the shadow of the long sweeping branches of the cedars. He doubted that there were any people taking refuge in Blue River. The church, which warehoused all of the resources that they had gathered for the community had burned to the ground a month previously, along with all of the precious food stocks. Still, he could not know for sure who might have come in the short time that he and his family were gone. Defensively he would assume that someone might be hanging out in one of the houses -- someone ahead who might be even more scared than himself; someone who also had a gun. The tension caused him to completely forget the limitations imposed by his wound.

He moved slowly toward the first collection of homes, spotting frequently to listen for sounds and to smell the air. All the houses looked the same from the outside: cold and abandoned. He peeked in a few windows, moving among them. None of them showed any evidence of recent occupation.

He did not have the time or the inclination to inspect every single house, though there were really not that many of them. He arrived at what was once the center of the community, marked now only by the burned out heap of the church. He scanned the open area before him. Nothing. That was good.

As he advanced toward the few houses that parallel the rail bed, he noticed that these all suffered from vandalism. Windows had been knocked out and doors left open. This included the last one he came to, his old home.

Upon entering Jarad was greeted with shards of broken glass and piles of human excrement on the front room floor. He just stared with disgust at the sight, before moving to examine the rest of the house. The raiders had rifled through everything, but found nothing of value. That was because there was nothing worth taking. Clothes had been dumped out of dressers and pulled from closets and strewn about, mostly it seemed for no other reason than to make a mess. Random windows were fractured and broken and the kids' games were thrown from the shelves, cards and playing pieces scattered everywhere. The same scene greeting him in the kitchen, as pots and pans now only served as obstacles on the floor. Seeing enough, he headed toward the bathroom.

Ignoring the mess in the small bathroom, he pulled out the bottom drawer of the vanity, lifting it off of its retainers and setting it gently to one side. Then reaching into the dark gap left behind, he felt around on the wooden base. He immediately found what he was searching for as his hand pulled out a single gold coin wrapped in a plastic sheath. There were nine more just like it. They were safe. He returned the coin and the drawer, but left the drawer as it was before and partly out, as if it had already been searched. Satisfied, he took a few more glances around the remains of his former home and then left, slamming the door shut behind him. He paused before his old Chevrolet station wagon that had reappeared from under its winter mantle of snow, but knew that it was no longer of value to him. It had no fuel and its capacitors were completely discharged. And what would he do with it otherwise? He headed back toward the snowmobile. He was done in Blue River.

*

The man remained hidden in the dark interior of the wood shed. He had just awoken from his night in the small dingy cabin and was set to build a fire when he heard the distinct sound of a door slamming shut. He froze in his steps. Then slowly he turned to face the source of the sound, peering from behind the wall and out of the doorless entry and across the clearing. He had been hanging out in this collection of houses because he found the pickings to be pretty good. Well, good enough for the time being; now that there was only himself. One was easier to feed than two.

He was curious, though, as to who this intruder might be. For a moment he became paranoid and wondered if this person was looking for him. Maybe a lawman had found Denny's body. "Damn, why did that fool have to push me?" he whispered to himself for what seemed to be the hundredth time. "He got what he deserved. And hell, there ain't no more cops."

The man was naturally cautious, some might say cowardly, so he waited quite a long time, watching and listening before leaving the protection of the old ramshackle shed. He moved slowly in the direction of the sound, using the shadows and the large trees as a screen. From behind a very large pine tree he first heard and then saw a man in the distance driving west to east on a snowmobile. The machine was very quiet, suggesting to the spying man that it was electric. The machine and the fellow driving it disappeared from sight and silence followed. Gaining courage, the hiding man quickly returned to the little cabin and retrieved his rifle and then slowly and stealthily moved toward the tracks made by the snowmobile.

He glanced at the path before him and traced it with his eyes to the east, suspecting that the man on the snowmobile was heading down to the rail bed. He was very familiar with the tracks, having just followed them up from Purcell a week previously. He had gotten himself recruited into joining a bunch of men from Purcell who were on their way to raid a place they called Junction. Well, they were supposed to have raided it anyhow, but the people there were waiting for them. It was trap! Too bad, they were all hoping to get something for their efforts – it had been a hell of a long hike.

He again looked at the tracks in the mud and snow, this time looking up toward the west. He wondered where the snowmobile had come from. He did not know what lay up in that direction, but he figured it would not hurt to find out. He had nothing better to do. But first he would make some breakfast. No need to go hiking without first filling the belly.

*

The sun had finally begun to burn off the morning's overcast sky, casting a warm caress across the room and against Myla's face. But she hardly noticed; she was already missing Jarad. She had been crying, but more out of frustration than missing her husband. Oh how she wished for a return to her old life. And her children; she worried endlessly about them. What sort of world were they to grow up in? What kind of future did they have? Maybe Jarad was right. Maybe they were living in a new kind of Stone Age. Life for her had become a roller-coaster and right now she felt at the bottom of a run and wondering where they were going next. She felt tired, mentally tired. No, exhausted was a better word. "God, I don't want to go back to Blue River," she prayed. "I don't want to go to Junction. I want to go back to Purcell, to my old job as an under-paid and under-appreciated nurse. And I want my house back. The old thing that is too dark, too cold, and too small. But it's mine. It's ours. Lord when will this end?"

She got up from the small divan in what they called the sun room and headed across the den toward the light that projected through the south-facing window. Her current bout of introspection had caused her to try and count her blessings: she was warm, she was fed, she was clean, but it wasn't enough. Strange, she thought. After she and her family had gotten to the Dome house she felt that their cares were over. Here, she knew, they could ride out whatever it was that had stormed into their world and which had strewn their lives about. But now Jarad wanted to head back to Junction. He wanted to know what had happened to their friends. She was afraid he would now want to move and live there.

"Oh Jarad....," she sighed. She stood by the picture window and looked over the valley to the south toward Purcell. She looked away as the bleakness she felt in her heart would not allow her to enjoy this moment within the caress of the warm rays pushing through the trees. Myla also wanted to know what had gone on in Junction; she, too, wanted to know what had happened to her friends, people that she had come to love like family. But she wasn't sure that she wanted to share in their struggles, their deprivations. Here she had all that she needed. Her children were safe, there was plenty of food, and there were no demands -- demands from others that she could never meet. After all, though she was a nurse they had expected her to be a doctor. She couldn't do it, but they wouldn't allow her to step off of that pedestal of expectations they had forced her upon. She knew Jarad felt the same, but still.....

But she was not of one mind and she was haunted by her own ambivalence. Was the Dome simply a gilded cage? What good is a sanctuary when it doesn't rescue you from your own thoughts, from your own misgivings and fears, from your own regrets? Perhaps these were the same feelings that the old man and woman who owned this home had wrestled with and ultimately lost to. Wasn't this shelter designed to be a refuge for their entire family, an ark to ride out some apocalyptic future? Where were their children, and their children's children? Were they trapped somewhere? Are they yet pining for the day when they will be reunited with a mother and father who had ceased to exist? They could not know that their parents had killed themselves; they had no way to know. That their dreams and hopes had become meaningless?

She turned from the window and leaned against it with her back, sighing heavily. No, Jarad was right she knew. They both needed to help their friends and to be reunited with them. She felt selfish for not wanting to leave the Dome. Perhaps they could bring the people, at least some of them, to here? But then what? They could not stay in the Dome indefinitely. And that was the gist of the problem Myla wrestled with. The Dome was not, nor never could be, an end in itself. It was simply a temporary sanctuary. They could not live here forever.

She went to check on her children. Annie was drawing in the family room. Even six months ago she and her brother might have been watching a movie, playing a computer game, or some other similar activity, but the televisor was down. Yes there was power to run the thing, but it still could not really function. This was because applications for the televisor, whether a game or a show, were all held on the web. People no longer kept libraries of movies or computer games in their homes, not even programs on their computers – everything was non-local. All functions for the televisor was via cloud computing and were held on off-locations servers, sometimes halfway around the world. Since the entire electrical system in the area, maybe the entire nation for all she knew was down there was no longer access to the web. Consequently, televisors were worthless.

Annie was a strong willed, independent spirit who was never shy about sharing an opinion, solicited or otherwise. She was pubescent and in love with Jimmy, a boy a couple years older than herself. She had only met Jimmy since her move to Blue River and her attendance at the makeshift community school held briefly in the church. Though both young, they had bonded together under the duress of the times. She frequently expressed her worries about Jimmy to her mother. She, too, wanted to travel back to Blue River or even Junction. The Dome was nice and she appreciated the many amenities it offered, but her thoughts were elsewhere.

Her brother, Cameron, was her alter ego. He was quite, unassuming, and always let his twin sister do the talking. His thoughts about the Dome or returning to Blue River or moving on to Junction were less clear. He had not voiced an opinion and no one had asked him. What did interest him was hunting and gadgets. He loved to be outdoors, rifle in hand. Otherwise, he would rather be tinkering with things. And that was exactly what he was doing as his mother entered his bedroom. She found him furiously rotating a small arm attached to some sort of electronic device.

"What's that?" Myla asked, with a mien of doubtful curiosity.

The boy looked up from his work and at his mother. "It's a radio," he replied matter-of-factly. "You charge the batteries by turning the crank." The little arm disappeared as Cameron swung it on its hinge and folded it back into itself. He then began to manipulate some buttons, causing static to emanate from a small speaker. Though it was faint, the static began to morph into voices and then music as he tried to home in on a specific frequency.

"How can that radio work? The grid is down," Myla asked her son. "Shouldn't all of the radio stations be down, too?"

"I don't know," he responded innocently. "All I know is that I can pick some stations after the sun goes down. The sun messes things up. It's better at night, though I had some stations really early this morning." He continued to stab at a little button again and again and swing the black box in space as if fishing for a radio wave, the long antenna dancing around him. "Listen," he said softly, excitement in his quiet voice.

Suddenly, in sharp tones a man's voice shot out of the little radio. Myla could not entirely understand what he was saying, but he spoke in the rapid narrative of a sportscaster. She kneeled near her son to better hear the faint voice that wavered in and out in strength.

"Sounds like a game of some kind," she said to him. "Hockey maybe, or basketball." They both listened for a few moments more before the voice was replaced by static.

"That is odd and doesn't make any sense. There shouldn't be any radio broadcasts. Where is it coming from?" she asked in a perplexed voice, speaking her thoughts more than asking a question.

Cameron shrugged his shoulders. "I don't know, but I think it's from someplace called Calvary."

"Calvary?" she asked. "I've never heard of a place called Calvary." She paused as she tried to sort out her thoughts. "Calvary is a place in Jerusalem, from a long time ago. You know, from the Bible. I can't think of any place today that goes by that name." Cameron shrugged his shoulders again and continued to play with the radio.

The little plastic box was now silent except for the occasional static or droning noise. Cameron was patient as he continued to push the different buttons, learning to operate the contraption through trial and error. Myla sat brooding, her mind trying to make sense of what her son had just told her.

"Calgary," she said with certainty. "I bet you meant Calgary."

Cameron cocked his head and looked at his mother. "Yah," he said in agreement. "Where's Calgary?"

"Calgary's in Alberta. Not far from here, across the border," she said.

"In Canada," he asked?

"Well, it was once part of Canada. Now it is its own place,

its own country. The Republic of Alberta. Calgary is one of their big cities," she told him. "You've probably been picking up some radio stations in Alberta."

"Then Alberta must be a nice place," he said

"Why's that?" his mother asked. "Why do you think Alberta is a nice place?"

"They got radio stations. That means that they got electricity. Their grid must not be down," he replied.

"You're right," she whispered. She got up from her knees and sat quietly next to her son as she pondered what he had just told her. They had radio stations, which meant that they still had electricity. But the grid was down where she lived. She assumed it was down in the entire country. Wait, she thought to herself. Of course! Alberta was a different country…and they had electricity. In her world they were clawing for survival and there they were playing hockey. Suddenly, her understanding of reality became clearer. Somewhere in this world life continued in a normal sort of way. And that somewhere was not that many miles away.

She gave her son a hug. "Thank you, Cameron!" she said effusively. "You just rocked my world."

Cameron looked up at his mother a third time. And again he shrugged. "You're welcome," he said.

***

Chapter 2

The run down to Junction was pretty straightforward as Jarad simply needed to follow the rail bed. He would have preferred to have taken the road, but timbers had fallen across the road over the course of the winter making it impassable – at least for vehicles.

The day held promise for being nice as the clouds thinned out and the late morning rays warmed his face. Still, Jarad carefully monitored the landscape around him, especially far ahead. He knew that the rail bed was a preferred route of travel, so he not only kept vigilance ahead; he routinely looked over his shoulder as well.

The snow was getting softer as he neared Junction and the marks caused by the passage of a large group of people a week earlier did much to disturb its integrity. It was weird for Jarad to be following in the tracks of the raiders. Spring was in the air, causing a further deterioration of the snow cover, causing the snowmobile to dig even deeper into the surface. He moved slowly along, though he would get there soon enough. He was only an hour or so out from Junction and he was both excited about seeing everyone and simultaneously dreading it.

Scouting out his path before him, Jarad noted what appeared to be an exposed patch of brightly colored rocks. Odd, he thought, though he knew it had to be something else. Moving closer toward the inscrutable mass it became discernable as clothing, the clothing of someone dead. He stopped the snowmobile and craned in his seat to take a look around. A cold shiver of vulnerability swept through him and he quickly scanned his surroundings. He then dismounted and approached the body. The corpse was laying face down. By the look of things Jarad estimated that the dead man had been there for at least a day, maybe two. The snow around the dead man was black with blood. It was apparent that he had been shot in the back.

Jarad again looked nervously around himself, searching the neighboring trees and banks of earth for movement or unusual sounds. He calmed himself by reasoning that that the killer was long gone. He noticed boot tracks in the snow and mud, barely distinct from and superimposed over those tracks left earlier by the raiders. What stood out was that these tracks moved in the opposite direction, toward Jarad and where he was now standing. He looked down again at the body and backtracked these fresher prints that had apparently been made by the dead man. About twenty yards further he encountered a spot of intermingled scuffs and prints, which to Jarad suggested a struggle between the man and another person. As he moved further down the rail bed there were two sets of prints, parallel and both heading into the tussle. It was as if two men were walking together before getting into a fight. The pair of tracks had come from the east, *after* the raiders had come through. It was all very confusing to him.

He returned to the body and searched the pockets of the jacket and pants for identification. There was none. He had no desire to turn the body over and see the dead man's face, so he let the body remain undisturbed. He returned to his sled. Then he swore. The body was in his way; there was no room to go around it. So he quickly returned to the corpse and grabbed the dead man's feet, dragging the dead man into the ditch and away from the shoulder of the rail bed. He then squatted down and rubbed his hands in a patch of snow, trying to remove the feeling of death from his skin.

Returning to the snowmobile he moved slowly pass the

body. Just as he was accelerating away a metallic reflection caught his eye. He knew somehow that he found the missing clue to the mystery. Lying in the snow about thirty yards from the dead man, Jarad stopped and retrieved a spent rifle casing. He also saw a set of very obvious boot tracks heading up toward the embankment and probably up to the road that sat further up the slope. Putting it all together, it appeared to Jarad that two men got in a scuffle. One man was knocked down and the other, the dead man, had walked on. His antagonist then shot him in the back and then scampered up the embankment to make a retreat. Jarad wondered where this other fellow had escaped to. He again glanced around himself. He was glad to get back on the snowmobile and head away from the scene.

He traveled a further thirty minutes or so when he began to hear the roar of rushing water as the rail bed swung next to Blue River, which gave the small town its name. The terrain began to become more level with the tracks as his path led him toward the flatter region east of the mountains. He knew that soon he would begin to see houses, cleared land, and farm pastures, especially as he neared the highway which met up with the tracks in Junction, hence its name.

Putting the unease of the dead man behind him, Jarad felt a growing sense of anxiety as he traveled toward the town. What would he find? What damage had the raiders visited upon the community? Were their deaths? Whose? Did the raiders steal all of their food? How would they receive him? Was he a deserter? Would he be given blame? He was making himself sick with worry. He even began to question the wisdom of continuing on. Perhaps ignorance was bliss.

The first structure he saw caused him to stop and stare. Jarad remembered his first time coming down the tracks going to Junction.

He was off to "rescue" his wife, not realizing that she did not need rescuing because she had gone willingly with a couple fellows from Junction in order to deliver a baby. That was his introduction to the folks living in that community. On his way down to Junction with his friend Genis, they had encountered a home constructed from two camp trailers cobbled together. He could still picture the little kids playing outside on that cold winter day, staring and then finally waving at him. Now, before him lay a burned out ruin of that pathetic structure. Had the raiders torched it? What had become of the children?

He pondered this as he continued eastward. He also wondered about the raiders. Perhaps he was being too assertive in his condemnation of the raiders. After all, they were former neighbors his hometown, Purcell. Nonetheless they had acted aggressively toward him and if he had not shot a couple of them in self defense during his escape to the Dome, he might himself be dead.

Soon more and more houses began to appear, the majority of them the second vacation homes of the wealthy. These wood and rock mansions dotted the ridge line which tumbled toward the river to the south and east. All of the houses appeared unoccupied and Jarad knew that most of them had already been stripped of any supplies they harbored by his friends at Junction. That was the only way for people to survive now: breaking into unoccupied homes and taking what was useful, whether food, clothing, firewood, or guns. Whatever could be carried and was of practical value was taken.

He knew that less than a half mile ahead was the home of Stanley Merton. At first it seemed that Stan had preternaturally anticipated the arrival of himself and Genis. He even had hosted them for their first night in Junction. It was only later that he learned that Myla had told her "captors" that her husband would be hot on their heels, so Stan was asked to head them off and put them up for the night. So Stan had stood vigil along the tracks until, just as expected, Jarad and Genis came along with the setting sun. Surprisingly Jarad and Genis agreed to follow Stan home and allow him to be their host. They had anticipated the worst when coming to Junction; Stan's kindness had mitigated that.

    Suddenly the stillness around him was rent by the explosion of a high-powered rifle. Jarad immediately tumbled off of the snowmobile and onto the sodden snow filling the ditch along the shoulder of the rail bed, embracing his rifle tightly against himself. Rolling to a stop, he sprang to his knees, bringing his rifle forward and up to his shoulder. He would not hesitate to shoot.

    A voice called out. "Who are you?" There was a pause and Jarad could sense movement on the rise near him. He tried to steady himself as the pain from his bruised ribs emanated up from his side, making it difficult to hold the rifle up. "Who are you?" the voice repeated. Jarad did not respond, but sat on his knees, breathing hard. He did not recognize the voice. He glanced around himself, trying to find a way to escape from his predicament. But the ambush point was well chosen. With the steep banks climbing up from the ditches on both sides, and the funnel-like trough behind him, he was trapped. He was unsure what to do.

    Surreally another man started to laugh. "Jarad, is that you?" he called out. Jarad recognized the voice. It was Benson, the fellow that collected solar cells for the community and who had rigged up the charging station for the snowmobiles.

    "Benson?" Jarad shouted, without standing up. Two smiling faces appeared in the sky above him. Jarad sighed and stood up, relief filling his mind. He reached up to the proffered hand and he was quickly tugged up and out of the ditch and back onto the rail bed. Another hand patted the caked snow from his back and sides. Both of the men were laughing.

"Jarad, it is good to see you. I thought it might have been you when I saw the sled. That is one of my toys – I'd know it anywhere. And sorry about the gun shot." He grinned apologetically. "We get bored, you know, watching the tracks and all. Got distracted by the card game…" Benson looked at him closely. "You've shaved. Wow. You must be living the life up there in Blue River. Don't you guys miss us down here?" he asked a hint of seriousness in his kind eyes.

Jarad looked at the two men. They were both holding deer rifles. Jarad did not know the other fellow. He looked at him warily as he responded to Benson. "Of course, I missed you people. That's why I'm here." He gave Benson a pat on the shoulder.

Benson returned the gesture and then pointed his thumb at the other man. "Jarad, this is Dev. He's a lost lamb from Montana. He joined up with us about three weeks ago."

Jarad shook hands with the younger man. He seemed to be a nice enough fellow, but something about his face triggered a memory in Jarad, as if he should know him. The man answered Jarad's unasked question. "I know you. You're a cop! Purcell." He explained that Jarad had arrested him once for a bar fight. The fellow shook his head. "That was a thousand years ago, it seems, and I was a lot dumber. Don't worry; I won't try to punch you again. I learned my lesson." He chuckled.

Jarad tried to laugh with him, but he was still energized with adrenaline. He was trying to settle himself.

Benson turned to check out the snowmobile. He checked the charge left in the batteries. "Maybe I'll ride into Junction with you and let Dev keep watch by himself." He looked at his partner. Then he pulled a radio from his belt and spoke into it. "This is Benson, anybody there?" he asked into the microphone of the small walkie-talkie. A voice responded though Jarad could not hear what was said. Benson responded. "Disregard that gun shot. No worries here. But Jarad is back, with one of the sleds…" he continued speaking as he turned away from the others and toward the sun, warming his face. He signed off and then turned back to Jarad.

"Let's go," he said. "We can both ride the sled. There's enough juice."

Both men mounted the snowmobile, though Benson took command of the controls. With a nod from Benson toward Dev they were off. Jarad was glad to not be driving. He wanted to be able to take a look around.

They had only traveled on for a moment before Jarad tapped on Benson's shoulder, indicating that he wanted him to stop. He pointed over at Stan Merton's house, appalled at what he saw. "What the hell happened there?" he asked with surprise in his voice, his hand pointing out the burned out remains of a home.

Benson shook his head in disgust and lament. He swore loudly as he declaimed the raiders. "They torched it! Why? I have no idea. We found Stan's body later, but we don't know if he was shot first or if he died in the fire. Either way, he's dead and they killed him. But good came of it. Because of the fires, this one and the one down the road, we knew that they were coming. We were ready for them! We'll talk later."

He again turned forward and they resumed their rush down the rail bed. Benson was going far faster than Jarad would have dared, but that suited Jarad just fine. His trepidation had eased and now he was excited.

Within minutes they were in Junction. Benson slowed and then guided the snowmobile over a crossing which brought the rails level with the road. He then jetted down a side street and then across a yard, finally arriving at the large shopping building where Jarad had originally gotten the machine some weeks past. Stepping off of the machine he took a look around. No welcoming committee, but then, they had just learned about his return. He suspected someone would seek him out soon.

A familiar voice was the first to greet him, followed by the form of a tall man with his hand in the air, waving a greeting. Jarad knew it was Otty though he couldn't see his face as he approached with his back to the bright early-afternoon sun. When he finally got closer the two men shook hands and then embraced. For Jarad it felt like being home.

Before speaking Jarad took a look at Otty. Though it had only been five or six weeks since he had seen him last, he already seemed older. He was obviously thinner and his beard had become quite a bit longer. Indeed, Jarad felt odd as he realized that all of the men he had seen were sporting great lengths of facial hair. He subconsciously rubbed his own chin, barely covered with a half-day's worth of stubble. Jarad also noted that Otty was also quite a bit grubbier than himself. Jarad had forgotten how difficult it had been to keep clean since his stay at the Dome. He felt conspicuous in his cleanliness.

"It's been a while, but I am glad that you are finally back," he said kindly. Otty's warm eyes glowed with satisfaction. Jarad could see that he had been obviously concerned about him. "Come, let's go sit and visit. We both got a lot of catching up to do."

They strolled in the growing warmth of what appeared to be a spectacular late-winter day. The brightness only added to the pleasantness of the moment. Otty pointed out a few things as they walked toward his quarters, a small and dilapidated single-wide mobile home. But nothing had really changed. The only difference was that Junction was now home to more people, as everyone had moved here from Blue River. Everyone, that is, except Jarad and his family. That would soon change.

Upon entering Jarad was greeted by Otty's wife, Ellie. She gave him a hug and then a second hug. She was so excited to see him. She asked about Myla and the kids, expressing sincere concern about their absence. Jarad reassured her that they were doing well. In fact, the irony was in that in some ways they were living better than any one of them had ever lived in their lifetimes.

"That nice, uh?" Otty asked, mildly incredulous.

"Yes, that nice," Jarad responded. Before he could explain about the Dome, Ellie asked him if he would like some tea.

"What, no coffee?" he laughed. Otty was famous for his consumption of the beverage.

"No," she replied, "I'm sorry to say that we have run out of coffee." Jarad could sense that the lack of coffee was not really humorous to Ellie. Perhaps it was indicative of the general want developing in the community. A moment of tension developed briefly in the room. Jarad was glad to break it.

He went on to explain how they ended up at the Dome, lifting his arm to indicate where he had been shot. Ellie had joined them at the small kitchen table and both of them were listening intently, gasping and sighing as the storyline ebbed and flowed. He described the Dome as a residence, how much food it had stored away, and the benefits of having electricity. "I have decided that the greatest thing in the world is hot water," he told them. He shook his head for emphasis.

Both Ellie and Otty asked a few more questions about the Dome, its previous occupants, and how Myla and the kids were doing. When the conversation lagged, Jarad jumped in with his long-anticipated apology. He needed to get it off of his chest.

"I'm sorry I wasn't here when the raiders came. And I'm sorry that I couldn't warn you. I never meant to abandon you folks and run away to the Dome. This has been eating at me."

Otty was looking at him as he spoke, or rather past him. He appeared to be thinking other thoughts as he listened to Jarad. But he heard Jarad clearly. "No one thought that you had run away. We were afraid that the raiders might have hurt you folks, as they came from that direction. But it all worked out okay. They were a rather inept group." Otty chuckled without smiling.

"How so," Jarad asked, now curious.

"I should probably let Peter tell you, as he was the hero that day, but I'll let him fill in the details."

Otty described the encounter with the raiders. For some reason they had set fire to two homes well before they got near Junction. The smoke alerted everyone in town that something was not right. James jumped on a snowmobile to find out what was going on and returned almost immediately. He reported a large group of armed men coming down the tracks. The warning from James allowed the people in Junction to take up defensive positions.

"But Peter had also been thinking –just like you – of this possibility that the raiders might sneak in the back door along the tracks during a new moon. He must have been reading your mind, Jarad. So he knew what to do."

Peter had formed the defensive line well north of the road and rail bed, allowing the raiders to get near to the community. No one fired a shot to give away their position; everything looked peaceful and open. Peter had also sent a handful of men to the west to outflank the raiders. He told them – on his signal – to make a lot of noise and to make it appear that there were more of them than there were. "James, Benson, and a bunch more were hootin' and a'hollerin' like a bunch of cowboys and Indians. It would have been hilarious if it weren't so darn serious," Otty explained.

"The raiders then began to fall back toward the highway which led to the bridge back to Purcell," he continued. "When Peter gave the word, we opened up from our line, a big noisy volley that went over their heads. I didn't want to shoot them, you know…." He looked at Jarad, his eyes twinkling as he relived the moment. "The raiders became panic stricken and began shooting every which way. They even shot two of their own men. Dead!" he said with emphasis. "Our only casualty, if you can call it that, was some bullet shards that hit Jimmy in the back of the head after a bullet splattered on the wall behind him. A lot of blood, but no lasting harm. Emma tried to dig out the pieces, but I'm afraid she did more harm than good. We miss Myla." Again, he looked at Jarad. He knew Jarad's feelings about the community's perception of Myla.

"Don't forget Stanley," Ellie reminded him.

"Oh, yes, forgive me," he said sadly. "Stan is dead. But we don't know if he was killed before they torched his home, or if he died as a result. But he was in such poor health. I can imagine that he had a heart attack…" He ended his story with a toss of his palms into the air. He was obviously done talking about the whole affair.

Jarad was relieved after hearing about the raiders. For him it was almost anti-climatic. So much worry and regret on his part, but it appeared for no reason. He sighed heavily in relief, not even aware that he was doing so.

"You tired?" Ellie asked him. "Have you had breakfast?"

"I'm fine," he said with a small smile. "I think that I'd like to go take a look around, if I could."

Otty waved toward the door. "Make yourself at home. You have the run of the place…"

All three got up and Jarad and Otty stepped outside. The rapidly melting snow glared harshly as it reflected the bright sun. Even the air began to feel warmer and Jarad's spirit rose within him. He had not taken the time to notice the passing of the season, and the prospects of spring, let alone summer, delighted him. Though there was still rain and cool weather ahead he knew that ultimately summer would be here. That will be nice, he told himself.

"I'll leave you to your own devices, Jarad. Just make yourself at home. Not everyone knows you're here, but they'll find out soon enough. Just keep your head down if you go out to the bridge. You'll find out why when you get there. I am sure you'll find Peter there too." He paused, "But you better take your rifle with you."

Jarad and Otty shook hands again and Otty took off toward the old realtor's office that they used as the community building. It was empty. So, he left to head out directly toward the bridge. Otty had piqued his curiosity. But he remembered his gun and hustled back to the garage and grabbed his rifle from its scabbard.

Returning outside, he cut through a couple yards and headed back across the tracks and down the old highway. In a small lot of land near the highway he noticed a series of earthen mounds arranged in an orderly fashion. Gravesites. These had become increasingly common in this new life he was living; indeed, he himself had dug his share of them the past few months.

He diverted his path to the makeshift cemetery. He noted the names painted on the wooden markers. He knew most of them, and a couple others he was less sure about. What he saw saddened him. Howard had died. That might explain Otty's demure state. Howard was his best friend. The other of note was the one tagged Emil Silverman. This one caused Jarad to think of the gold coins that he left hidden in his old cabin. Emil had entrusted them to Jarad to give to his son, if that day were ever to come. It was all that Emil and Sarah had left in the world. Now they were both dead. Jarad would not fail them.

The last two graves were fairly recent. Jarad realized that of the two grave markers, he knew one of the names: James Cook. He searched his mind trying to remember how he knew that name. Then it came to him. James Cook was that big happy fellow who always worked the graveyard shift at the Conoco minimart. James always got him his coffee. So James was a raider. Such were the times, he mused.

He turned away from the graves and headed back toward the bridge. He regained the road and passed over the tracks, following a well worn path that headed toward his destination. As he moved along he heard in the distance the report of a small caliber gun. This caused him to pause for a moment, his rifle instinctively being brought to the ready. The shots continued to ring out regularly though intermittently as he got closer to the bridge, which was still a good quarter mile distant. He supposed that he would discover soon enough what was going on.

As he walked along Jarad tried to make sense of what Otty had shared with him, trying to read between the lines, so to speak. He was sure that food stocks were low, but that was to be expected. He was confident that the folks at Junction had themselves raided every home in practical distance. But that was probably the limit of their supply line, as there were few homes and no settlements much past Junction. Except for the Luddite Colony, but they were pretty poor folks. Purcell was itself about just as far off the beaten path as anyone wanted to go, and Junction was even further yet. Only National Forest land lay beyond.

Howard was dead, which meant no more communication with that contact in Central America via the shortwave. Jarad wondered why Howard hadn't tried other channels, or stations, or whatever it was they were called. Why only that Spanish-speaking contact? Although Howard knew Spanish somewhat, he would be the first to admit he was not fluent. Otty knew a little, too, but even less than Howard and not enough to be meaningful.

And Emil was gone. Jarad didn't know what he would do with that bullion if he could not locate Emil's son. He decided to ask Otty; maybe he had some information about Emil's family. Not that it mattered much right now.

The shooting continued, which Jarad found exceedingly strange. It increased in loudness as he neared the bridge, the rifle shots echoing among the hills. The river was audible now, too, though the water was not very busy underneath the bridge. Though the canyon was deep where the bridge spanned the gorge, the river would not really get busy until late spring and the snow in the mountains began to melt. Then it would rage.

He had not traveled more than another hundred yards before he came upon a couple men with binoculars, standing among some tall firs to the side of the road. They were Genis and Peter. They began to bombard him with questions and greetings.

"Look who the cat dragged in! We heard you were in town. How the hell are you, Jarad! Hey, keep your head down! Here, come on up before they peg you in the head. I don't want you dead now that you've finally gotten here alive." It was Peter, who reached down and pulled Jarad up to them. Jarad had first met Peter when he was one of Myla's patients at the county hospital. In fact, one of Myla's last patients before events took a turn for the worst and they had to flee Purcell for the cabin in Blue River. Peter had settled in Junction about a year ago, after retiring from Homeland Security. Actually Jarad had met him in that capacity many years earlier when Peter was making a tour of the northern border between Canada and the United States. The breakup of Canada into Quebec and Alberta had sent reverberations through Congress with the fear that terrorist groups would use the tumult to sneak into the country. But that was a long time ago.

Jarad shook his hand, trying not to wince under Peter's strong grip. Jarad observed that the man was still physically fit, despite his age. "It is good to be back, let me tell you," he said to them. Genis, too, shook his hand, but far more gently than had Peter. "How is married life?" he asked the man, who had married Emma only a few weeks back.

"Grand, absolutely grand," he said with a wink, "even in spite of the deprivations, the lack of food, and the constant fear of raiders!" He smiled at his own cynicism. "If you can look beyond those minor issues, life couldn't be better." Genis was the heart of the community, even though he had only recently moved from Blue River. He was vivacious and everyone's favorite son, especially for the older folks. A lifelong bachelor, he fell in love with Emma when he went with Jarad to rescue Myla. Emma was a fortunate consequence for him and a stunning redhead, to boot. Jarad could appreciate his comments, especially from certain perspectives.

The men began to pepper him with questions, until another shot was fired from across the bridge. This time the bullet hit near the trees that Genis and Peter were hiding behind as the sniper across the way zeroed in on their position. The men crouched lower. "First off, tell me what's going on with the popgun?" he said, pointing his thumb toward the sound of the noise. The men led him back to a safer location in the trees.

"Just some ass from Purcell thinking he's tough," Genis said, spitting on the ground. He pulled his binoculars up to peer across the expanse of the bridge and toward a rock ledge that overlooked the road. "I guess they're pissed at us for messing up their big raid and are trying to let us know how dangerous they really are – with a twenty-two!" He laughed sourly. "Idiots."

"I wouldn't downplay it, Genis. Ever been hit with a .22 long rifle?" Peter asked. "I suspect that they want to keep us on our toes and that they are still there, still dangerous, and that they haven't forgotten about us. And a twenty-two is a lot cheaper to waste shots with than a deer rifle. Just don't get hit, especially in the head. It could kill you just as soon as something bigger."

"How long has this been going on?" Jarad asked, peering across the gorge toward the gunman. "How many of them are there?"

"Oh, they started a couple days ago," Peter answered. "They've been taking pot shots at those of us who've been manning the barrier that we set up to block their access across the bridge. They don't like it. It looks like they're trying to keep us from fortifying. It's harassing fire and so far it's been working."

"Point them out to me," Jarad said. Genis pointed toward a stand of trees near an embankment, the same rocky ledge that Genis had just panned with is binoculars. He kept describing details until Jarad could see where he was indicating. "I see 'em," he said flatly. "Watch this." He flicked the setting of his assault rifle to three-round burst and pulled it up to his shoulder. He didn't have a scope, but then he didn't need one. He hoped that this show of firepower would have an effect. Genis and Peter both watched with their binoculars.

Taking aim at the shadows about three hundred yards away, Jarad squeezed off two short bursts. The mountains reverberated with the harsh staccato, the echoes chasing themselves down the canyon. Pulling the gun down from his shoulder, Jarad could see someone scrambling down the embankment, making haste for coverage.

"Bam! You got 'em, Jarad," Genis said flatly, still holding the binoculars to his face. He pulled them down and looked at Jarad. "He ain't dead, but I think you might have nicked 'im. Either way, both of them are scrambling." His face busted open with a sudden smile. "I know it's not funny," he said with a chuckle.

Jarad smiled too. "Good, I'm glad they stopped," he said. "That was my intention." He flicked the safety back on his rifle and slung it back around his shoulder. He was done with it for now.

"Okay, I am now ready for questions. Hey, Genis, do you still have any of that beer?"

***

Chapter 3

Jarad had a lot of catching up to do; at least it seemed so to him. He was able to do so at an impromptu public meeting. When word got out that he was in Junction, people came by the dozens to see him. Soon there was no longer any place to sit at Peter's house and people were finding room on the floor or simply standing in the corners and against the walls. This reunion proved fortuitous for Jarad because not only was he able to tell his story and to share his feelings, he was able to ask his own questions.

First, he learned that almost all of the older folks who moved to Junction from Blue River had died. Pneumonia was the primary killer, but Emma also shared that almost all of them seemed to give up hope and did not even try to fight the disease. They just lay in bed and allowed themselves to simply drift off to permanent sleep. She did not understand it. Of the twenty-two people who had come to Junction from Blue River, only fifteen remained. Jarad discovered that the graveyard that he visited this morning was a second site – the first was already filled up.

Second, the United States had seemed to have imploded. According to what Howard had shared from his limited shortwave communications, the country had apparently devolved into five or six separate parts. There was some confusion as to what had transpired. Neither Howard's Spanish nor his contact's English were good enough to be more definitive on what was going on. What was known was that Texas had declared itself a republic along with Oklahoma. California had also seceded from the union, but was currently fighting a defensive war with Mexico, who had invaded and annexed both Arizona and New Mexico. The states in the Mississippi valley seemed to have formed a temporary union, called Mississippia, and Canada had invaded and taken control of many of the north-central and northeastern states. Ironically, the southern states that one time in history formed the Confederacy were now laying claim to the title of the United States. So the good old USA still existed, albeit in a hyphenated southern form. The status of many of the Rocky Mountain and Pacific Northwest states was still unknown.

Jarad's head began to swim as he tried to take all of this in. Events were becoming increasingly unpredictable, even bizarre. It was one thing to face the death of a friend, another completely to face the death of your country. He didn't know what to say. He was at a loss for words. The others told him that they too suffered from a spell of disorientation, but that after a while it would all make sense. The growing hostility between the states and the federal government the past few decades, exacerbated by the inept management of the national economy and the growing power of the military and Wall Street business interests, logically led to secessionist movements. The collapse of the electrical grid simply served as the trigger.

"And what caused this collapse? Has anyone figured that out?" Jarad asked, perplexed.

Peter answered after a long pause. "Well, who knows for sure? I mean, who knows about anything for sure, but it seems that Abrahamson was involved in that…you know, General Abrahamson, our national savior?" he said sarcastically.

Jarad nodded. He knew Abrahamson, who had taken control of the federal government after Congress gave up the reigns when the president was assassinated, again. No one wanted to be president, etc. "Yah, I know about him. So, what happened?"

"It appears that he shut down the grid as a show of power. When the various states began threatening to secede and form their own national governments, he threw the switch. Electrical power became the political pawn for cooperation. You do what he said and you got your power back. If you didn't, then you'd just sit there in darkness while nature took its course."

"Bastard," someone muttered.

"Well, I suppose so, but hell's fire, this was a long time coming. People had long ago lost faith in the feds. Washington D. C. was so patently a money racket that politicians didn't even try to hide it. It was a circus! And the military became just one more special-interest group – I know! The hell with 'em! I'm glad to see it coming."

Voices echoed Peter's sentiments. Jarad did not respond. He was lost in thought. He realized that now they truly were on their own. Previously when he had time to think about the future, those times when he had a moment to catch his breath in the whirlwind of life he had been living the past few months, he always figured that eventually things would return to normal. The power would come back on and he would go back to that life he had always lived. But now he realized that this was not possible.

"So, what's next?" he asked no one in particular. "What's next?"

Otty cleared his throat, indicating that he wanted to talk. Jarad respected Otty and not simply because he was the only pastor in town, as well as the *de facto* leader of the Blue River community. He was in Jarad's estimation a really good and intelligent man and who had earned everyone's respect. "I think that we are all at a stage where we have more important concerns than what nationality we might be. You know that I taught history at the university for much of my adult life. And if history taught me anything, it is that empires rise and fall. And they can fall practically overnight. We are living through that process. But we don't have the luxury of pondering those questions right now. We are in a struggle for survival, and friends…." He paused to quickly look around the room at people's eyes. "We have more urgent concerns than what flag we should be saluting. We need food. And right now, we barely have enough to get us through the summer. And that is on slim rations, too."

"What about the Dome?" Jarad asked. "It has tons of food. Literally tons." He looked at Genis and Peter. "Is there a way to get that food down here? It's not that far from here."

"Yes!" Benson shouted out, from behind the crowd. He was standing furthest back, near the kitchen. "We could use my old wood hauler. It's probably got more than enough diesel stashed away for a trip. And if I can charge the capacitors…probably not all the way, mind you, but some; we might even manage a second trip. We could get that food down here!" he said enthusiastically, which drew a hurrah from the group.

Voices began to rise as new plans were proposed, people calling out ideas, voicing concerns, solutions to problems, or simply encouragement. Otty stood and clapped his hands, bringing the attention back to himself.

"That is all good and well. We need to get that food. That is marvelous, and thank you Jarad for the idea. But…what then? How long will this food last, people? Another couple months? Three, four, five months? Then what? We are simply prolonging the inevitable. I am not saying that we need to come to a solution today. But the fact remains, by this time next year we…." He stopped talking, his hands falling to his side. "We will need to address this, but let's do so at another time," he said softly. "Let's get that food at the Dome, Jarad, and then let's get your family down here, too." He sat down again, his thoughtful mien in stark contrast to the smiles and optimism around him.

*

The small man wiped his face with his sleeve, smearing the sauce from the canned spaghetti across his scabby cheeks. He was obviously unhealthy, suffering from some sort of malnourishment. Right now, though, he was content. He was full and he felt safe, at least safer than he had in a long time. And he was glad to be rid of Denny. He was kind of glad that he shot him; he had it coming. He knew that if Denny was with him right now, he'd have taken the spaghetti away and eaten it himself…and laughing at him the whole time. He hated Denny, but Denny was his only friend. The man scoffed at that thought and then giggled. "Denny's dead," he said in a sing-song. "And I got the spaghetti…"

When he finished he tossed the can to the floor and wiped his hands on the front of his shirt. Then he rubbed his nose with the same sleeve and stood up. He grabbed his rifle and pulled on an old baseball cap. He also grabbed his canvas haversack. He was going to check out the snowmobile tracks, but he didn't go anywhere without his haversack. He hoped that he did not have to go far, because he liked his new home and he did not want to leave it unoccupied. He wanted to make sure no squatters moved in while he was gone.

It was already late morning and the day had become warm and sunny and this delighted him. He was tired of the cold and looked forward to summer, though it was still months away. He stopped and slowly spied the area around himself, listening for unusual sounds or movements. All he heard was the chattering of birds and the bark of a chipmunk in the distance. He moved on.

The snowmobile path was easy to follow. He walked on past the last house as he left Blue River behind and hiked toward the rise that led to west. He had never been up this way, even before the grid had failed and everyone's world had changed. He actually preferred this new world. At first it was tough, but he now felt stronger and more of a man than any other time in his life. Now he didn't have to grovel for work and take what others would give him. No more dish washing and calling himself lucky! For the first time he could take what he wanted because he had a gun; and he wasn't afraid to use it. Just ask Denny! He laughed at his own joke, his hoarse cackle filling the stillness around him.

As he followed the path he wondered who that man was and what he was doing this far out from Purcell. The only logical conclusion he could make was that the man was local and lived in the area. He was probably out foraging like everyone else, breaking into empty homes and taking the supplies. But he was on a snowmobile and the small man knew that those old electric machines had very limited ranges. That thought filled him with excitement, because it proved to him that he was local; that his home might be very near. He kissed his rifle and danced a little jig. He was going to find this guy's house and stake it out and then ambush him when he returned. He would get all the loot – not only in the man's house and all that he would be bringing back from his day of foraging. Easy, easy, easy, the grubby man thought to himself.

The grade marked by the snowmobile trail became increasingly steep and the man soon realized that he was going to have to earn this treasure trove, but the thought of rich loot – food especially -- was motivation enough.

After an hour he found a dry shaded spot to rest. He was too warm to want to sit in the sun. Even though he was resting, he still actively monitored the area around him. He was not going to be surprised suddenly by somebody. He wondered if that man on the sled was going to be gone long. Probably not, he reasoned. Those old electrics could only go so far. This realization caused him to get up and hurry down the path. He needed to be in position before the man showed up. He just knew that the man's house – he imagined it to be a mansion – could not be too much further.

After a few more hours of continuous uphill hiking he began to question if he had made a mistake. The sun indicated that it was well into the afternoon and it would become dark before he could have made it back to his previous night's shelter. And it would get cold. He didn't like the cold. But he was able to cast doubt aside when he spied a fence post. A fence post in the wilderness could only mean one thing: a farm house. He was closing in on his target.

Reenergized, he pushed up the path again, which now began to level off. The fence seemed to go on forever, but then changed from one of plastic picket to stone. Ooh, he thought to himself, this'll be a fancy place! He came to an iron gate that was partially open, the snowmobile track splitting the mushy snow in the gap. He grew more anxious and cautious. He peered into the dimness of the grove of trees that sheltered the driveway with their shadows. Instead of following the tracks down the driveway, he moved parallel to the fence. He would approach from an angle, assuming that the house was directly ahead of him. But he had to hurry. It was getting dark and he needed to be ready. He might only get one shot.

He came upon the house, a grey form in the trees. Quickly he found a place where two young fir trees were competing for the same patch of open space, pushing their branches together toward their centers. Their crossing boughs created a dry, shady spot from where the man could easily monitor both the house and the front drive. As he sat to take his position, he realized that the house was huge, far bigger than he would have imagined. It was a bizarre place, an oversize concrete dome, sitting incongruently in the middle of a forest on a perch overlooking the valley below. These people had money! He had stumbled upon a gold mine and it was all his. But were there other people inside? The thought worried him. For some reason he had assumed that the man on the snowmobile was alone. How stupid! It was too late to turn around now. But the more he considered the half-sphere in front on him the more he desired to possess it. All he had to do was get inside and eliminate any people.

It was dark now and the man remained still. His haversack contained snack food, gloves, and a sweater, so he could stay the night if he chose. He imagined that the darkness was playing into his hand because not only was his position even more obscured, but the man on the snowmobile would have to use his light in order to find his way back. All he had to do was to put a bullet right above the headlight. Bam! Man's dead and he gets the fancy house.

Lights were coming on in the home and the look was magical to him. He had forgotten how wonderful electric lights were and how they so easily and quickly displaced the darkness. He felt a chill shiver through his body as he considered the warmth being enjoyed within that tall dark dome. At that moment he wanted to be in there more than anything else in the world.

Unless the lights were set to come on automatically, there must be others inside the Dome turning them on. His supposition was confirmed when he saw shadows move before some upper windows, momentarily making the light dance. He couldn't see the people from the angle he was at, but the very fact that there was more than one person in the building created new problems for him to consider.

Before he could muster up a plan, a door opened toward the rear of the house, almost in front of him. Indeed the light escaping from the open door briefly exposed him, but the door closed almost as quickly as it opened. To his dismay he realized that a dog had been let out of the house.

He cussed quietly to himself, but remained frozen in position. He was unsure what to do next as he knew that the dog would find him quick. He hoped that it was not something nasty like a pit bull or Rottweiler. He was not particularly afraid of dogs, but they could be a serious problem when defending their turf. And he knew that he was the intruder.

All at once an idea came to him and he immediately put into play. He jumped out of his overhang of a shelter and charged the dog, who was quietly investigating something in the snow. The dog jumped with a yelp at the rapid and unexpected approach of the strange man. The animal quickly scrambled away for a dozen yards before turning to face the interloper. But the man had no interest in the dog and quit the chase as quickly as he had begun it. Instead, he spun toward the house and pasted himself against the wall, immediately next to the door which had been open just a few moments before. The man was gambling that the dog would begin making a fuss and that someone in the house would investigate.

As if on cue, the dog let loose with a staccato of barks as he caught wind of the strange person standing next to his home. He moved stiff-legged in a sweeping arc before the man, alternately growling and barking, but didn't approach any closer. The man realized that the dog was not going to bite him, so he made a lunge toward the animal. The dog again jumped back and dashed away for a couple yards before again squaring himself and barking furiously.

The change in the window light sweeping the trees confirmed that someone had come to take a look at the dog and then disappeared again. He thought that he could feel against the wall footsteps descending a stairwell somewhere inside the house. Gripping his rifle he waited for the door to jut open. Just as it did, he shoved it apart with his shoulder and forced himself into the house, knocking down a girl in the process – he could tell by her gasp of surprise. She then let out a scream as the man grabbed for her arm. He gripped it painfully tight as he pulled her to her feet. Then he spun her around and hooked her neck in the crook of his arm, his elbow projecting forward. He didn't know where to go, so he dragged her to the stairwell, prompting her with blows from his knee. She held onto his arm, gasping for air, unable to scream. Her feet struggled to find traction as the man alternately lifted her by the neck and prodding her stabs in the back. The dog continued barking manically behind them, keeping his distance in the open doorway.

The man paused and craned his head to see what dangers might be above in the stairwell, but none were apparent. He then leveled his rifle before him like a lance before advancing. Using the girl as a shield, he hoped to get the first shot off at anyone that appeared.

The top landing opened up to a large, well-lit room. On any other occasion the man would have been impressed, if not cowed, by the display of opulence set before him, but now he only had eyes for danger. The room was empty. He savagely kicked the girl in the back with his knee and directed her forward toward the adjoining room. She cried out in a choking gasp of pain and clung to his arm, struggling for breath.

As they entered the room an older boy jumped up from a

couch, his face frozen in disbelief. He shouted out, "mom!" before bolting from the room. Good, the man thought to himself: two children and a woman. He could easily deal with this. He steadied his gun. He'd let mama come to him.

A woman approached. She cradled in her hands a pistol, which she directed at the man, but heedless to her own danger. Concerned only for her daughter, the woman had negligently exposed herself. She was exactly where the man had wanted her to be.

He steadied his gun, aimed down the barrel and pulled the trigger. Nothing happened. He had forgotten to chamber a round! He allowed the now unconscious girl to fall to the floor, freeing his left arm to grab the rifle in order to load a round. He reached up with his right hand to pull back the bolt when the room exploded with a thunder clap. He felt an overwhelming blow to his upper thigh that knocked him to the carpet. He did not feel pain so much as surprise and an intense burning. He had been shot!

He ignored the woman and made for the stairs, but it was difficult to stand, let alone walk. He hobbled to the top step, but could not command his legs and he tumbled down the length of the staircase. Suddenly, he felt another crushing blow to his shoulder as the woman above peppered the stairwell with shots.

He was manic with fear and was somehow able to open the door and rush out into the darkness. Fear still compelled him and he was oblivious to the dog that snatched a bite on his one good leg, maneuver that again caused him to tumble. Adrenaline pushed him forward and he disappeared into the embrace of the darkness around him.

*

Myla stood at the top of the stairwell and continued trying to fire the gun, but the pistol refusing to respond. She had spent all the cartridges. She ran down the stairs, still holding the gun as if ready to fire, before dropping it on the floor. Her dog was sniffing the blood at the base of the stairs, whining. Ignoring him she pulled the door shut and bolted the lock fast. She knew that they would be safe once that door was secured.

She then quickly returned up the stairs and rushed to the side of her daughter. Cameron was already by her, helping her to sit up. "It's alright," he cooed softly to his sister, "he's gone. He's gone." Myla threw herself to the floor and embraced her daughter, crying convulsively as she buried her daughter's face into her chest. The girl was crying too, but in gasps.

The three sat together on the floor for a few more minutes before Myla began to inspect her daughter for wounds. Finding nothing serious, she knew that the girl would be sore in the morning and the bruising on her lower back would spread – overall she appeared to be fine. It could have been worse, tragically so. Myla said a prayer of thanks and Cameron helped his mother get Annie to her feet. She led them to her bedroom. They would all share the same bed tonight. Indeed, after this, they might very well share the same bed for many nights to come. All were thoroughly traumatized.

Myla cared nothing for the blood on the carpet and the stairwell. She was done. Now she wanted out of the Dome. All of her prior longings for the place evaporated with the violence of that evening. She lay in bed with her daughter and son and awaited the coming of the morning sun. It would be a long night.

***

Chapter 4

"This old beater gonna make it?" Jarad asked in jest. The big Dodge four-wheel drive one-ton truck was set up to haul wood and it had evidently hauled more than its fair share the past couple-hundred-thousand miles. But Jarad had no doubt it could make the trip, assuming other problems didn't develop. One was fuel. Benson had long ago siphoned as many fuel tanks as he could find, but as a rule they were either empty or almost so. When the power failed, so did the fuel station pumps, so people were left high and dry. Jarad thought that they were sure to find fuel at the Dome.

"She's a goer," Benson said enthusiastically. He loved this old truck and it had made him a lot of money in the past many years. He could haul almost anything that needed to be moved and he never could cut too much firewood for it to transport for sale. Firewood had become the fuel of choice for most country folk. Natural gas and propane were either too costly or no longer available and electricity, though the most convenient and commonly used, was still not as cheap as firewood. That suited Benson just fine, because besides being a welder and roustabout, he loved to cut and haul wood. He was a man of the forest.

Though there were a lot of volunteers wanting to go up to the Dome, mostly out of curiosity, it was determined that for maximum payload fewer men were better than more. In addition there were three people at the Dome who needed seats for the trip back. In the end it came down to Benson, who owned the truck and knew it best, Jarad, and Jimmy who were picked to go. While only sixteen years old, Jimmy was big enough to do heavy work and his father did not particularly want him doing guard duty – it was too dangerous. So Jimmy went in his stead. Jimmy was also a bit bored, too old to do this, too young to do that, so Jarad found him practically begging to be taken along. Jarad also knew Jimmy's ulterior reason: he was in love with his daughter Annie.

They pulled out with two chainsaws and a trailer, their route the only road to Blue River. The road was certainly passable with what little snow still covered it; and the truck had aggressive traction tires, all four of which Benson had lashed with snow chains. It was only the possibility of fallen trees that would make the going slow. But the men were ready; especially Jarad who felt energized this morning. He did not like being away from Myla, though he knew that the Dome was impenetrable. He was sure that his family was safe.

The sound of the Dodge heading through the little community and onto the highway drew people from their homes. People stood in their doorways or from windows watching the spectacle of the truck – the winding of the engine and the husky rumble from the exhaust – which evoked memories of a time that seemed from the distant past, though it was not. Benson and Jarad did not realize that they were making a scene, but waved at the few folks that they saw watching them motor past.

The road was mostly gravel and dirt and very thin snow, speckled with potholes filled to the brim with earth-colored water. Any snow that covered the road was easily penetrated by the truck, which left behind mired tracks. The tire chains hummed discordantly, spewing grime in little rooster tails as the truck sped westward.

Their first obstacle was not a fallen tree but a mud slide,

which spewed rocks and oozing dirt from the embankment onto the road. The men had not anticipated this and realized that a more sizable slide would literally stop them in their tracks. They did not have access to a backhoe to dig away a large slide. Fortunately this one only covered a single lane and Benson was able to maneuver around it, using the far shoulder as part of his lane. He told Jarad and Jimmy to keep their fingers crossed, that they would not meet anything more serious.

Within a mile or two of Blue River they were finally forced to pull out the saws and cut through a pair of small tamaracks that lay perfectly perpendicular to the road. Benson hated rolling the cut sections of the tree into the ditch. He would have preferred tossing them in the back of the trailer to be used as firewood back at Junction. But they had more valuable cargo to haul.

Driving through Blue River was like driving through a ghost town. No, it was more personal than that. It was a poignant reminder of the transience of life, that all of men's efforts for permanence were ultimately up the whims of fate or the plans of God. Either way, the end result was the same. Jimmy especially seemed to be effected by the slow climb through the sepulcher of a community. Blue River had always been his home. It would probably never be again. He simply stared silently out the window as the cold and empty homes passed by. Regardless of sentiments, they left Blue River quickly because the community, even at the snail's pace speed of the truck, was so small. But they would have time to reflect at least three more times, for they still had to make another round trip. But first things first, Jarad thought to himself; let's get to the Dome – seven miles to go.

No sooner did they leave the community that the truck began to jerk about as if the engine was being starved for fuel. The electric motor began cutting in and out as if the diesel motor could not decide whether to run or not. "Damn it!" Benson exclaimed. "What the hell now?" He revved the motor a couple times before it smoothed out. "Come on baby, hold together. We're almost there," he said.

"What's wrong?" Jarad asked. "Is she gonna make it?"

"Yah, I think so," Benson said less than confidently. "But I think the fuel pump is having issues….won't be the first time. She should hold," he said. "I hope."

Once the truck seemed to settle in again, they began to follow the snowmobile tracks that Jarad had made just two days previous. Though the weather was warm and was taking its toll on the snow, plenty remained to see where the snowmobile had traveled. In fact, as they climbed up toward the Dome on the tree-shaded road, the amount of snow slightly increased. It was Benson that pointed out the pair of foot prints superimposed over the tread marks.

"Whose boot prints are those?" Benson asked, curious.

"Huh?" Jarad asked, not sure that he had understood Benson correctly. "Boot prints?"

"There, in the tracks. You didn't break down did you and have to hoof it back to the Dome?" Benson asked him.

"Can we stop and look?" he asked the older man. "I got a bad feeling about this." Benson simply stopped the truck in the middle of the road and all three men got out of the cab.

They inspected the tracks. It was obvious that someone had followed Jarad's path and whoever it might have been was marching directly to the Dome. The size of the print suggested a man.

"I got a bad feeling about this," Jarad said, his voice tinged with anxiety. He stopped moving for a moment as his mind wheeled with an idea. "I think I know who it is!" he said with surety.

"Who?" Benson asked. "Who is it Jarad?"

"No, no," Jarad responded. "I don't know who he is, but I think I know who he is…" He was making no sense, as his pulse quickened and a sense of danger was aroused in him. "Let's go, I'll explain on the way."

The three men jumped back in the truck, Benson and Jimmy now both infected with Jarad's sense of urgency. Jarad explained about the dead body he had found along the tracks two days earlier, and how he surmised that some one – possibly a companion – had shot him in the back, killing him. But he knew nothing about this other man except that he had climbed the embankment away from the rail bed.

"Two men! Seriously!" Benson exclaimed. "So that's what happened to them. I'll be damned."

"Who?" Jarad asked earnestly.

Benson explained that during the raid, two men from the group of raiders were separated from the main body and retreated back up the rail bed. No one paid them any concern. It was assumed that they would simply head back to Purcell the same way they had originally come, following the tracks. It was the long route, but they wisely didn't want to face the guns at Junction. Evidently there was a problem between the two of them and one shot the other.

"The body is still there?" Jimmy asked, listening intently.

Jarad looked over his shoulder at the boy. "Yes," he said. "Why?"

"No reason," he said, a bit defensively. "I was just curious."

Benson snorted. "There's lots of bodies out there. Lots of them. After a while I hated to break into homes when we were scrounging for supplies. Everybody killing themselves. Hell, I've seen babies…" He paused, turning away, his eyes misting up.

Jarad did not say a word, because he knew what Benson was

feeling. Still, he wished the truck would move more quickly; he felt a growing sense of unease. But, he reminded himself, the Dome was a virtual fortress. A lone man would not likely be able to get into it. Not likely...

A fence line appeared and Jarad knew that they were close. Soon the stone work appeared and then the truck came to a rest before an iron gate – the truck could not be able to make it through the half-closed opening. With a chain the truck could easily pull the gate completely open, but Jarad did not want to take the time right then and there. He opened the cab door and jumped out, heading up the lane to the Dome. Odd, he thought to himself as he ran and slipped along, where are the man's tracks? Jimmy followed right behind him.

Arriving at the huge white hulk of a structure, Jarad ran to the front door and grabbed the twin knobs. The door was fastened tight. Good, he thought himself, good. He ran to the right side of the house, to the door that the family used as its primary entrance into the edifice. There he found a sight that took his breath away.

A swath of scarlet drew a path from the closed door and toward the forest. Jarad's heart began to pound in his chest, the sound seeming to fill his ears. He became dazed and stood, staring, in a stupor. His mind was wrestling with the possibilities of what this all meant. Jimmy, too, was stunned. He had never seen so much human blood and the sight repulsed him. He stood immobile, his eyes fixed on the horror before him, as if mimicking Jarad.

Suddenly Jarad began to scream. He seemed to have gone mad. The sound released Jimmy from his daze and he found Jarad pounding crazily against a metal door, screaming out his wife's name, "Myla, MYLA!" again and again. He then ran to the rear of the building, cupping his mouth as he continued shouting until he was hoarse. Then he fell to his knees and began to sob. He feared for the worse.

If there was ever a time in Jarad's life when he believed that he heard an angel's voice, it was right then. No sooner had he fallen to the snow when a woman's voice called out from above, evidently from an out-of-sight window.

"Jarad? Jarad, is that you?" the voice asked. It was Myla.

"Myla!" Jarad called out loudly, springing to his feet. "Myla, are you okay?" He ran back to the door.

In what seemed to Jarad like an eternity, the bolt to the metal door was released and the door opened. Myla stepped out and was immediately embraced by her husband, both of them crying into the other's shoulder. The nightmare proved to be a passing squall. All was well.

Myla broke the embrace of her husband and guided him by the arm into the house. She noticed Jimmy and gave him a tear-streaked smile. "Hi Jimmy," she said with a loud sniff, and then beckoned him to follow them.

The gore in the stairwell and the blood sticking to his boots was almost too much for the boy, but he dwelt with it by focusing his eyes upon Myla and Jarad as they climbed the stairs. But there was also blood on the stairs, so he had to elevate his visage even higher. He began to feel a bit queasy, but he kept things together by concentrating on his steps and toward making it to the landing at the top. His journey was interrupted by Cameron, who met his father halfway up the staircase. Seeing his son, Jarad embraced him strongly against himself, greeting him with a fresh set of tears.

Once he made it to the top, Jimmy found the house to be quite impressive, the most beautiful home he had ever been in. It was even nicer than the fanciest mansions that they had raided in both Blue River and Junction. The only detraction was the blood-imbued carpeting at the opening between the two rooms. He sat down on a couch. He was feeling ill.

Myla explained to her husband what had transpired that night as she led him to his daughter. She was awake in the bed and greeted her father with a smile, lifting her arms to hold her father. Jarad sat beside her and drew her near to himself, and a third set of tears flowed. He breathed heavily into her hairs, sobbing. He didn't want to let her go.

After their embrace, Annie rolled over to show her father her back. Three dark purple and brown bruises grew outward from her lower back. Seeing them caused anger to begin to flow in Jarad's veins, but he let it go. Enough of that, he knew subconsciously. Everyone is safe.

Jarad lifted himself up from the bed and noticed a face peeking into the room through the bedroom door. It was Jimmy. The boy's eyes met with Annie's and she shyly pulled her covers up to her shoulders, but she smiled which encourage him to enter the room.

"I'm glad you're okay," he said, his cheeks turning ruddy.

"Thank you," she responded. She then held out her hands to him and he knelt over her and gave her a brief hug.

"Guess what?" she said with conspiratorially. "We're moving to Junction." She looked into Jimmy's face, seeking his reaction.

He smiled so broadly that his face hurt, but he couldn't help himself. "I know," he said, not even attempting to hide his pleasure. "Your dad told me." He reached his hand toward her and she held it, the two staring into each other's eyes. Myla found the scene endearing, Jarad found it troubling. He left them to their own devices, and took Cameron by the shoulder. He'd visit with his son for a while.

The two sat down in the large family room down the hall from the bedrooms. He was going to ask his son how he felt and what else, beyond the obvious, had gone on since he was gone. But no sooner did they begin to converse when Benson stepped into the room.

"I found you!" he said to Jarad, giving Cameron a wink and seemingly oblivious to the drama that had unfolded. "This is quite a place; I can see why you were enjoying yourself." He sat down on the leather loveseat opposite Cameron and Jarad. "By the way, I found the body of that guy. Poor fool, didn't stand a chance. Looks like he got pegged a couple times. Both wounds pretty nasty. Bled to death. I'm surprised he made it as far as he did. I assume it was your wife? Hell of a shot, I should say. Gutsy, gutsy woman."

Jarad didn't say a word. He really didn't want to hear all the gory details, especially in front of his son. But Benson sure found it interesting.

"So, show me around this place," he said to Jarad. "And especially the food. Let's get this show on the road."

*

It hardly took them anytime at all to load the first cargo of food. Loading the truck and trailer was a nice diversion from the earlier tension. For Jarad the work felt good, though his wound slowed him down. But he believed that he was truly contributing to the needs of the community and at one level he felt that he was repaying Junction for any troubles that his earlier absence might have caused. Though no one even hinted at this possibility, Jarad knew it to be true in his heart. He realized that Junction needed both he and Myla and it was wrong to not have moved down there earlier.

But then, perhaps he was second guessing himself. If they had moved down to Junction with everyone else in Blue River, they would not have ever discovered the Dome and the current supplies it was giving them.

While the men loaded the truck and trailer, Myla packed up their personal effects and other supplies. She would accompany the men back for the second load, as she knew that there were many things that would prove to be essential in Junction, such as medical supplies. She was glad to be leaving the Dome, which sort of surprised her. Just a day ago she was saddened by the thought of moving away and from the security it represented. But her feelings about Alberta changed everything. She was pregnant and did not want to deliver the baby in the Dome, nor for that matter in Junction. She wanted to get to Alberta and Junction was simply a means to that end. It wasn't that she did not hold the needs of the community dear to her heart. She did. But she was also going to be a mother for the third time. She had to think of her child. Now she only needed to let Jarad know. She would do so when the proper time presented itself.

After they had loaded the truck, Benson went to inspect the Mercedes in the garage. He hoped to siphon it of fuel, thereby increasing the number of loads he could make in his truck. Unfortunately there was less fuel than he had hoped – the previous tenets had not thought of all contingencies after all. They neglected to stock up on fuel for their car. Granted, they could still have charged up the capacitors for local trips, but an engine was needed for extended travel. Maybe they had decided that they would not be going anywhere. Benson figured that it was more likely that they got caught off guard by the power outage like everyone else. He could not even find a spare fuel tank of diesel. So he siphoned what he could and added it to his truck. With luck, they might make three trips. There was enough food to warrant the effort.

At last they were leaving. The truck had plenty of room for everyone, including the dog. Champ loved going for rides and it had been so long since he had had the opportunity to do so that he began to yodel. Annie laughed so hard at this that she almost began to cry, though this was probably a trigger for the release of tension. Jarad was sure she was suffering from some trauma. It surprised him that everyone in his family was glad to be rid of the Dome. That was strange to him. He saw it as the perfect stronghold and refuge.

The ride back was quick, especially since it was mostly downhill. No one said a word while going through Blue River. Jarad supposed everyone was adapting. He knew that he was.

The return to Junction did not find Jarad, Benson, and Jimmy being welcomed home as conquering heroes, but a small group of people was there to greet Myla and the kids and to admire the food. Myla hugged and chatted with some of the ladies before wandering off with a couple of them. Someone was ill and needed her attention and she did not think twice about going. Jarad watched her disappear from sight, realizing that nothing had changed. She was now again Myla the doctor, instead of Myla the nurse. He shook his head.

They quickly unloaded the food and had enough time that same day to make a second trip. The return trip also went exceedingly well, so much so that Jarad proposed a third trip. There was still more food to be had, but they decided to wait until the next day for the third trip. First, Benson wasn't sure that they had enough fuel to make it all the way there and back and he didn't trust the fuel pump – which he had no way to replace. Second, if they did find themselves alongside the road, it was better to do so early in a day than as the sun was setting. And he could charge the capacitors over night. But the all agreed that they could not leave that food where it was. As desperate as they were, that would have been ludicrous. Indeed, even if they did not have the truck, it would have been worth their while to bring it all down by hand, or sled, or wagon – whatever it took. Such were the times.

That next day they were successful in getting off one more load, but it would prove to be their final one in the truck. Benson did not know for sure, but he thought that the fuel pump had given up the ghost. Benson was able to recharge the capacitors at the Dome, and he determined that if they left the trailer behind they should just make it home.

During their final pass through Blue River Jarad had Benson pause for a few moments before the old family cabin. He told him that he had to grab something. While everyone else waited in the truck, Jarad rushed in and grabbed the gold coins, putting them in his leg pockets. To eliminate curiosity, he took the cribbage board and a set of playing cards from the dining room cabinet. He waved the board at his friends when he returned. "This is practically a family heirloom," he told them honestly, "and I wasn't about to leave it behind. Who knows when I might be able to return to Blue River?"

Benson was almost right – he was off by a half mile. The truck ran out of juice and now sat dead in the road. It took most of the able-body population of Junction to haul their trove from the truck to the community storage, but the folks were glad to help. The food was the most wonderful sight to them.

Finally, the last load of food was stashed away in the community center. In fact, there was so much that they had to store the excess in the garage of a neighboring house. They did better than they had hoped and there was more food than Jarad had originally supposed. But they knew that they would not let the food left at the

Dome sit there indefinitely, even if they had to haul it to Junction on their backs. It was worth the effort to increase their larder.

Jarad and Myla had a pick of residences for their new home. There were so many abandoned homes in the area that they had many to choose from. They chose one with three bedrooms and with, most important of all, a wood stove. They would not survive the coming winter without one. Myla didn't say a word.

Toward sunset Peter and Genis came to visit Jarad. They wanted Jarad's thoughts about how to end the harassing fire across the bridge from the Purcell raiders for once and for all. "They're back, of course. I wish I could call in an air strike, like back in the day," Genis said.

Peter shook his head in agreement with Genis. "I wish it were that simple. It would solve our problem, maybe, once and for all. It seems that our friends across the river are planning something, though I wish I was a fly and could buzz over there and listen in."

That gave Jarad an idea and he realized that he knew instantly what to do. He suggested that they attack the raider position and capture the two of them. "There's always a pair of them, right?" he asked.

Peter said that attacking across the bridge would be a bit rash and someone would bound to end up dead, or seriously wounded. A direct assault would be dangerous. Jarad said that they misunderstood him. He meant a covert mission at night. They could cross the bridge under the cover of darkness and surprise the men at the crack of dawn.

Genis agreed with Jarad and thought that his idea was doable, but he suspected that the men probably had a night vision scope. They would see the crossing as clearly as if it were daylight. "True," Jarad agreed, "but do you honestly think that these fellows would be monitoring the bridge at three in the morning?"

The men looked at each other. No, they didn't think so; those guys with the .22s were not professional soldiers. So then it was decided. The evening after next they would make the crossing and see what bad guys they could rustle up.

*

Myla was unpacking the last of her luggage, settling her family into their new home. But she hardly looked at the house as more than a temporary stay, as if she were a traveler simply passing through for an extended stay in a rental, because that was the way she truly felt. As the kids had gone off to reacquaint themselves with their friends and Jarad was doing whatever it was that Jarad did, she considered her immediate plans.

She wanted to get Cameron's little crank-up radio going so she could listen to some Albertan radio stations and perhaps catch up on the news. Second, she needed to tell Jarad her plans, the sooner the better, because she was not going to back down on this decision. Third, she estimated that she was about four months along in her pregnancy. That meant that she wanted to be at her destination, wherever it was, within four months at the latest. There was no way on earth that she was going to be traveling on foot that final month. The thought made her snort. "No way in hell," she said aloud to the walls.

***

Chapter 5

Jarad was excited about the prospects of crossing the bridge and raising a "little Cain" among the raiders. Though he understood the situation that the raiders were in – everyone was in the same desperate boat – he found their methodologies brutal and unnecessary. Like Otty was fond of saying, "If they would only ask, we would help them. But as they continually try to take, we need to resist them." Jarad found himself loathing the raiders, even though they were his former neighbors and community members in Purcell. Or so he assumed them to be.

"Jarad, I suppose I should've thought of this before now, but how do'ya know that we won't come upon a whole lot of guys?" Genis asked barely above a whisper. "I mean, there might be more than the two we've been seeing."

It sounded to Jarad's ears that Genis was getting nervous and having second thoughts. Jarad couldn't blame him; neither of them had ever done anything like this before. "Think about it, Genis. Put them in our shoes. Do we ever have more than two people manning a barricade?"

He paused in thought for a moment. Jarad could just make out his face in the darkness. "Humph," he grunted. "I suppose you're right. I just hope that they're asleep and not setting to bushwhack us. I guess I'm just a little nervous…"

"Fingers crossed," Jarad whispered. They were playing the odds and Jarad knew it. But he didn't have any other solutions, nor did anyone else.

Jarad was the first to sprint over to the barricade. Their barrier was not really very significant, as the raiders discovered when they passed over the bridge just four weeks before and who demolished it in their panic to get away after being ambushed in Junction. That was the reason they set up the barrage of harassing gun fire – to keep the men at Junction from reinforcing their barricade and making it more formidable than it currently was: a series of stacks of logs laid horizontally against an A-frame girder, fronted by a couple of abandoned cars. The people at Junction were anxious to improve it with something more substantial, but they could not until the "snipers" were taken care of; thus, this covert mission by Jarad, Genis, and Peter.

Genis and Peter followed Jarad, one after the other. Once they were all in place, Jarad peeked through a gap in the structure. The bridge seemed to be far longer now than it did during the day, but he knew this was not true. He was simply subconsciously acknowledging that the next phase was the most dangerous for him. He now had to rush down that bridge and toward the raider encampment and without any structure to hide behind should he be seen.

Without a word he weaved between a gap in the staggered grid work of logs and dashed pass the shot up cars and down the bridge, as silently as he could. He hugged the guardrail simply because it made him feel less exposed. After what seemed to be an eternity, he made it to the far end, where he rolled up against an aggregate of boulders and large rocks that formed an embankment on the highway.

He did not signal the other men, because he knew that they could not see him. And they were not using radios – for fear that a chance sound would give away their position. They were simply following one after the other, knowing that gunfire would indicate failure and signal a retreat. After Jarad disappeared in the darkness, Genis counted out thirty seconds and then, he too, dashed into the night.

Within a minute all three men were again together, Peter still breathing heavily as he was the last to join them. "Ready?" Jarad asked in a whisper. The other two men grunted acknowledgement and the half-standing men moved down the highway and toward the path up toward their target on the bluff above the road.

As Jarad had hoped, the path was obvious. He and Genis immediately moved up the dark trail, while Peter hunkered down in a defensive position off to the side. He was assigned to keep guard in case there were other men out and about. He would let Genis and Jarad know there was trouble simply by firing away. He was going to shoot first and ask questions later or, as he thought to himself, not ask questions at all. If it moved, he was going to shoot at it.

Jarad moved slowly up the path. He was not in a hurry. He also did not want to lose Genis, who was so close that Jarad could hear him breathing. He moved forward a few steps and then would stop, listening for any sound in the inky stillness. The two dark forms moved in synchronicity: up, forward, crouch, pause, listen…up, forward, crouch, pause, listen…

Adrenaline kept the two men from feeling the exhaustion that normally would have been settling into their calves. But both felt nothing, neither the cool breeze sweeping against their faces nor the heat building up under their heavy dark jackets. They were only focused on sounds of the night, their position relative to the path, and the position of their rifles.

The trail suddenly leveled off, indicating to Jarad that they were probably near their target. He was about to begin a new cycle of movement up the path when he heard the distinct sound of a zipper being manipulated – perhaps only a half-dozen or so yards ahead. Someone was doing loudly manipulating a zipper, whether a tent or a sleeping bag. It didn't matter which. For Jarad the sound indicated the location of the men, or at least one of them, and that fact that he was awake.

Jarad paused a moment to let Genis catch up to him and then motioned their preset signal that a target had been located – the two men then quickly and quietly moved themselves off of the path and into the dark underbrush. In the near distance they heard a man cough followed by a long, drawn out yawn. Jarad was tense, but he knew that he and Genis still had the advantage. He would wait for the man to settle down again before continuing forward.

The two listened as the man continued to move about, but only making the barest of sounds. Then Jarad realized that the man was walking down the path, directly toward him. Jarad wanted to slip the safety off on his rifle, but he was afraid that the man might hear the click of the tang and be alerted to their presence. He just waited, practically holding his breath.

Looking up from his concealment Jarad could make out against the night sky the head and shoulders of the man. He was looking around, but not with deliberation. The dark silhouette stood directly in front of Jarad, but was seemingly oblivious to Jarad's presence. The man turned away from the path and in a moment Jarad understood why the man had gotten up. He was peeing!

Jarad stood up and waited for the man to finish. After a short time the man turned around and found himself face to face with Jarad. The man was too shocked to say anything and before he could make a sound Jarad swiped the man's face with the butt of his rifle. He crumpled to the ground, piling up against Jarad's legs. Jarad stepped back and the man completed his collapse. Jarad knew the man was either out cold or dead. He did not have time to care which.

Jarad then moved quickly though silently to where his victim had come from. This was a gamble on his part, but he wanted to find the man's companion in case the man he struck woke up or began to make sounds. Jarad felt he had the advantage and wanted to keep it.

He spotted what appeared to be a tent, large enough only for a single person. Looking intently, Jarad surmised that it had an open flap. He glanced around himself, noting a fire pit that had gone cold. Next to it was another tent, similar in size to the other. This one was fastened up tight.

Jarad tried to decide what to do. He could establish his presence and wake the sleeping man, but he knew that the fellow was probably sleeping with his gun. Who knew what he might do? Or he could wait until the man also had to respond to the call of nature. This seemed simplest and was the route he chose to take.

He quietly returned to the man he had struck down. Genis was already near him. Kneeling down, he cupped his hands over Genis's ear and whispered his plan. "There's another guy in a tent, still sleeping. I want to wait for him to wake up on his own. Let's hogtie this guy and gag him. Can you do that?"

Genis whispered a yes and pulled a couple oversized zip-ties from a pouch. He used these to tie the unconscious man's hands behind him and his two ankles together. He then got out a roll of duct tape and, as silently as he could, he pulled off enough tape to encircle the man's head. He wrapped it around the man's mouth and head, effectively gagging him.

Jarad returned to the little encampment and settled down for the wait. The tension he was feeling subsided when he heard sounds of snoring emanating from the nylon fabric before him. Someone was enjoying his slumber. After Genis joined him, he moved out to the overlook that the men used to observe the bridge. Under different conditions, Jarad would have enjoyed the view, even during this early spring night. He was anxious to get back across the bridge, but he knew that it was most practical to be patient. He returned to the camp.

After a couple hours the sun began to pierce the eastern horizon, though none of them could see it from their redoubt. But the changing colors in the sky were obvious, dawn was upon them. As anticipated, the change in ambient light awoke the sleeping man and Jarad began to hear the sounds of stirring. The man sounded like he was getting dressed. Then Jarad noticed a few tugs at the tent and the exterior zipper began to race down toward the bottom of its track. The man was getting out of his tent.

The man looked out of the tent and instantly noticed Jarad, or more importantly, the gun barrel pointed directly at is face. Jarad wanted to say something smart-alecky but decided against it. He just stared at the man, down the length of the barrel.

"We ain't got no money," he said, sticking both of his hands out of the flap and into the morning air. He stumbled out of the tent as he tried to both stand up and exit his nylon shelter, before stepping onto the dew-dampened ground in his socks.

"We don't want your money," Jarad said. "Where'd we spend it?"

The man didn't respond. He was thirty-something in age and very thin. He apparently had not been eating well lately. Jarad did not recognize his face. The man just looked at Jarad and Genis in the early growing light, not saying a word. Then he noticed the empty tent behind Jarad and he began to look around for his friend.

"Where's Jon?" he asked. "The other guy…" He looked at Jarad and James accusingly. "You killed him?" he asked, fear growing his face. "Man, you ain't gonna kill me, too, are ya…?"

"No, we're not gonna kill anyone," Genis said. He smiled at Jarad as he toyed with the man and then glared back at him. "Unless we gotta," he warned in what Jarad knew to be a mock threat.

The morning air was unsettled by a low groan that increased in volume and intensity. All three men turned toward the figure that still lay on the path a couple yards from the encampment. Genis went over to him and pulled out his knife. That man had opened his eyes and now stared with horror as Genis approached him with the exposed blade. He began to thrash around on the ground, trying to escape the approaching threat.

"Just settle down, settle down," he said to the man, resting his arm and weight on the man's shoulder. I'm just gonna cut your feet loose."

Hearing that, the man stopped moving and waited patiently as James slipped the blade between his ankles and pulled it through the plastic band. With his feet now free, James helped the man to a standing position. Even though it was still low-light conditions, James could see the damage done to the man's face by Jarad's rifle butt. A scrape on his temple area was superimposed over a large purple bruise. James whistled to himself when he looked at the man and shook his head. He knew that the poor fellow was probably suffering from a nasty headache. But the fear evident in his eyes probably mitigated any pain he might be feeling at that moment. James felt pity on both of the men. He found them to be quite pathetic.

James directed the man back to the encampment and in moments he was standing next to his partner. Jarad asked Genis to cut the bands on the man's wrists. "Why?" he asked. Genis did not trust any of them and would have preferred if they were both bound up tight.

"So he can zip up his pants," Jarad said, indicating the man's crotch with his rifle. James looked down and instantly understood what Jarad was pointing at. The man had not had a chance to finish his morning chore, so to speak, before Jarad had popped him across the face. James cut the man's wrist bands and he instantly arranged himself, zipping his pants up fast. Afterward he began to remove the duct tape from his head. It appeared to be a painful process, especially considering the head wound he had suffered. The man groaned loudly as he pulled the sticky fabric from his face.

Jarad suspected, but did not know for sure, how many men there were in the immediate area, so he began to interview the men in a circuitous fashion. "So, where are the rest of the guys? We know that there are more than just the two of you," he asked calmly but with a hint of severity. The men looked at each other, as if each waiting on the other to answer. Finally the shorter of the two, the one without the huge bruise on his cheek, spoke up. "There's only us two. There's always only two. Sometimes only one. There ain't no others," he replied.

"Why are you people here? Why are you camping out? Odd place to be camping, don't cha' think?" he asked, a bit sarcastically.

The men finally realized that Jarad and Genis were not robbers, but had another purpose for holding them at gun point. But it was too early in the morning and they were, in their current situation, too emotionally disadvantaged to consider alternative possibilities. They just wanted to be done with this and be out from under Jarad's stare, both his eyes and his gun.

"We're watching the bridge," the smaller man answered.

"That's all we do; watch the bridge."

"And take pot shots at us!" Genis interjected accusingly. Then the men came to the realization that Jarad and Genis were from Junction. They again looked at each other and then they began to argue with each other in whispers.

"What?" Genis asked. "Quit jabbering and answer my question. Why do you keep taking pot shots at us?"

"We gotta," said the smaller man again. "We gotta, those are our orders. We gotta keep you people from reinforcing your roadblock."

Jarad jumped in with a question before Genis could continue. What the man said got his curiosity up. "Who ordered you? Who's the boss?" he calmly asked the two of them.

The smaller man paused again, considering his words. He must not have considered the information to be especially meaningful because he was direct in his response. "The chief," he said.

"The chief…" Jarad responded. "Does the chief have a name?"

"Bronsky, but we just call him 'chief'," he said, neutrally.

Jarad had never heard the name. He glanced over at James, who only gave him a shrug of the shoulders. Bronsky…it meant nothing to him.

"So, who is this 'Bronsky'," he asked, continuing his probing.

"One bad hombre!" the man said, whistling. "He's one bad dude. He's like some escaped convict or something, but that man is wicked!" The man swung his head at some thought. "He'll kill a man in a heartbeat," he said knowingly. "Even a woman." He whistled again. Great, Jarad thought to himself, the raiders are being led by a psychopath.

"So tell me, why do you people gotta keep us from building up our barricade on the bridge? Why do you care?" Jarad asked. He knew that this was the crucial question.

"The chief told us too. He knows that you people up there got all sorts of food. All sorts. Tons! We all know this," the shorter man said. Then he got almost surly. "You people don't know what you got comin'! No sir, you ain't got no idea."

"What do you mean by that?" Jarad asked softly, not trying to make his question a demand. He wanted to keep this chatterbox chattering.

"We know you got that food. We know it. And the chief has got a plan. We're gonna come and take it from you people and a whole army of people like you won't be able to stop us. We're gonna waltz right over that bridge."

"How so? We'll stop you. We'll blockade the bridge," Jarad insisted, baiting him. The other man started to get restless. He couldn't talk clearly because of his jaw, so he had been grunting at this partner and now he began to nudge him sharply against his ribs, trying to make him be quiet. But the shorter man liked playing the big man with Jarad. Jarad looked over at Genis.

"Genis, take this guy outta my sight. I don't like lookin' at him anymore." He stared grimly at the taller man, making him cower a bit. Genis motioned with his rifle for the man to move down the path, Jarad playing the macho hard-ass card. "And Genis, if he moves, shoot 'em. Just shoot him, 'em" he repeated for emphasis. As Genis led him away, he hoped that Genis understood that he was not serious. He hoped to God that Genis knew that he was bluffing.

Jarad moved to his left so that the shorter man had to turn to face him, causing him to put his back to the others. "So tell me, how are you people going to take our food? We were ready for you when you came up the rail bed, we'll be ready for you when you come across the bridge. Anyhow, we don't have any extra food, we're starving."

With that the man began to laugh. "Starving? You people got tons of food. TONS! I know. I heard it. Some dome. You got dome food! We all know it."

So that was it. There was a spy in their midst at Junction. Here it was only two days since they had gotten the food from the Dome and this scrawny fellow knew about it. But Jarad didn't flinch.

"Pretty good, I got to hand you that! You got one on us. But we're not gonna give it up. Not without a fight. And we're ready for you or anyone else."

The man laughed again. "No sir, you ain't. We got a tank. We got a tank and there ain't no way to stop a tank unless you got another tank. And you don't have a tank. I KNOW you don't got a tank. You don't even got enough fuel to spit!" He laughed again.

"A tank?" Jarad said doubtfully. "No way."

The man gave Jarad an exaggerated shrug. "You'll find out soon enough, yes sir. Soon enough. Like in two days or so," he said, practically smug.

"Two days…come on, you're telling me a story," he said, to bait the man.

"I ain't saying nothing more. You can kill me, and I ain't gonna say no more. But you go ahead, build the biggest, baddest roadblock you can and I tell you what, it ain't gonna matter." With that the man shut his mouth and quit responding to Jarad's questioning.

"Alright, let's go," he told the man sharply. He indicated the way with his gun. "Head down the path." Soon all four of them were heading toward the bottom. When they reached the end they were met by Pete. Raising his hand to keep Peter from speaking, Jarad told his two captives to sit down. He asked Genis and Peter to both keep their guns pointed at the men and then he returned to the encampment.

He searched through the men's tents and it wasn't long before he discovered what it was that he was searching for: a walkie-talkie. Someone had been sharing Junction "secrets" with the raiders. And he had his suspicions as to who it was. He slipped the radio into a pocket and then gathered up what guns he could find and the ammunition, putting the shells into his small backpack. Then he returned to the others.

No one had moved in the few minutes he was gone. He looked at the two sitting men you stared up at him expectantly.

"Go, get outta here," he told them pointing down the highway with a sweeping motion of his hand. "Get!" he shouted at them.

The two men sprang to their feet and began trotting south, both of them barefoot. The further they got the quicker they ran and soon they were practically sprinting, periodically looking over their shoulders. They were trying to get out of rifle range. When they figured out that they were not going to be shot at, they slowed down to a jog and then a walk. Jarad could see them arguing in the distance.

"I see that you two were successful," Peter said, pointing his head in the direction of the two men. "Good work."

"No, it's worse than you can imagine," Jarad responded languidly. He reached into his pocket and pulled out the little walkie-talkie. "They know about the food we got from the Dome.

They know everything they could possibly know about us. We got ourselves a spy."

Both Peter and Genis were aghast. They both stared stone-faced at Jarad. "And there's more. They are planning on a huge raid, in two days. And they got themselves a tank."

"A tank?" Genis scoffed. "You're gonna believe those two dimwits that they got a tank?"

"No, I doubt that it is a real military tank. It's probably a narco-tank, you know, one of those one-ton trucks covered in heavy steel plate. Something like that. But it just as well be a real tank." He pulled his baseball cap off and scratched his head. He was tired and he began to feel the ache in his legs. He was done for the day, but he still had to meet with Otty and the others. And they had to flush out that spy. He handed each man one of the extra rifles he had gotten from the encampment. He let them share the load.

As the three men walked back across the bridge, Jarad shared what he had learned from the talkative man. All three of them would periodically look over their shoulder as they walked toward safety. They still felt vulnerable, perhaps even more so now.

When the men got back to Junction they all headed for the community building. They knew that they had to share right away what they had learned that morning with the Committee. Plus, they were all in need for some breakfast. First their report, then each would return to his home for something to eat.

But as they neared the community building in the distance, they noticed a great number of people outside the building, adults and children. As they got nearer it became evident that everyone was having an outdoor potluck. There were people of all ages sitting around makeshift tables and eating. At least it appeared that they were eating. It didn't seem right, though, because it was not a particularly nice day for a potluck and it was still quite early in the morning. In addition, none of the men had heard anything about such an event.

When they were within shouting distance, the men could see the people far more clearly. Jarad wanted to stop and rub his eyes, for surely they were deceiving him. The majority of the people appeared to be Amish! This was too bizarre for Jarad and he honestly wondered if he was hallucinating.

"Luddites!" Genis exclaimed. "I'll be damned, Luddites. What in the world…"

"Luddites, of course," Jarad agreed. It had been a long time since he'd run into them. Some members of the community were using fire pits to cook up meals and others were helping to serve, spooning out the food from a chow line. He headed for a familiar face among the tables, the two others in tow.

Elaine Stevenson greeted them as the three men approached. She swung her head faintly back and forth with a bright smile but a grim look in her eyes. "We got visitors," she said without enthusiasm. "And it looks like they will be staying with us indefinitely." She smiled at the people sitting near her as they listened to the conversation. They looked up at the three men with kind expressions, but no words of greeting. To Jarad they looked all the world like Amish farmers.

"Indefinitely?" Peter asked, a bit perturbed. "What's the occasion?"

"Well, our neighbors here got forced out of their commune a day ago. It seems that we are not the only ones having trouble with raiders."

Genis was not shy. He ignored the conversation and went directly to the chow line. He was hungry and wanted some breakfast. But Jarad still had some unfinished business. "Peter, can you come with me?" he asked firmly.

"Of course," he said. "Are we going to take care of that other problem?" Jarad nodded.

They first went to the shop to see Benson. Benson was always repairing or building something, in this case it appeared to be some electric component, probably for one of the solar cells. He greeted the two men as the entered his shop. "Hello gentlemen. And a fine morning it is," he said in a faux-Irish accent.

Jarad gave him a nod. He was angry, but he wanted to keep his anger focused where it belonged. "Is Dev around?"

"Dev?" Benson said. "I suppose so, but I don't know exactly where? Why?"

"Reasons," Peter said, hoping to keep Jarad from getting hasty. "Where does Dev live? I mean, where does he bunk?" he asked Benson.

Benson's face was neutral, but his eyes held a hint of curiosity. He was curious why anyone, let along these two men, would be asking about Dev.

"Well, right here, at the top of the shop. I got an apartment up there, you know." He led the men up a set of stairs and to the door that led to the apartment. It was locked. Benson knocked on it, but there was no response.

Jarad told them to step aside and proceeded to kick the door open. The door flung inward and fragments of wood flew every which way, littering the floor. Benson was aghast to the damage to his door, but his curiosity become even more intense.

The room was empty, so Jarad and Peter began rifling through the room, searching drawers and the man's personal effects. It didn't take them long to find what they were looking for. Peter called out from the little bathroom, holding the evidence in his hand. It was a walkie-talkie, identical to the one that Jarad took from the raider's camp that very same morning.

"Where'd you find it?" Jarad asked, surprised at how quickly Peter discovered it. "He hid it in one of the most obvious hiding places you might imagine." He pointed to the empty space where the bottom vanity drawer had been removed, which Peter had set in the bathtub. "Evidently Dev was not particularly bright, because he hid the radio underneath here. As if no one would look!" He laughed. Jarad laughed too, but only at himself.

***

Chapter 6

Jarad sat with Otty, Peter, James, Elaine and John Stevenson, Myla, Emma, and Genis, sharing with them to the *nth* detail what he had learned from the men that they had captured that morning. He also told them about Dev. After a search, it was apparent that the man had disappeared. He was obviously in a hurry as he had not taken the incriminating evidence: the walkie-talkie.

"This is exhausting!" Myla exclaimed. "It seems that we are forever going from the frying pan into the fire." She looked around the room. "I'm sorry, I don't mean to sound so self-absorbed. I guess I am still caught up with my own issues."

Otty looked at her kindly. "It's okay. We are all undoubtedly sharing similar thoughts. These are troubling times. But what we need to do now, and I mean now, is to come up with a collective solution."

John Stevenson spoke: "I just don't know what we can do to build up the barricade enough to stop what seems to be coming. We have no heavy equipment. We have no fuel. And we surely don't have the firepower to stop their tank. Maybe we should go on the offensive and try to negotiate with these people."

"No, sorry John, I don't think that is a good idea. As I stated before, this Bronsky is a nut. He sounds like a certified psychopath. Negotiating will be a sign of weakness. He'll take all of our food and still try to slaughter us!"

"So what do we do?" Elaine practically shouted. "How do you stop a psychopath?"

"We have to somehow make the bridge impassable," Peter piped up. "We have to somehow make that bridge so they can't get across. Damn, I wish we had a front loader, we could cover that thing with rock!"

"Well, rock might stop the tank, but it isn't going to stop people," Jarad reminded him. "I suppose we can keep them down with constant rifle fire."

"And they'll do the same. And then we have a war of attrition. Who runs out of bullets first? Or worse yet, you runs out of men able to wield a rifle?" Otty added.

Abruptly a hand slapped a table and all eyes turned to Genis. He began to laugh, rolling his head back as he did so. "I got the perfect solution and it is a DOOZY!" he shouted. He looked around the room, relishing the moment. "But I will need a little help," he said, rubbing the palms of his hands together, menacingly.

*

"How far," Jarad asked, again, as the men were all assembling next to the community building.

"Two miles, more or less," Genis responded. He was the last to be ready as he had to scrounge up backpacks and haversacks for some of the volunteers. But he could not get as many men as he wanted because there was unease in the community with all the Luddites, so some men asked to remain behind to provide a presence. Just in case. Though the Luddites were avowed pacifists, they were very odd and were not particularly approachable. They were also not invited to participate in this exercise.

Genis stood counting the men around him. They all smiled at him as he tallied each one for he was wearing an old green military helmet, which was obviously one or two sized too large. "It belonged to my great-grandfather," he said. But in spite of his comical appearance, he was serious. Seven men, he thought to himself, hopefully that'll be enough. Well, five men and two big boys, he corrected himself. "Let's get going," he said with a wave of his hand and the small band rambled off to the north and down the highway. Their destination was a small warehouse located at the Denex quarry.

Genis had worked at the quarry on and off over the course of the past ten years. It was seasonal work and the last few years had been slow, but he knew – hoped actually, but he did not tell anyone his doubts – that the quarry's supply of explosives would be there. Quarries use a lot of explosives in their operations and these particular explosives would be perfect for what Genis had in mind. He was going to blow the bridge to "kingdom come," as he liked to phrase it. That should stop the raiders, because it would make it impossible for them to cross the Blue River.

The highway they were marching on cut north for many miles before turning east toward Montana. There were few homes out this direction and no communities. A person might travel to Montana along this route for scores of miles before meeting up with another living soul. The road was narrow and rife with potholes, but once it descended from the main pass and out of the mountains little communities began to reappear on the Montana side of the border.

The men were excited, but not nearly as much as Cameron and Jimmy. They were not only keyed into participating in an adventure with the men, but they were looking forward to the final result. The thought of demolishing the bridge in a paroxysm of a chemical reaction was for them an extremely exciting proposition – a once in a lifetime event.

Jarad was anxious. Not because he would soon be carrying twenty or thirty pounds of high explosives on his back. Rather, it was what their dilemma would be if these explosives failed. Genis admitted that he had never set up or set off explosives. He had no training in their use. He had always been an observer. But Benson said that he could help him rig up the electrical charge necessary to set off the blasting caps. Benson, too, had worked at the quarry on occasion and did a lot of metal fabrication work for them. He was also confident that they could pull off the demolition of the bridge. "It's not rocket science," he gruffly told a doubtful Jarad. "You set out the explosives, you add the blasting caps, you hardwire them to a battery and "kaboom," down comes the bridge. Simple as that." Jarad hoped so! This had to work; otherwise they were in serious trouble. There was no plan B and tomorrow was the day!

The metal shed was an old Quonset hut from who-knows-how many years ago and though the door was secured with a pair of dead bolts, it could not resist the railroad tie the men used as a battering ram. The shed was filled with boring machines, spare parts, explosives, and sundry other items used in quarry mining. Genis pointed out what he wanted and counted out the number of cases needed. He also grabbed a couple cases of blasting caps, wiring and a small white box that he called detonator.

The men loaded up their backpacks, but the material was quite bulky and heavy. Genis also heard a few men mutter whispers of trepidation about carrying high explosives on their backs. Genis just laughed at them. "It's perfectly safe," he assured them. He then dropped to the floor the case he was holding. "BOOM!" he yelled, as the men all jumped. One screamed. Genis laughed so hard he had to sit down.

They resumed filling their packs, chiding each other for being afraid. They took what they could and left a lot behind, though most of it was probably not usable as Genis grabbed all of the blasting caps.

The trip back was slower but no less exciting. Now that they had the explosives, the demolition of the bridge was that much closer. Jimmy and Cameron spent the entire time describing what was to come, trying to outdo the other with outlandish possibilities. They were having a good time, hardly feeling the weight that they were carrying.

Jarad, too, contemplated the task before them. He knew that destroying the bridge would not solve all of their problems. The rail bed was still an access point and he was sure that Bronsky would direct his men down this route again, assuming the bridge became inoperable. He was not sure that they could do to stymie movement along the rails, but he hoped that something could be done. He was out of ideas.

All the men were tired from hauling the heavy weights. They had to stop once on the return route so people could get a respite from their loads. But while they were still a good distance from their destination, they began to hear gunfire in the distance, toward the town. The men began to hurry their pace, their packs bouncing on their backs. The closer they got near Junction the louder the shots became, intensifying everyone's concern. It became clear that they were approaching a firefight.

"What the hell!" Jarad shouted out as he realized the implications of what was occurring. But when they finally approached the town it became apparent where the action was. He and the others ran down the highway toward the bridgehead, their rifles raised to the ready. Ahead, he saw one man kneeling down and taking a shot across the bridge. Other gunfire emanated to his left, out of sight.

When Jarad neared the bridge he spotted Peter directing

men, all of whom were hunkered down in defensive positions. When Peter turned and saw Jarad and the others approach, he shouted at them and gave the motion for them to get down to protect themselves. The distinctive sound of bullets whizzing overhead explained why, causing Jarad and those near him to flinch. Jarad felt his bowels move. He really, really hated being shot at.

"What's going on," he asked as he moved close to Peter. Peter set an arm on his shoulder and spoke into his ear, trying to get above the din of rifle fire.

"The raiders are here a day early. I suspect that Bronsky got wind of our little maneuver and realized that his man spilled the beans, so he evidently wanted to get a jump on us."

Jarad nodded and then looked across the bridge. The log barricade that was to be shifted toward the center of the span was only partially complete. Jarad would learn later that gun fire from raiders had sent the Luddite helpers scrambling. They would have to work with what they had, which wasn't much.

Genis looked across at the meager barrier he was supposed to set the explosives up against. He let loose a long chain of curses. He did not want to venture out onto the bridge. The thought of doing so sent a shudder down his back, but he would. He had the men set their explosives-laden backpacks behind an old concrete Jersey barrier to protect them from an errant bullet. He had also sent Jimmy to get a specific wheeled dolly from Benson's shop. He had a plan. He went over to Jarad and Peter and told them what he had in mind.

"I'm gonna stack the explosives onto a cart and push them out to the far barrier. I think that there's enough cover to allow me to do what I need to do. I'll need you to figure out some sort of coverage so I can make a dash out there without getting shot. Can you do that?" he asked. Peter shouted at him something about quadrants. He said fine and then scooted back in a near crawl to the Jersey barrier. It would serve as his bunker while he assembled the wiring for the explosives.

It took a few minutes, but Jimmy finally returned with the low heavy cart. "Perfect," Genis told him as he looked up from his work, his helmet tilted jauntily, like a scene out a World War II picture book. He was splicing wires. "Does your father know that you're here?" he asked sternly. Jimmy ignored him, pretending to not hear. He was watching the action unfold on the bridge. Genis looked around himself for another volunteer and saw a likely candidate in John Everson, a member of the town committee. "John," he shouted above the din. The man turned when he heard his name being called. He saw Genis, who motioned him over with his head.

"John," he said when the man got near, "help me out by emptying those packs and stacking the cases onto that dolly. Can you do that for me?" The man nodded and went right to work. Within five minutes he had a stack of explosives assembled on the dolly, ready to go. Genis opened the top case and exposed the sticks of explosives and began preparing them for use. He was attaching the blasting caps.

Jarad came over to check on him. "How much longer, Genis?" he asked. Genis by now was unrolling wire. He looked at his handiwork and shrugged. "Two minutes," he said.

He was done even sooner than that. He tried to pull the cart, but it was too heavy. Seeing his predicament, John came over and between the two of them they were able to maneuver it. Ready, Genis signaled to Peter, who shouted at the men. Peter had organized them into quadrants, each handful of men responsible for a specific section of the far bridge. When he gave the command, these men would open up a barrage of covering fire, keeping the raiders pinned down while Genis and John pulled the cart into position.

Peter shouted, "Ready…fire!" A burst of gun fire exploded from the ranks of the Junction line, like a Civil War reenactment. The guns on the opposite end of the bridge fell silent, though no one on the Junction side could hear that.

John and Genis made for the center of the bridge. They completely disregarded the danger they were in, they simply pushed and pulled as fast as they could, Genis holding his helmet down with his free hand. Within moments they were behind the barrier, both lying down, the cart of explosives between them, Genis working furiously with the wiring. Peter had stopped the covering fire. The men needed to save ammunition. They were not finished yet.

No sooner had Peter spoken when he heard the distinctive mechanical sound of a tracked vehicle approaching. Everyone stared down the length of the bridge to see a large, black machine slowly approaching the bridge, its exhaust letting loose puffs of black and blue smoke. Everyone realized that they were looking at the "tank" that they had been warned about. It was a monster bulldozer with metal plating covering the radiator, engine cowling, and the cab. *Klack, klack, klack* it sounded, its engine roaring as it came down the highway and began to cross onto the bridge. Its flanks were covered with spray-painted Aryan-nation swastikas.

"Oh, my lord!" Jarad exclaimed. "How do we stop that?"

Emma and Myla had just appeared, coming up to Jarad with the approach of the tank. He jumped as Myla laid a hand on him. "What the hell…you're gonna get shot!" he shouted at them, pulling them both down. "Why are you here?" he asked them, severely.

"Why are you here?" Myla retorted. "We've come to help." Jarad sighed, angry, but he knew Myla would not budge. He moved them back to a more protected position, but the sound of the tank drew their collective attention. All of them could not help but watch the monster machine slowly working itself toward the barrier, its wide and heavy plow down and scrapping the road surface, making a horrendous scraping sound, like some demonic creature. It was apparent to everyone that the barrier was no match for the tank.

Jarad got an idea and turned to his wife. "We need Molotov cocktails," he told her urgently. He explained to the two women what they were and how they were made. "Can you make some up, quick like?" he asked, his eyes betraying his fear. He knew that what he had planned would take all the courage he could muster.

They said they could. Myla turned to Cameron and Jimmy and told them to go find some sort of fuel, anything that would burn – gasoline, diesel; she didn't care what it was. They took off quickly. The women talked for a brief moment and they too headed off, though in different directions.

All four had returned within a minutes and were soon making bombs. Emma had scavenged a case of vinegar bottles from the pantry, pouring out the contents on to the ground. They were the only glass bottles she could think of. The boys then filled them with gasoline from a small plastic fuel can. The gasoline was chainsaw fuel. Myla then stuffed the filled bottles with cotton rags that she had scavenged from dish towels and t-shirts. The majority of the cloth hung out of the throat of the bottles. She then doused the fabric with same fuel.

"Jarad," she shouted at her husband, who had gone forward to sit next to Peter. When he looked at her she held up of the bombs. He rushed over and grabbed four of them. "Are these right?" she asked.

"I don't know," he said quickly, "I've never made them

before. I'm sure that they work," he said before heading back to Peter. Peter had passed the word along to prepare the men for another volley of covering fire. He looked at Jarad as he shouted out his command, nodding for him to go. Another enfilade of rifle fire erupted as Jarad dashed forward in a crouch, his arms holding tightly his homemade grenades.

Jarad headed directly for Genis and John. They had completed their task and were ready to return, but were now waiting on Jarad. They had heard the tank, but had not dared to peek above the log barricade. Jarad arrived and kneeled next to John, carefully setting down his cargo. He needed room to maneuver.

He pulled a lighter from his pocket, grabbing one of the glass grenades. He peered over the barricade, quickly scanning the terrain in front of him before pulling his head back down. He had seen what he needed to see. Lighting one of the rags, he threw the homemade grenade overhead as far as he could. He then did the same with the other three. He turned to signal Peter, his hands to his side, palms up. He was asking how it looked. Peter gave him an okay sign and the three men then saw Peter raise his hand. They could not hear his voice, but they did hear and feel the subsequent barrage that resulted. Jarad, John, and Genis made a dash for safety.

John immediately fell, one of his feet tangled in the wiring. Genis and Jarad quickly stopped, returned, and both of them pulled him up by the arms in a single smooth motion. The three men then ran quickly back to the far end of the bridge, Genis unrolling great loops of wiring as he went. He slid behind the concrete barrier and quickly attaching the wires to the white box – the detonator. He flicked the safety switch, gave the signal, and then stabbed the large red plunger with the heel of his hand. The silence was deafening. Nothing happened!

Genis jumped up, enraged, his hands clenched at his sides. He looked across the bridge toward the stack of explosives, wondering what had gone wrong. But a moment later he collapsed to the ground, causing Emma to scream out his name and rush to his side. A bullet had deflected off of his helmet, saving his life but knocking him unconscious.

John knew what had happened. He realized that his foot had tugged pretty hard on the wire, probably pulling it out from the charge. He rushed over to Peter and explained. Peter nodded his head and raised his hand again, shouting at his men. With the third barrage, John rushed back toward the center of the bridge, but halfway to his goal he again tumbled down. Propping himself up on an elbow, he reached toward his leg and felt with his hand. Holding it up, it saw it soaked in red. John had been hit in the leg with a bullet.

Jared made a move to go be with him, but Peter grabbed his sleeve and pointed at the wounded man. He was waving at them that he was alright and they watched him painfully crawl the rest of the way to the stack of explosives, placing himself tightly up against the cart. Jarad and others stared anxiously at the scene as the tank, which had been temporarily rebuffed by the curtain of fire caused by the Molotov cocktails, had realized the lack of threat this effort posed and soon resumed its relentless course toward the barrier.

The tank met and easily pushed the first and then second wrecked automobiles that served as the vanguard of the barrier. Forcing them forward, the tank advanced on the wooden structure. When the weight of the cars met the barrier there was a brief halt in the tanks advance, as its treads dug into the road surface for traction. A huge cloud of black exhaust curled upward and the driver of the tank forced the tank forward against the resistance. The logs could not resist and in a lurch the entire barrier slowly began to move backward and toward John, who seemed strangely indifferent to the impending threat. He continued to work on the wiring.

He had evidently found the problem and corrected it, because in a thunderclap the entire span disintegrated, showering the immediately area in dust and debris. Even the tank could not resist the force and it was tossed backward onto its roof, finally resting upside down on a precipice of shattered concrete.

Gun fire came to an immediate halt, replaced with the sounds of coughing and hurrahs. The cheering continued until people suddenly comprehended the price that John Everson had just paid for his community. It was not realized until later that when Genis had been knocked unconscious, the detonator had remained primed. John had reattached a live wire to the priming charge, creating a circuit – a circuit which ended both his life and the life of the bridge.

Jarad and the others stood dazed, not only by the explosion but by John's sacrifice. Everyone had seen much death in the past few months, but no one had seen anything like this. The initial joy over the destruction of the bridge was soon replaced by a sense of loss and a lament over John's death. This cast a pall over any thought of celebration at their victory.

The raiders were stunned. For the second time they had been resoundingly defeated. Most began to leave, heading down the highway back to Purcell. A recalcitrant few fired off shots towards Junction, as if in defiance to their obvious failure. Others helped wounded comrades, evacuating them to the rear. But before long, no one remained. Only the dead.

*

Surprisingly, the only death was that of John. A few suffered from gun shot wounds, but none of them serious. Genis had regained his consciousness, but was suffering from a serious headache. He rued the fact that he had missed the explosion. But he had held back some explosive charges and blasting caps in reserve. He knew he would need it later.

Elaine did not take news of her husband's death well. She was already bereft of her children, both of whom had long lived out of state and whom she had lost contact with, and now she was alone. She had heard the explosion, which drew her and others to the bridge. But she did not realize the heroic role John played until Peter told her. She was wondering why everyone was staring at her after she first arrived.

Now she wanted to be alone. She returned to her house, followed by Myla and Emma – all of them in tears. Myla and Emma feared for the worst. A typical outcome of John's death would be for Elaine to kill herself. That was how most people dealt with loneliness since the collapse of the grid. But she told both women that she just wanted to be alone, to cry, and to come to grips with her new reality. She promised not to do anything rash.

The Luddites, too, were impacted by the destruction of the bridge and the violence that led up to it. The firefight between the two groups and the destruction of the bridge confirmed their religious belief that the outside world was insane and that non-Luddites would always use their technology to kill others. They neither witnessed the destruction of the bridge, nor cared to see it. They remained in their homes.

Many of the Junction people lingered for a long time at the foot of the bridge. The destruction of the span and the subsequent break in the link to the highway on the other side had a profound effect on their psyches. It was as if many of them were coming to grips with the enormity of their situation, that they were now even more isolated from Purcell. This was both good – they now felt safer than they had in months – and bad – they had severed a link with the outside world.

Myla and Jarad returned home. Jarad was exhausted from the day and he wanted nothing more than to rest and think of different things. A game of cards was the perfect remedy. Plus, the death of John was unsettling. Jarad kept seeing in his mind's eye the struggling figure lying awkwardly and painfully on the bridge, working furiously to repair the electrical circuit that ensured his death. John seemed oblivious to the danger posed by the tank, intent on one thing: getting the wire repaired for the explosives. The more Jarad considered it, the more convinced he had become that John knew that the explosives would detonate. The thought sobered him.

As he sat with his wife at the small table in their "home," Jarad knew something was eating at his wife. She seemed pensive, as if her mind was filled with different thoughts while she made small talk with her husband.

"Okay, Myla, what's up?" he asked her with a chuckle while dealing out the cards. "I can tell that you're thinking about something. Is it the baby?"

She looked up from her hand and crinkled her eyebrows, her face a bit dour. "Yes," she said, "I mean no...yes and no." She snorted softy through her nose. "Sort of...I guess both."

Jarad smiled again. "That's clear as mud," he said teasingly. I'm glad you know your own mind." He laughed again, trying to prompt his wife into smiling, but it was not working. She was getting upset.

He set down his cards and pushed the cribbage board to the side. He had his wife do the same and then he took both of her hands into his own from across the table. Then he told her to close her eyes and he would read her mind. She sighed heavily, which told Jarad that she was not in the mood for a silly game. But he insisted, so to make him happy she closed her eyes and waited on him.

Jarad started to play the role of soothsayer, trying to sound mysterious. "I see darkness…long roads ahead…traveling…hope in the distance…many miles to Alberta…"

"Jarad!" she shouted and pulled her hands away, and then reached over and slapped him playfully on the arm. She was trying to look hurt by again furrowing her brows, but the twinkle in her eyes and an irrepressible little smile betrayed her. "How'd you know!" she insisted.

He played along and gave her a smug look, but then reached over and grabbed her hands again. "Because we're thinking the same thoughts. Cameron told me all about the radio and what he shared with you – and what you told him. I think it is pretty obvious that Alberta is where we need to be."

She smiled, relief written all over her face. She picked up her cards and repositioned the cribbage board between them. She reviewed her hand and tossed two to the side. "My crib," she reminded him. She then paused and looked deeply into his eyes. "I love you, my special man," she said softly.

Jarad tossed two more cards onto her pair. "I know you do, baby," he said. "And I love you, too." He laid down a card face up. It was a jack. "Ten," he said.

She looked at her cards before tossing out an eight. "Eighteen," she responded. "So when do you want to leave?"

He followed up with another jack. "Twenty-eight," he said. "Tomorrow isn't soon enough."

She immediately followed his face card with a four. "Thirty-one, my points, and I couldn't agree with you more."

Chapter 7

Otty was normally a very optimistic person; indeed, sometimes to a fault. He was a man of faith and he acted out that faith everyday, with every person, and in every situation he seemed to encounter. This practice had served him in good stead, especially in regards to the last few months. Then he had to endure the collapse of society as he knew it, physical threats upon his own life, deprivation, even the suicide of his daughter. But now, that faith was being challenged like it had never before. It was not that he did not believe God could help them, he just did not understand how – for as far as he could see, they had hit the wall.

"I want to begin our meeting today to express my gratitude to all involved in the destruction of the bridge yesterday. It solved one of our most pressing problems," Otty began. Others seconded his words and that moment of victory was savored again by the people present. When the murmuring waned, he resumed his dialogue.

"Jarad," he said, nodding in his direction, "and Benson gave us some breathing room. Were it not for their efforts to bring down that food from the Dome, we would be in dire straights. But now, instead of a food supply counted in weeks, we can count it in months."

"But," he continued, "and that is a very big but, again, we only have a food supply of a few months. And that is still with padding it with whatever we can continue to scrounge up or harvest from the land around us. It doesn't change our fundamental situation.

We are going to run out of food. And now with the Luddites..." He paused. People knew what the Luddites represented: more mouths to feed and consequently less food for later.

"Then let's boot 'em out," Serena said emphatically. Serena was filling in for Elaine, who was not up to meeting with the committee so soon after her husband's death. Serena had sat on the committee until just a few weeks ago, when she gave up her chair to Elaine. This was a common practice and allowed for everyone to have an opportunity to serve on the board. "We didn't invite 'em," she continued, "like we did the Blue River folks and we aren't obligated to take care of 'em. And they bring nothing to the table. They're just a bunch of polygamist pagans anyhow!"

Otty discretely sighed. He did not like such talk. Serena was right, the Luddites were pagans, in that they worshiped the earth, personified as Gaea, and they did practice polygamy. But they were also human beings. Otty would never condone forcing them out, and now he had to state that clearly and kill this idea before it gained currency.

"No," he said a bit more forcefully than was his custom. "That would not be very Christ-like. I don't agree with the customs and practices of the Luddites, as probably most of you don't agree, but they are still people, flesh and blood like you and me. No, we will simply have to find some other solution."

Serena did not agree with Otty and she conveyed this by entwining her arms and looking away. Otty knew that many people in the community would side with Serena on this issue. He just wished that he could formulate an idea, but his well had run dry it seemed.

Myla raised her voice; she had her own ideas. "Why can't we grow our own food? It is still early in the spring; we still have time to put in gardens. This seems like an obvious solution to me." Others nodded. Why could this not be done? Folks here routinely raised gardens.

Otty, too, had been giving this some thought and long ago realized that it was not as easy as it sounded. "Yes, we could and should grow some gardens. But our needs are more longer term than that. First off, it will be difficult to make it through the summer, let alone before our gardens were ready. But let's say that we did make it through the summer and we all raised gardens. Can we grow enough surplus to store? To get us through, what, six months of winter and then into the spring? And then through another summer? Our next harvest would not be for an entire year! Can we last that long? I doubt it. Second, can we preserve our extra food, assuming that there is enough to store? I talked with both John and Elaine about this just the other day and Elaine was of the opinion that there was not enough canning supplies to put up food for one family, let alone all of our families. So what do we do? Dry it? How can we preserve it? And what about grain? We would have no grain, no flour, no bread. It's not as if we're like the Luddites who can grow...." Otty stopped abruptly in mid-sentence. He stared at the far wall, as he wrestled with a thought. Slowly, his demeanor changed from one of despair to that of hopefulness. He actually smiled.

"May the Lord forgive me," he began, shaking his head. "I don't mind confessing to you folks that I thought that the good Lord had abandoned us. But instead, he had again provided for our care." He looked up at his friends, looking into their eyes. "Can't you see it? The Luddites aren't the problem, they're the solution. The Luddites can grow more food than they can eat. The Luddites can help *us*!"

It took a moment for Otty's words to settle in, but then a general sigh of understanding rose from the table. Even Serena had to admit that he was right. A new sense of optimism began to permeate the people, as well as one of relief. Hope was at hand and life would continue. As Otty had pointed out earlier, the destruction of the bridge solved one big problem, but it didn't solve their most pressing problem. It now appeared that even this most important problem of all finally had a solution.

It went without saying that the people of Junction began to look at the Luddites with new eyes. Before, they were accepted as odd little folks, who dressed like the Amish and eschewed anything that was powered, whether by electricity or fuel. In fact, their religious tenets viewed such things as evil. Instead, they worshiped the earth, viewing it as their mother. Their community had evolved from a radical interpretation – and implementation – of the early environmental movement from the 1960s, beginning as communes and then, in time, into full-fledged colonies of farmers. They grew or raised everything they needed and sold the surplus, converting the cash into more land. They were ardent pacifists, a policy which did not always serve them well, and which led some people to take advantage of their gentle nature. They were also separatists and viewed the outside world with fear and mistrust. They were good neighbors, but exceedingly private. They were indifferent toward government, but did pay their taxes. And as polygamy was legalized many years previously, they no longer had to hide that aspect of their world.

The meeting had come to such a high note that Myla and Jarad did not want to ruin it by sharing their plans to leave Junction and travel to Alberta. Instead, as the meeting adjourned they motioned for Otty to stay behind so they could talk to him privately. This was a common thing – Otty was always in demand, so no one thought anything more of the matter. After everyone had left, Jarad broke the news. "We're leaving, Otty. We want to head for Alberta."

They explained their reasoning to him. After his initial shock, he nodded in understanding, though disappointment was evident on his face. But he understood. "If I were in your shoes I would probably make the same decision," he consoled them. "Still, that is going to be quite a trip. It is a long ways to Alberta. But we'll help in anyway we can." The men shook hands and as Otty turned to leave, he told the two of them to let Peter know their plans. "I think that he'd find this news very interesting. I can't tell you any more than that, but I think that you should talk with him." Jarad promised him that he would. Jarad and Myla were filled with ambivalence: glad to have shared the news, but saddened about leaving the community for a second time. And both regretted the disappointment on Otty's face. They felt that they owed a great debt to both him and the people of Junction. But that did not change their minds; they still needed to go.

They were also curious about Otty's recommendation in regards to Peter. "We have nothing going on this morning, let's go see him." Myla said. Jarad agreed, so as they left the community center they steered themselves in the direction of Peter's house. Peter had been at the meeting, but he had had wandered away with everyone else. Myla and Jarad assumed he would have returned to his house. He had, and he let them in with a knock.

"Welcome," he said with honest delight. "I'm so glad you've come by for a visit. Can I get you some tea...I mean, coffee? Now that we got coffee again," he said with a wink to Jarad.

Peter Rafferty was a small man, older – in his early sixties – but active and robust. He was not married, but Jarad did not know if he had been in his past. He also did not seem to have any children; at least, he never referred to any. What Jarad did know was that he had some military training, which Jarad assumed to be as an officer, and he had retired from Homeland Security. Other than that he knew little more. He did respect Peter and found him to be fearless, but also accommodating. He could lead men, but did not always need to be the one in command. He always seemed to see the big-picture and kept things in perspective. That included himself; he was a modest man.

They sat at the kitchen table as Peter boiled up some water on the wood stove. The house was very neat. Peter did not live like the stereotypical bachelor. He also shaved regularly, if not everyday, one of the few men in Junction to keep up the practice.

He chatted about Myla's children, commenting especially about how bravely Cameron performed the other day at the bridge. He did notice. He also inquired about Annie's health, for he was also aware of how she had been brutalized by the invader at the Dome. He sighed deeply as he, for a moment, tried to imagine how frightful that whole affair must have been. Without realizing it he had patted Myla's hand in sympathy. When the teapot whistled he dismissed himself to make coffee. He poured the water into a meticulously clean coffee press before returning to his guests.

"So, what brings you two to come and visit this old man?" he asked with his gentle though piercing blue eyes.

"We were talking to Otty after the meeting this morning and...we shared with him some...important news," Jarad began, a bit hesitantly, "and he suggested that we come share it with you." Before Peter could so much as nod in acknowledgment, Myla got right to the point. "We're going to Alberta," she said matter-of-fact. "He thought that this fact might interest you."

"Cut to the chase, eh Myla?" He laughed. "Ah, Alberta." He paused as he considered that. "Why, Alberta, might I ask?"

"I'm pregnant," Myla responded. She explained that she delivered her first two kids – the twins – via c-section. She knew as a nurse that a normal birth after a c-section could be problematic. "I don't mind having a birth the old-fashion way. In fact, I'd prefer it. But I can't risk a ruptured uterus. Quite honestly, that is a death sentence for both me and my child. And the thought terrifies me," she admitted. She shuddered almost imperceptibly. She took Jarad's hand and clenched it firmly. This was the first Jarad had heard about her fears. He knew the facts, but he had not known the fears. He squeezed her hand in return.

"That's both wise and understandable," Peter agreed. "So how are we going to get there?"

"We?" Jarad replied. "Is that a rhetorical 'we' or an 'us' we? Do you want to go to Alberta, too?"

"Yes, me too," he said softly. "I've got friends there and I've got family there...a son." He explained that he had once lived with a woman for many years, but they never contracted in marriage. They had one child, a boy also named Peter. But in time the two of them sort of drifted away from each other and it was only a matter of time before they separated. She left him, moved across the country, and then followed some fellow back to Alberta. His son now lived there. He is married, has a family... "In fact, I was getting set to go visit him and then I slipped on that ice and ended up in the hospital with a broken butt bone!"

"Coccyx," Myla laughed. She remembered that well. That was the first time she had met him, right before they had to flee Purcell. It was also where Peter and Jarad got reacquainted. Jarad had not remembered him, but Peter remembered Jarad.

"I've been wanting to, even planning to, visit Alberta ever since." He cocked his head and gave Myla an inquisitive look.

"Why still, why Alberta? Why did you decide on Alberta?"

Myla told Peter the story about the wind-up radio that her son had discovered at the Dome. "I think that it's more of a toy than anything, but he did get it to work and the strongest stations, in fact the only stations, came out of Alberta. To me, that says a lot."

"Yes, you're probably right. One would assume that if things were fine elsewhere, you would've picked them up on the radio as well. I never thought of that."

He changed the subject and began to talk about a map. "I got a route planned out. Want to see it?" he asked, hope shading his eyes.

"Absolutely," Jarad said. "Absolutely, please!"

As he fetched his map Peter rambled on about how he had not kept it a secret that he was eventually going to Alberta, it had always come down to when. "We've been busy, haven't we?" he said to his guests as he retook his seat. "Especially since you folks moved here. You must've brought the excitement with you."

He opened up the road atlas to a well-read section. He traced with his finger a route that had long been analyzed and considered. Peter had invested a lot of time and thought in his plan. "It's about 400 miles if we go by road, but I would like to avoid the roads. Too dangerous," he said, laying out the path and indicating the highways they could take. Jarad seconded his thoughts about the highways. They would be dangerous, far too dangerous to traverse. But that would only leave the railway. The rails also had the advantage of having gentler grades.

Jarad mentioned that. "So, that leaves the rails, I suppose." Peter nodded silently and knowingly.

"Not only that, but it is far more direct path. Look..." he said, again outlining the route with his finger. There was a faint line on the map that looked like a road but was far more direct toward their destination – almost directly east and west.

"So how many miles by the tracks?" Jarad asked?

"Three hundred," he responded, "more or less."

"That's still a long ways," Jarad lamented. He shook his head and glanced at his wife. "Especially for a pregnant woman." He quickly calculated in his head that if they could make fifteen miles a day, which was asking a lot, it would still take them 20 days. Could they carry enough food, he wondered.

Peter sat back and looked at Jarad. "What kind of car you got?" he asked him.

Jarad and Myla both looked at him, quizzically. That's an odd question, he thought, but he answered anyway. "A Chevy," he said.

"Chevy what?" Peter asked again. "A big Chevy, small Chevy, fat Chevy, skinny Chevy…what? There're a lot of Chevys."

"A Chevy Volt," he responded, "A station wagon, second generation. Kind of older…"

"Perfect!" Peter said. "A newer one would be too small." He snorted, "Everything is getting smaller."

"Why do you ask about our car?" Myla wondered aloud. "You yourself said that the highways were too dangerous."

He pointed his finger at her for emphasis. "Myla I've thought about this again and again. And this'll sound crazy to you, but I've seen it done….more than once." He recalled for them that he had served in the US Army; his last tour of duty was in Syria during the Third Gulf War. "Or maybe it was the Fourth or the Fifth," he said sarcastically. "But this became a means of travel on the rails." He explained how one guy got the idea of driving his car on the rails. He had taken off the tires and set the car directly on the wheels, each wheel straddling a rail. "They went like stink and you don't have to steer! Pretty soon, you'd see them everywhere. Even the hostiles were using them."

"And even if we can't use your car, we can find one with the right dimensions. The wider the wheel the better. It only has to span the rails, whether it rides on the center or the outer or inner edge of the wheel – it just doesn't matter,'" he repeated with cadence. "The point is, with a full tank and a full charge on the capacitors, we could easily make that run in a single day."

A single day! That sounded like a miracle to both Jarad and Myla. There was one glaring problem though: fuel. The Chevy had about a fourteen or fifteen gallon tank. That was a huge amount of fuel.

"Diesel," Jarad said. "We need a lot of fuel."

"That's the caveat," Peter agreed. "We can't even think about leaving until we can scrounge up the fuel."

They talked a little more as they finished their coffee. They were all hopeful, but understood that nothing was going to be easy.

"Plus, we got to deal with the Luddites," Jarad reminded him.

"Yes, I suppose it would be unseemly to leave the people of Junction until that problem was settled, too." Peter agreed. "But," he said, tapping his temple with a finger, "we got a plan. Let's keep it under our hats for now."

"Umm…" Jarad paused. "Can I let Benson know? He's sort of the keeper of the fuel. The truck we used to get that food out of the Dome still has some in its tank – we didn't use it all because the fuel pump failed and we were able to top off the charge on the truck at the Dome. Maybe I can convince him to let me have what's left."

Peter hemmed and hawed. "I suppose so. But I don't know

how cooperative he'll be. I guess it's worth a shot. And we gotta let people know sometime. Besides Benson, let's not tell anyone else…yet."

"Agreed," both Myla and Jarad said. They got up to leave.

*

Jarad went in search of Benson, and was surprised to not find him at his shop. That seemed to be the only place the man ever went. He was not at his home neither. Unsure where to turn next, he was finally directed to the man by a neighbor who had seen him earlier that morning, walking out toward the truck with his toolbox in hand. As Jarad approached the truck out the road leading to Blue River, he could see the hood raised in the distance. He found his man.

But Benson was not under the hood; instead Jarad could only see the man's two legs sticking out from under the left rear of the truck. Jarad called to him.

"Hey Benson, how's it going under there? What'd you find out on the truck?" he called out, squatting down along side the truck.

Benson did not move, but kept on doing whatever it was he was doing. "Doggone fuel pump. Just what I'd thought it would be." He stopped and dragged himself out from under the truck. He had been lying on cardboard – an opened and extended piece of what had once been a large box, now spread under the truck to protect him from the dampness and the snow underneath. He sat up.

"It's electric, so that makes it easier to replace. I can probably swap it out with just about any pump I can scavenge from any one of the rigs parked around here. With any luck, I'll have this thing going in a day or two," he said, wiping his hands on an old tattered piece of cloth. He winked at Jarad. "Then you and me can go get that trailer and the rest of the food. Wouldn't that be something," he said with enthusiasm.

Jarad smiled weakly at him, though his eyes did not join in. That was not what he was hoping to hear. Actually, as he hiked out the half mile to the truck he was hoping to find Benson in a foul mood, indicating that he was not able to get the truck up and running. But the opposite had occurred; Benson would have it back on the road.

"That's great, Benson," Jarad said, trying to sound sincere. "But I was hoping to ask a favor of you, but I suppose it's a moot point now."

"What's that?" he asked, sitting back against a tire and taking a break. He looked at Jarad and cocked his head slightly to the side, curious.

"I wanted to siphon out the fuel from the truck. I need it for a special trip," he said. He went on to explain his plans about Alberta, mentioning that Peter was going to come along too. They planned on leaving as soon as he could find some fuel.

Benson seemed less than impressed. "So what you're saying is that you're gonna bail on Junction a second time? Is that it? Leave us to fend for ourselves? Again?" He shook his head negative and stared past Jarad, as if not even seeing him. "Nope, not this time. I ain't gonna help ya," he said. "This fuel is for the people of Junction. And I'm gonna use it to get that food. I'm not gonna let it be wasted on you 'cause you wanna get the hell outta here." He looked at Jarad in the eyes with anger and defiance. "We all want to get outta here," he whispered. "Now if you had a plan for that, maybe I'd help. But I ain't gonna help you to turn your back on everybody else." With that he spat on the ground and crawled back under the truck.

Jarad felt himself slipping into a rage. He grabbed the cuffs of Benson's legs and pulled him out from under the truck with a lurch. He then grabbed him by the lapels of his coveralls and picked him up to a standing position, shoving his face practically against the old man's whiskered grimace.

"Listen to me, you bastard," he shouted. "I am not turning my back on no one, you hear me? But I sure as hell am not gonna let my wife die by hanging around here and twiddling my thumbs, because of pompous asses like you."

Jarad released his grip, resisting an impulse to push him to the ground. He stared at the man for a moment longer and then turned on his heels and headed back toward Junction. He was done, now more than ever determined to leave – and to leave for good. He only needed to find the fuel.

*

"So the sun's going down…show me how this thing works," Jarad said, handing the radio to his son. Jarad knew he could probably figure out how to use the radio himself, but he also recognized that his son was proud about discovering the radio and figuring out how it worked. Jarad was simply being a good father and helping his son find success. And he needed a positive distraction after his confrontation with Benson earlier in the day.

Cameron took the radio from his father and deftly pulled the little crank out from the end of it. He then gave it a measured number of spins before folding it back into its original position. It seemed to disappear. He then pulled out the long, collapsible metal antenna. He looked about himself to find the largest window and he moved to that side of the room, positioning the antenna toward the glass and seating himself on the small couch positioned underneath it. He had already found a few favorite stations, which he had added to the radio's channel memory, setting them up as pre-set stations. Whenever he pushed in the pre-set code a new station would come live on the speaker. He could change pre-set stations or search for new ones. After watching him a bit, Jarad changed his mind. He realized that he would have quickly lost patience trying to work the contraption. This gave him a new appreciation for his son.

"Wow, you're amazing," he said, giving him a push on the shoulder. Cameron smiled as he rocked on the seat because of his father playful handling, but not taking his eyes or hands off of the radio. He was enjoying himself showing his father the radio. He knew it was more difficult than it looked, but he was patient with such things.

"Pick a station and let's listen. It's been a long time since I've sat and listened to a radio." He moved closer to his son, sharing the small couch with him, his arm around his son's shoulders. He listened keenly to the broadcast. It was an advertisement for a restaurant – a steak house! Oh, how he wanted to be there! The thought of a big, juicy, sizzling steak was almost too much for him. "How'd you like to go out for a steak? Wouldn't that be sweet?" he asked him.

His son's eyes grew big as he pondered his father's question. "Don't I wish!" he said. "And I'd like to play hockey, too….that's what I'd like to do."

"Hockey? Why hockey?" his father asked. He had never before shown interest in any sport, especially hockey. Jarad rolled his eyes mockingly. "Hockey!" he repeated.

"I've been listening to the games every night. They're having junior hockey play offs in Calgary. Kids just a little older than me. That'd be cool."

"What else is there to listen to?" his father asked. Cameron selected the strongest signals, which he knew by heart. There really were not that many choices available and most of them were not all that interesting – just what a person would expect to find on the public airwaves. There were a few stations dedicated to music of various types, one to sports, and a couple more that seemed general interest or talk shows. What Jarad found the most compelling about these stations was how "normal" they were. He now better understood Myla's desire to go to Alberta. It seemed like a place that had been spared the tumult of his world. People were attending hockey games in Calgary! That meant participants and spectators, which meant movement and commerce…and electricity.

"That is really cool," he said to his son. "Good job!" His son beamed at his affirmation. Cameron was getting big, Jarad had to admit. In fact, he seemed to be getting older, quicker. Such were the times and there was little Jarad could do about it. This is the world his children had inherited.

"Tell me, are all the stations from Alberta. Can you find any stations that are not from Alberta?" he asked his son. Jarad understood that these local stations had a limited range, and it was only because of an atmospheric effect that he really didn't understand – and which came into play only after the sun fell behind the horizon – they even received these broadcasts from Alberta. But there were other places just as close as Alberta – British Columbia, Washington, Montana, and a handful of other adjoining states – that should be as readily accessible on this radio. But they were absent. It was this absence of radio stations that Jarad found as important as the ones that they were listening to right now.

"I want to go to Alberta and so does mom," Cameron said. He looked over at his father, searching his eyes. Jarad knew that Cameron wanted his opinion on the matter.

"Well, we gotta go, you know that," he told his son. Instead of being excited, he simply acknowledged with a nod what his father had just said. Both Cameron and Annie were well aware of their mother's condition and her need to bare the baby in a hospital. And they both understood the necessity of the upcoming trip, as well as the perils it posed for them. But he was still ready and willing to go.

"I can't wait," he said honestly. "I'm ready when you are." He snuggled closer to his father, whether as a show of support for the decisions his father and mother had to make, or because the thought of the upcoming journey worried him. Or perhaps both. Jarad could not know, but he relished this intimacy with his child. He loved them both so very much. He wished that he did not have to drag them through the potentially perilous situations ahead, but he had no other choice. They were a family and families shared such things, together.

"How far away is Alberta," he asked his dad. "And how are we gonna get there? Walk?"

He explained to Cameron what his mother and he had discussed with Peter Rafferty. The boy's eyes lit up with the prospect of driving their car down the railroad tracks. He found it humorous. But then his countenance became more serious when his father told them the entire trip, at least at this point, was delayed until they could find enough diesel fuel to fill the tank of their car. He knew that the lack of fuel was a problem in Junction, or else they would not have left that food behind in the dome.

"I know where we can find diesel dad!" Cameron practically yelled. "I bet that there is a ton of it there, too!"

His dad didn't respond. He was not sure if Cameron was being serious or just jabbering nonsense like a boy. His hunch was the latter, so he played the patsy. "And where might that be?" he asked in mock somberness.

"Seriously, dad, I know where fuel is. I kept waiting for that thing to explode, but it never did. Then James told me that diesel doesn't blow up like gasoline. So it's still there!"

"What are you talking about, son? What's still there…where?" he asked, now a bit more serious.

"The tank! That big tank-thing that the raiders made. When the bridge blew up the tank almost blew up too. I kept waiting for it to explode…" He made explosion noises with his mouth, fluttering his fingers to simulate debris thrown into the air. He dropped his hands and mimed dejection. "But it never did."

Jarad was without words. His son was right. There might be a hundred gallons of diesel in there; more than enough for himself and the community. "Hot damn!" he shouted, leaping to his feet and swinging a fist into the air. He gave Cameron an exceptionally long and tight hug

"You are brilliant!" he told the boy. He went out of the room to tell his wife, but he paused at the doorway. "Let's keep it a secret, okay?"

"Okay, dad," he said softly. Jarad knew that he could trust him.

***

Chapter 8

"I talked with Elder Jonathan and we discussed this at length and I've come to a decision," Otty said, his voice unusually assertive. "I'd like to handle this one myself."

Jarad blanched at Otty's words. "Does that mean what I think it means?" he thought to himself. But Peter beat Jarad to the question.

"What d'ya mean by 'handling this' yourself?" he asked. Peter's face was neutral and questioning. His intention was not to put Otty on the spot or to challenge him. He might disagree with Otty on occasion, but he had enough sense of self to discuss issues with him as they appeared. Otty accepted Peter's question for its face value.

Otty furrowed his eyebrows and held his breath, which was characteristic of him when he was carefully choosing his words. He knew that everyone in the room wanted to be involved in "rescuing" the Luddite colony from the squatters who had taken control of it. And, undoubtedly, all would be opposed to his plan, but he was determined to do this his way. That is, with minimum risk to the others. He had already discussed this with his wife Ellie…

"Hear me out before you respond," he said to the attentive eyes before him. He felt like a lord surrounded by his vassal knights, each willing to fight and defend him, each eager to do his bidding. But sometimes a lord has to fight his own battles. "Many of you in this room have willingly risked life and limb for our community. This is noble, indeed the noblest deed a person can do. As we are reminded in the Scriptures, that there is no greater love a man can have for his friends than to lay down his life for them. And some have paid that ultimate price, so that others of us didn't have to. That we could go on living. It's time that I'm the one who puts his life on the line."

"You wanna die?" James asked, taking his words literally. "You're confusing me, Otty. What are you saying?"

"No, gosh!" he said, shaking his head. He paused to get a fresh start. "I have a plan to get the squatters off of the Luddite property and to get the Luddites – as we've talked about – back on their farms and getting back to the work of raising food. But we need to act quickly."

He explained his plan. He wanted to take as many armed men as could be mustered, even any women that were willing. He wanted a highly visible show of force. He would lead the little army up to the colony, though they would avoid any direct fighting. The show of force was simply that, a show. He would be the one who would approach the squatters with a white flag and unarmed to explain to them that they needed to surrender.

Peter laughed out loud! Realizing his *faux pas* he turned bright red and was instantly apologetic, though he couldn't hide his amusement. "You're gonna ask them to surrender? Why would you be carrying the flag?"

"Good point," Otty acknowledged, smiling at the irony of his proposal. "Then let's call it a flag of truce. I got to get their attention and get them to talk with me. I got to carry something! They'll understand the white flag. I want to get them to understand that we are many and that they are few, that they can't hold the colony. If they're reasonable they'll understand that leaving the Luddite's place is their best bet. I'm going to try to convince them to leave – not surrender, but leave."

James raised his hand before speaking. It was one of his habits that many of the other committee members adopted. "And if they refuse to leave?" he asked, raising the question that was on everyone else's minds.

Otty shrugged. "I'm hoping it won't come down to that. If my plan goes as I hope, and pray, there won't be any need to find out that answer."

"So there's no plan B," James ventured.

"Sure there's a plan B," Otty countered. "But I just don't know what it is yet." He smiled again. He was confident his plan would work.

People began talking among themselves about Otty's plan, discussing the ins and outs of his proposal. They knew that Otty would be open to any suggestions.

Jarad now raised his hand. "We could offer them the Dome," he said. This suggestion brought all talking to a stop. He looked around himself as his words had gotten everyone's attention, but he did not as much as shrug. This was evidently not a popular suggestion.

"No, no, no! There's still a lot of food up there," said Benson emphatically. "I don't think that we should just throw it away." He sat back and crossed his arms, shaking his head as if in disbelief. "That would be dumb!" he barked.

Jarad's anger began to rise again in him, but he choked back a response. He also blushed, but with anger rather than embarrassment. He had avoided Benson when the group assembled, sitting as far from him as he could. He sat silent for a few moments before continuing.

"It's a carrot and a fair trade," he responded to everyone else

112 | Crossroad of Shadows

in the room and not directly to Benson. "Think about it: they get the Dome and what food remains there and we get the Luddite colony. And, no violence. They can leave and know that their situation won't be desperate, at least not in the short term."

Benson calmed down a bit. He hadn't considered that. Benson had become sufficiently jaded by the changes in the world that might did make right. Jarad was reminding him that there were alternate solutions.

Otty redirected the conversation. "That is my sentiment, too, Jarad. Everyone is just trying to survive. I think that these folks at the colony would be less inclined to leave if they were tossed out on the street, so to speak."

"So what's your time frame?" Peter asked. "I think that sooner is better than later."

"Yup, I agree. How about tomorrow?" Otty asked everyone in the room. No one objected so Otty ran with his initiative.

"Great," he said, "let's all meet here again shortly after sunrise, after everyone's had a chance to eat some breakfast. It'll be a long day. Oh, and everyone bring a gun; anything that'll make some noise, the louder the better." With that, he dismissed the group.

*

The day was clear but cold. The warming trend that had removed the last white traces of winter had apparently taken the day off. Myla had reluctantly agreed to allow Cameron to accompany his father to the colony. She rued that her son had to grow up in a world where violence was a solution, but she had no alternatives. Indeed, she herself had actively participated in violence – making Molotov cocktails. She just asked Jarad to make sure that he was safe and did not have to participate in any fighting. Jarad knew that Myla would not have a good day; she would not rest until Cameron was safely back in Junction.

Jarad had given Cameron a 22-caliber rifle to carry, the one that he had taken from the Junction raider whom he had captured before the bridge was destroyed. As far as firepower went, it was pretty meager, but the gun had heft to it and Cameron was pleased.

Jarad pondered the change in the weather as he and Cameron walked toward the rendezvous point. He thought that cooler weather was better than warmer, as they had a seven-mile hike ahead of them – each way. It would be better to not have to fight the heat, at least as much heat has could be expected at that latitude in early April. Anyhow, Jarad thought it was April. He was losing track of time, at least as it was formally measured out by a calendar.

Cameron was delighted to see Jimmy when they arrived at the community building. Jimmy was not only Annie's boyfriend, but he was developing into Cameron's best friend too. Jimmy was bearing a shotgun. His dad said that it would make a lot more noise than a rifle. Cameron agreed, instantly wishing that he had something more formidable than the little twenty-two.

Cameron pointed out to Jimmy the two Luddite fellows standing next to the assembling group of men. Cameron stared at their odd appearance with their hand-sewn trousers being held up by button suspenders, their course shirts, and their wide-brimmed hats. Even though the Luddites had been living in Junction for a week now, they had kept themselves secluded. They had chosen to live in a collection of abandoned homes further from Junction rather than closer. Their self-imposed isolation and odd appearance had made them the objects of gossip.

"Did you know," Jimmy whispered to Cameron, "that some Luddite men have more than one wife?" He looked at Cameron with a bemused smile, his eyes twinkling in the morning rays.

Cameron thought about this new information for a moment, partly with uncertainty about its veracity and partly with the adolescent fascination about sexuality. He was curious. "Do they all sleep in the same bed?" he chortled, trying to suppress a laugh.

Jimmy got wide-eyed with the thought. "I'd guess so," he said. Both the boys giggled, Cameron's voice cracking and squeaking, betraying the onset of puberty. The boys had plenty to talk about as their march to colony began. Cameron began to wonder aloud what it would take to become a Luddite.

Six months ago, a fourteen mile hike would have been a physical impossibility for most anyone in Junction, or anywhere else for that matter. But among the many changes wrought by this new upside-down world they all lived in was increased physical vitality. With the near complete absence of motorized vehicles people had to walk to where they needed to go, or simply not go at all. Consequently virtually everyone had become physically inured to the demands of a more physically demanding life and obesity had become a thing of the past. In many ways people were healthier than before the collapse of the grid, assuming that they were getting enough to eat and had access to an adequate variety of foods to eat. Malnourishment was a chronic problem for many people.

It was hoped that the trek to the colony would be uneventful. Otty, Jarad, Peter, and others worked out the details of their confrontation with the squatters as they moved along the highway to the north. The group of armed men soon passed the quarry where they had recently gotten the explosives to destroy the bridge. They still had a long ways to go. After an hour the group took a ten-minute break before moving on.

People began to get wary as they moved further from Junction. It was not that any of them were unfamiliar with the area north of Junction – they were. It was that so much had changed in the past half-year that no one knew what to expect. It was not anticipated that they would encounter any people along the highway, but who was to know who may have moved into the area in search of supplies? After all, had not the Luddites encountered this exact situation?

The two Luddite men walked together, but apart from the rest of the group. They were the object of continuous interest to Cameron and Jimmy, who pondered many things about them, even their boots. The boys moved their discussion about Luddites to the boots, fascinated by the idea of homemade footwear. "How do you make books?" Cameron wondered aloud. The boys discussed this, each with their own theory, a path of inquiry that led them to examine almost every aspect of their own lives and how they sustained themselves. After a bit of time, the lives of the Luddites seemed to be the less anomalous than their own. The Luddites might not have been able to work a televisor, but they could grow their own food. And right now, that seemed to be the better skill.

The group of armed men continued to make short breaks with each passing hour. Finally, three and a half hours later the posse neared its objective. The optimists in the group were excited, whereas the pessimists were less so, but all were sobered by the seriousness of the moment.

The people toward the front noticed that the two Luddite men were talking intently with Otty. Otty then talked to others and word was passed back to the rest of the group that they would begin to encounter Luddite land the next half-mile or less; everyone was to keep their eyes peeled, their mouths shut, and their guns on safety. No use of firearms unless told otherwise.

It became apparent when the group had met up with the

Luddite property because it was cleared of trees. Notably the tilled areas were relatively small plots, outlined by wide swaths of weedy, overgrown strips, so unlike modern practices were every square inch of land was under cultivation.

A short distance away a pair of horses whinnied, drawing the attention of the armed men toward the statue-like animals who stared from across the field at the intruders. Cameron noticed that it was the sight of the horses that caused the Luddite men to openly show emotion as both men now sported small grins. Thinking back, Cameron did recall that Luddites seemed to never show any emotion, whether happy or otherwise. He wondered why this was. The smiles on the Luddite men seemed incongruous.

The group of men began to pass small dark houses, all covered with cedar shakes – both their roofs and exterior walls. Each was framed in still-dormant flower beds and some had rather large barren vegetable patches next to them.

They walked on for almost another mile before they came to a halt, everyone puddling together before a sweeping turn in the highway. Word was passed that they were now approaching the houses where the squatters were known to have occupied. They could not approach them without being seen. The group of men remained loosely assembled, anxiously biding their time like a group of students waiting outside school before the first day of classes.

Otty, Jarad, Peter, and James stood in earnest discussion, each man periodically throwing an unsure glance toward the houses. A Luddite man was questioned by the leaders, but he was unsure exactly who was where, only sure that the homes down the dirty path were the correct ones. At least they were a week ago. There appeared to be no movement in them, even this late in the day. A donkey brayed somewhere behind them, at some distant Luddite homestead, causing some of the Junction men to laugh quietly.

Jarad was uneasy. He did not like the layout of the situation. They could not approach from the long driveway because their movement would be obvious. But then he had an idea and proposed it to Otty.

"Let's see if there is a way around the back of those two houses by cutting across a field or something. Maybe I can take some men behind that a way," he proposed. "Peter or James could come around the other way." He indicated these movements of men by drawing an arc in the air with an outstretched arm.

The four leaders again talked with older Luddite man, who then in turn conversed with his kinsman. The younger man nodded as the older man spoke in quite tones. Hierarchy by age was an important value among the Luddites. The older man then spoke to Otty, who also nodded in affirmation. Otty motioned to the others to come and speak with him.

"Ganahan agrees with Jarad. He thinks that it might be easier if some of the men approach along a crossroad that cuts through the fields behind that rise." He drew a map in the wet ground with the toe of his boot. "If you two follow Dunstan," he continued, pointing at Jarad and Peter and referring to the younger of the Luddite men, "he'll guide you where you need to go." He looked down again at his makeshift map in the dirt. "You, Jarad, can take your men and set up position here." He marked an arc that traced a third of an invisible circle around the houses. "Peter, you can cover this area." He dragged his foot to connect the first arc with a second, covering another third of the encirclement. "And James will cover the remainder." His foot completed the circle. "Sound okay?"

The men agreed and then the discussion turned to timing. It was felt that Jarad and Peter should keep visual contact with Otty.

They also quickly worked out a set of signals. When ready they would gesture to Otty that they were in position. He would then take it from there.

Jarad, Peter, and over half the men retreated back down the highway following Dunstan. The younger Luddite man would guide the contingent into position behind the houses, both of which were within a stone's throw of the other.

In about fifteen minutes Otty saw the men moving off to the left as they passed over the crest of a field. Shortly thereafter Otty was able to see Jarad to his left and Peter to his right, both signaling that they were ready. James had already spread out his assigned group of men behind Otty. The houses were now effectively encircled.

Otty had butterflies! All eyes were now on him, at least those that could see. He was very nervous inside, though outwardly he was as poised as usual. As he set off toward the squatter's houses, he felt exposed and vulnerable. This was his intention; he didn't want the squatters to feel threatened. In fact, he was unarmed and had purposely removed his jacket to suggest that he was not concealing anything. He also carried a long stick to which a large white handkerchief had been attached like a flag. Though Peter had ribbed him over his carrying a white flag, Otty had not thought of an alternative and he did not want to approach the squatters empty-handed. Then they might simply mistake him for a lone vagrant. No, he had a message to deliver and he wanted to convey that intent.

The closer he got the more naked and alone he felt. The gravel path he trod was not really a driveway. The Luddites did not use motor vehicles. Instead, this narrow, weed-covered path was only wide enough to accommodate a horse-drawn buggy or wagon. He walked in one of two parallel ruts. He could imagine rifle cross hairs centered on his chest as he neared his destination. He did not like the feeling.

He stopped about thirty feet from the main entrance and shouted out a greeting. "Hello in there…is anyone home?" He was greeted by utter silence, which filled him with relief and dread: relief that maybe the people had left, which would make their task much easier; dread that their silence might lead to a violent confrontation, which he strongly wanted to avoid.

After a few moments he called out a second time. "Hello. We know that there are people living here and I want to talk with you…I am unarmed…I only want to talk."

A sound came from the nearest house, the one he was facing. It was the sound of a door being pulled open. Otty could see the hand-hewn door crack open just wide enough for someone to speak through, or to level a rifle.

"Then speak!" the voice said. It was a woman and she sounded profoundly nervous.

A sense of relief again came upon Otty and he sighed loudly, betraying the tension he felt. He had made contact, which identified where the squatters were, and they had chosen to speak with a human's voice rather than that of a rifle.

"Good day, ma'am!" he said in as normal of a tone that he could generate, as if their meeting was perfectly normal. "My name is Otty Oleson. Maybe we know each other? I was the pastor at Blue River Church, now I'm here representing the people of Junction."

There was a long pause before the woman responded. "What do you want?" she asked. It seemed to Otty that she was giving voice to someone else's questions.

"I'll be blunt and direct. We want you to leave this property.

It belongs to the Luddites. I am here to make you folks a deal. The Luddites are now living with us in Junction, but they would like their homes back. Who can blame them? We intend to help them and, quite honestly, you can't stop us. But we don't want any violence. There is only a handful of you, but many of us." He was growing hoarse shouting out his words, so he resumed his slow approach toward the house. "I'm coming forward a bit," he said loudly, "or I'm gonna lose my voice."

As he shuffled a few yards closer to the house, Otty eerily felt that he was being watched by more than one pair of eyes. The woman had not answered him, but Otty knew that he did not want to lose this link through the door. If that door were to close, things would become far more difficult.

Otty glimpsed some sort of activity in the shadows and the door moved open a bit wider on its hinges. Then a man's voice called out to him. "You're bluffing," he said gruffly. This is progress, he thought to himself. He could also sense fear in the man's voice.

"Why should I bluff? This is a serious matter," Otty said calmly. "We are offering you another sanctuary, what we call the Dome." He described the Dome to them, making it attractive, but not too much so. If it were so wonderful, they'd wonder why he didn't live there. "We offer you safe passage there. We simply want to take back what belongs to our friends the Luddites and are prepared to use force, if necessary. You folks are surrounded. You can't escape. I don't tell you this to scare you, but to show how serious we are. But we don't want violence."

Otty could hear more sounds behind the partially opened door. He thought that he heard the hushed tones of an ongoing argument. It appeared that the people in the house were not of one opinion.

Before the man could respond, Otty took the initiative. Maybe the people need help making up their mind. "Let me prove to you the predicament you are in," he said. "Listen!" With that he turned around and signaled to James, who in turn signaled to Jarad and Peter. Afterward, he turned again to face the house. In a few moments the first gun shot rang out. As signaled, the early afternoon was punctuated by the sound of rhythmic rifle fire, like a string of loud but slow firecrackers. The blast of gunfire steadily circled around the house, counting out the proof of firepower that Otty warned them about. Sometimes the gunshots were powerful blasts, others bordered on being faint, but each shot added certitude to Otty's position and the precariousness of their own.

After the last shot had been fired, Otty struck again quickly: "I will give you ten minutes to decide." With that, he stuck the pole bearing the white flag into the ground and retraced his steps down the path. He took up a position alongside James. He motioned to Peter and Jarad to maintain position and wait. Both men knew that Otty would at one point give them an ultimatum. This was that time; now it was a matter of watching and waiting. Word was passed along the line: reload, but wait; no shooting, unless told; this might take a while.

Evidently the show of force was very convincing. Within a couple minutes two women and two men stepped out of the house, all of them lugging suitcases, the men also carrying rifles. They seemed unsure what to do as they looked nervously about themselves, like sheep in a strange new pasture. They slowly moved toward the pole affixed with the white flag. The leading man then pulled it from the ground and waved it rapidly in the air, indicating to all the hidden men that he posed no threat. The group then moved slowly down the two parallel ruts and toward the highway.

As they approached Otty, he could see that one of the women was particularly agitated. She kept tugging at the one man's arm and looking over her shoulder. She was crying, often pausing to yell back at the house. Otty could not make out her words, mostly because of her sobbing. Evidently there was still one person back in the house. She even dropped her luggage and ran toward the house, pausing midway and shouting out a name. She then returned to the man, crying profusely, trying to talk but being reduced to mere babbling.

Otty looked at the squatters. The winter had not been good to them, as they were filthy and unkempt. They did not appear to have been eating well as evident by the pallor of their skin. He felt pity for them; not the sentiment that he thought he would have. They appeared to be in quite a pathetic state, emotionally and physically.

They approached Otty, seemingly only seeing him and not the armed men around and behind him. The lead man spoke to Otty. There was a problem. Yes, there was another person still in the house. It was the woman's younger brother and he was not well in the head. The woman's brother did not want to leave the security of the house, believing that he could fight off the armed challengers.

"Great!" Otty said in frustration. Why must there always be hitch, he thought to himself. Now what should he do? He had not planned for this: an armed face-off with a nut – a nut with a gun.

James chimed in. He had listened to the conversation between Otty and squatters and understood the problem. He had a solution. "This is easy," he said, holding up what he called his "deer rifle." It was a large black bolt-action rifle with an exceptionally long barrel and topped with an oversized scope. "I don't tell people this because, well, it's nobody's business and…I don't like to talk about it. I'm not proud of it, but…I was a snipe in the service. I…" he paused and looked down at his feet before resuming, "I was good at what I did."

He looked severely across the field that separated them from the house. "Piece of cake," he said confidently. "As soon as that fellow so much as peeks through the curtains I can drill 'im with a shot. One shot. Problem solved."

With that the upset woman again dropped her large bag and fled the group, racing back up the path and toward the house. She was crying hysterically and screaming out her brother's name in loud, wailing shrieks. She grabbed the now closed door, but in her hysteria had difficulty in operating the primitive latch. She tried to open it with her hands and then, frustrated, began pounding on it with her palms, crying and shouting. It opened suddenly and she practically tumbled in.

Everyone who could see from the road stared at the dark rectangle of the open doorway, imagining the unfolding drama within the house.

The two squatter men began their own argument. Evidently the young man within the house was a point of contention. One of the men wanted to leave him behind, the other defended the actions of the woman. Their words ended as quickly as they had begun – neither had the energy to continue it.

The woman had won her battle. She reappeared in the doorway, victoriously dragging out by his hand a man who appeared afraid of daylight. But once drawn from the house, he seemed to resign himself to his fate. He never once more looked around himself, keeping his eyes planted directly before him and down toward the path, both of his hands clinging tightly to his sister's arm, his rifle slung around his back.

Otty was relieved. Once the woman and the young man joined their friends, he signaled Jarad and Peter. They acknowledged his go-ahead, Jarad further indicating that they'd meet him and the others along the road.

The two Luddite men were very pleased with the outcome, as evidenced by their broad smiles, but they remained silent. They overtly avoided the squatters, not even wanting to look at them.

Otty had some of his men disarm the squatters. The three men readily gave up their guns. Otty then directed the captives to be the first down the road and toward the highway, the rest following behind. In a few minutes the small group more than doubled in size as it met up with Peter and Jarad and their men. The two squatter men looked at each other, each trying to gauge the tacit thoughts of the other. It seemed that they were relieved that they did not choose their other option.

Otty watched the squatters shuffle before their captors. He felt sympathy for them. He realized that they were as much victims of circumstances as any of them and he was curious to hear their stories. Their clothing was filthy and mismatched in size and fashion, suggesting that they had to forage for replacement items as opportunities allowed. They all needed a good scrubbing, as their body odor was obvious and it seemed that weeks had passed since any of them had a bath – maybe months.

As they walked along Otty positioned himself to question the squatters. They seemed to be completely cowed and their emotions conveyed neither relief, nor fear, nor optimism. Nothing. They seemed resigned. Even the woman, who minutes earlier had been crying hysterically, had become, like her mentally disturbed brother, dispirited automatons. He began talking with the two men, as they were closest to him. Once he got them talking, they seemed to be unable to stop. It was cathartic.

He learned that the two pairs were unrelated but longtime friends. Both couples were "partnered," a term which meant though they considered themselves to be life mates, they did not think marriage to be relevant nor necessary. The five of them had traveled together on a road trip to the Pacific Ocean with an extended stay in Seattle. They were all from Iowa, and only one of them had previously been to the West Coast. When they were on their way back home, they hurried to make Glacier National Park, before it closed for the season. It was there they became trapped when the grid failed. No one would help them, so in time they had to break into homes and stores to get the supplies that they needed. That is how they ended up with the rifles, though none of them were hunters nor had served in the military, so it took them a while to figure out how the guns functioned.

They had an old tourist map that they were using to try to backtrack to Spokane, Washington, but they did not get far on foot before winter came. They were heading for Spokane because it was the closest large city and they figured that from there they might find help to get back to Iowa. They were all extremely anxious to get to Spokane because they were desperate to fly out and get back home; they had left children in the care of relatives. When the man mentioned that fact to Otty one of the women began to weep silently to herself.

With the onset of that early winter, they had to hole up in the first decent dwelling that they had come to, but it was too small for all of them. They did their best to get through those months, but it was very difficult for them and the younger man began to have mental issues, which made the close proximity even more trying. By spring they had run out of food and that was how they found the

Luddite colony. "We all damn near went crazy with worry and hunger. If we hadn't happened upon those Amish people, we'd probably all be dead," the one man opined.

Otty explained to the squatters the difference between the Amish and the Luddites, though they didn't find the information particularly interesting. "Why did you chase the Luddites away?" he asked them. The other man responded to the question.

"We didn't mean to!" he asserted. "I tell you, we seemed to have waited forever for that damn snow to clear so we could get back on the road. When we finally got out we were so hungry we couldn't think of anything else. We were obsessed! When we came upon the Amish people…I mean Luddite…we were so happy. These were good people, we figured. They'd help us. But they didn't. They told us to go away!" The man looked around to find the two Luddite men. Locating them, he spat on the ground. The Luddites ignored him.

"We explained our problem. We begged them for help…just something to eat! But they kept slamming their doors in our faces. What were we supposed to do? Hell's fire! I couldn't take it no more, so I kicked in a door and demanded food. Just to get us down the road. I didn't care anymore. They could've killed me for all I cared. Hell, we were dying anyways! What would you have done?" Otty could see the anger building up in the man as he relived the frustration of that confrontation with the Luddites. Otty found the man's account fascinating. He revealed a side of the Luddites that Otty had not imagined. He supposed that the Luddites were as scared as the man was obviously crazed. He looked again at the fellow…he could understand why the Luddites would have been afraid of him, indeed all of them. But, that still didn't excuse not helping people who were simply asking for basic assistance. He would ask Ganahan when the opportunity presented itself.

Otty also knew that he could not blame the squatters for their actions. He had often pondered how he would have fared if things had turned out more poorly than they had after the grid failed. He was so glad that his brother Karl had sent him that warning. He wanted to thank him for the heads-up. He wondered if he would ever see him again.

"And then the strangest thing happened; the strangest thing in my life, I figure. The Luddite people…they just started to leave! We didn't touch 'em…we hardly talked to 'em…but maybe they thought we had the plague or something, because they gathered up a few things – bam!" he smacked his palms together, "and they were down the road. We couldn't figure that one out."

The man looked at Otty, wondering if he believed his story. The man seemed tired, mentally adrift. Talking appeared to help him to psychologically collect himself, but he had endured so much the past few months that it would not be a surprise to Otty if they all "went over the edge" emotionally, so to speak. Otty did not doubt the man's interpretation of events, but he also knew that there were two sides, two perspectives, to every story.

The man became quiet and sullen and none of the other squatters seemed inclined to talk. Especially the women, they seemed too…well… forlorn, Otty thought to himself. But he could understand that feeling. When his own daughter, Breann, committed suicide just a few months back, he lost something deep and meaningful in his spirit. Something that nothing else could replace; something that even time could not heal. If it were not for his two lovely grandchildren that he and Ellie were now raising, he might have fallen into deep despair. Now he could not, he had children to care for.

Crowds move in amorphous ways – shifting and stretching and coalescing – like a flock of birds. Whereas Otty and the squatters began at the front of the pack, in time they had drifted toward the center as younger legs moved more quickly. Soon the group had reorganized itself by age: the younger toward the front, the older toward the rear. But the two Luddites never complied with this natural pattern; they remained aloof and separate, though they did not try to avoid Otty. He was their one concession to mixing with the world.

During one of their hourly breaks, Otty took the opportunity to ask Ganahan the reasoning behind the Luddites abandoning their colony. He did not share with the older Luddite man what the squatter fellow had told him. He did not want the Luddite man to get defensive. Now that he had heard the squatters' perspective, he naturally was curious as to the Luddites' view. For Ganahan, to explain to Otty the Luddite reaction to the squatters required a quick introduction to Luddite beliefs. "Our mother, Gaea, teaches us that anger is unnatural. It is irrational and therefore can not be calmed with rational words. Trying to reason with irrational people only leads them to violence. Our mother instructs with the storms: storms are violent and cause damage, or at the very least great fear. What good comes from storms? Do you prefer storms or gentle days? Gentle days, of course! It is then that we till our fields, plant and harvest our crops, and enjoy our days. When it storms we seek shelter. When these angry people came into our colony, they were a storm. They were irrational, so we sought shelter. We knew our mother would provide for us. That is how we found you." He smiled at Otty and gently nodded his head in thanks.

Otty could understand Ganahan's analogy of irrational human behavior and stormy weather, but it seemed to him too simplistic. Human behavior was far more complex, and probably more unpredictable, than the weather. Otty could understand the logic in the Luddites response to the violent threats of the squatters; after all they were devout pacifists. But as he pondered this behavior, he came to the realization that the Luddites more likely had simply fallen victim to panic, if not mass hysteria. After one family ran off because of the violent threats of the squatters, so did others, and then soon all of them had. But it seemed to him that this compulsion would make the Luddites easy to manipulate. Perhaps that explains why the Luddites as a movement had not proved to be very successful. Otty wondered how other groups – at least those superficially similar to the Luddites, such as the Amish – handled similar situations.

The group moved steadily though increasingly at a slower pace. People were getting tired. The return was a hike in itself, but the toll of the adrenaline rush caused by the excitement of meeting up with the squatters added to the level of fatigue. Conversations died off with each passing mile and the hourly breaks were often silent. People now just wanted to get home and be done with this adventure.

The quarry appeared on their left, indicating that they were nearing Junction. The pace picked up slightly. Otty pondered what to do with the squatters. He was not able to determine from talking with them what they wanted to do. When he explained the advantages of the Dome, it fell on deaf ears. Their only interest was getting to Spokane. He presumed that they would need to stay in Junction for at least a couple days to clean up, etc. But he realized that what was logical and sensible to him, may not be so for them.

A short distance ahead a gunshot rang out, driving everyone to the ditches. A couple voices were hollering up ahead, but they were too far to be discernible. Then two fellows began to laugh and word was passed back that Tyler Johnson had shot a deer. This was a fortuitous find and no one blamed him taking the deer down. In the environs around Junction people had thinned, some might say decimated, the local deer and elk populations. There was simply no other source of meat. What few cattle that were raised in the area had long been butchered and consumed. Otty wondered if the Luddites raised beef.

As the people regrouped and resumed their march down the highway, they came upon Tyler and Genis butchering the deer. Genis was fast with a blade and those who knew him were confident that he'd have the deer carcass gutted and hanging within minutes. "Good shot, Tyler," someone good-naturedly shouted out. "Venison tonight?" another voice asked. "I'm heading to Tyler's tonight," a third voice chimed in.

Tyler looked up from the deer, a steaming gut pile lying languidly and shiny next to him. He smiled broadly. "Party tonight!" he shouted back at onlookers. "Party?" someone asked. Tyler raised his blood-covered hands to simulated dancing. "Celebration…for today!" he crowed.

Eyebrows were raised. Of course, the people needed to celebrate their "victory" over the squatters. Otty realized that the victory was the fact that everyone came back alive, including himself. He said a brief, silent prayer of thanks to God. He hoped that he would not have to risk his life again for a very long time, if ever. When he spied the old rundown service station ahead, he knew that he was almost home. "Nap time," he shouted out to any and everyone. His words were greeted with hoots.

***

Chapter 9

Tyler Johnson's anticipated celebration fell a little flat that evening. To the wonder of most everyone in Junction, the Luddites began to return to their homes that very same afternoon. Elder Jonathan explained to Otty that the people were concerned about their animals and the good news was the only excuse that they needed to head back to their homes. After all, it was only a seven-mile hike. Even Ganahan and Dunstan had made the trip with the rest of the Luddites, in spite of already having gone there and back that same day. Otty and Elder Jonathan shook hands, the only thanks the people of Junction would receive for their hospitality. Elder Jonathan did confirm that he would be expecting some Junction people to come work with the Luddites. He said that he looked forward to that opportunity. Otty silently hoped so.

Fortunately, the exit of the Luddites made it simple to find residences for the squatters. Some found it peculiar that they insisted on remaining together in one house. Many thought that they would have preferred to finally find some privacy, but that was not the case. Perhaps the paranoia of the younger man was a reflection of a collective one. But they had been through hell, so perhaps they found comfort in each other's company.

Jarad remained home for a couple days to get his strength back, but he hated having "down time." He had things to do, but Myla insisted that he sit still for a bit. She was right, he knew, but it was nonetheless a challenge. Fortunately it rained the next two days, which made outdoor activity less than inviting. He and Myla ended up playing countless hands of cribbage and they even taught their kids to play pinochle with them. And when Jimmy came by to visit, they played a stack of board games. They had so much fun that Jarad actually did not want it to end.

It was during this time that Myla had her first quickening. She felt the baby move! This was very exciting for her, but it also gave her a sense of urgency. Jarad knew that her "nesting" instincts were coming to the fore and she would soon become unbearable. She would need some stability in her life and any sort of anchor to give her a sense of permanence. In other words, Alberta better come sooner than later.

He met up with Genis that evening. He assured Jarad that he had things well in hand. They had discussed their plans earlier for getting the fuel from the raiders' tank, but Jarad had to defer to Genis. Not only did he seem to have the advantage in strategy, but his plan was playing into his strengths. Jarad had no counter solutions to propose. Genis was such a jack-of-all-trades and, in Jarad's opinion, a master of them all, that he also had a plethora of ideas. And Genis's current plan was as good as they came. He'd be ready in the morning.

*

Genis explained it again. He knew that Jarad was doubtful, but that was after he told Genis about his fear of heights. "Okay," he said patiently, "I've done this a million times. It's easy and I know you can do it. Hell, I'd go across the river with you, but who do you trust on this side? Exactly!" He grinned, patting himself on his chest.

When Cameron shared his idea about the diesel fuel still trapped in the raiders' "tank," Jarad was roused to action. He could not move quickly enough to retrieve that fuel – here was the answer to their prayers. But getting that fuel was going to be a challenge, as it was on the wrong end of a now missing bridge. The destruction of the span had removed approximately twenty yards of concrete and rebar and the broken ends that reached vainly across the gorge were badly damaged and structurally unsound. In other words, a person could not walk out toward the ends of what remained of the bridge as they were liable to give way. Genis had devised a clever way to get around this problem, though it made Jarad uncomfortable, actually terrified. It involved heights and he did not like this one bit!

Genis's idea was for Jarad to cross over the river by way of a ford a couple miles downstream from Junction. The crossing of the river would still entail a descent down into the gorge, wading across the river and a climb up the other side, but it was doable. Once Jarad had crossed, he'd follow the high ground back up toward the highway and the remains of the bridge. Then the work would begin.

Genis would fire an arrow across the chasm to Jarad. Jarad would retrieve the arrow and the string attached to it. Attached to the string will be a rope and attached to the rope will be a wire cable. After pulling the cable across the divide, Jarad would then fasten the end to a secure anchor, such as a large tree. He carried a pair of clamps in his pack plus other tools for this purpose. Genis explained to him where he would need to position the anchor point: slightly lower than the anchor point on the north side of the bridge, thereby creating a minimal downward slope. When this was done Genis would begin sending fuel cans attached to pulleys down the "zip line," as he called to it. Afterward he himself would cross over and help Jarad siphon the fuel.

When they had the fuel cans full, they would then reposition the end of the cable higher up the hillside, creating a reverse slope toward the Junction end of the bridge. Genis would zip himself across and then wait for Jarad to return the now-full fuel cans. When the fuel was safely across, Jarad would attach himself to the cable and shuttle himself over the gorge as Genis did. That would be the hard part for Jarad!

"I've done this sort of thing countless times," he assured Jarad.

"Yes, I know," Jarad responded sarcastically, "a million times."

Despite his fear, Jarad would gladly use the zip line if it meant that they would get that much closer to Alberta. Myla's belly was growing! Genis promised him that they could accomplish his plan all in one day – "Once I get all the stuff together," he said.

*

They took off the following day: Jarad, Genis, Cameron, and the squatters; the eight of them heading down the rail bed. Peter had given the squatters a map to guide them to Spokane. This was all the help they wanted or needed. Genis and Cameron were coming along because Genis was still planning on creating a rock slide to bury the tracks. It was hoped that this barrier would keep the raiders from planning a second assault down the rail bed with another one of their "tanks." The rock slide would not deter men on foot, but it would slow them down. Either way it was a proactive way to keep Junction protected. Genis had the perfect place in mind: a rock wall with a natural overhang that faced a long, steep, slope of scree. Cameron came along to help Genis carry the explosives and other items needed for his work, plus a little company.

It was still early in the morning and the sun had not yet crested the ridge lines that surrounded the community. Though the ground was still damp from the prior two days of rain, the morning held promise of dry weather, at least early on.

Jarad carried a small backpack full of the tools and other equipment he would need for his work that day. Genis had explained how to use each item until Jarad felt confident. It was actually pretty straightforward and Jarad did not think he would have any problems. Besides the equipment Jarad also packed a plastic bottle of water, some snacks for lunch, and his pistol. He had wrapped the gun in two re-sealable plastic bags and then strapped it into his holster. He didn't want to end up on the "bad guy's" side of the river without a weapon. And since he'd be scaling a steep slope or two, he did not want to pack his rifle. He could also still shoot the gun through the plastic.

The squatters were amazingly resilient and determined. They had a single-minded determination to make their way to Spokane and to then fly out to Iowa. No one in Junction had the heart or courage to tell them that they were only going to be marooned in Spokane, assuming that they actually made it there. But as Myla pointed out, this mania for Spokane was indicative of their fragile mental state, both individually and collectively. "They're nuts," as Jarad had said so succinctly.

They moved down the tracks, the squatters taking the lead. They were moving surprisingly quick, as if after a prize. They were refreshed after three days of eating and sleeping, but evidently not much else. They apparently had a complete disregard for their personal hygiene, as clued by their powerful body odor and the greasy, stringy hair that covered their heads. Cameron backed off a couple steps behind them so as to avoid their stench. As Genis had whispered to Jarad, the squatters made the Luddites seem normal.

After an hour they neared the place where Jarad had encountered the dead man who had been shot in the back. He had not warned anyone about the body, hoping that by now the body had been dragged off by scavengers. He peered down the tracks when he could and did not notice anything usual. His assumption proved correct. When they passed the spot where the corpse had lay, there was nothing remaining but a couple small scraps of clothing – nothing to cause anyone to take note of. He moved on without a word.

The rail bed then began to pull away from the river gorge and toward the mountains. Jarad would separate from the group at this point. He, Genis, and Cameron briefly paused while they reviewed their plan. "This won't take but a few minutes," he said, pantomiming a detonator in his hands. "Hopefully it'll work. Cameron and I are simply going to place the explosives at the base of the wall, light the fuses, and run like hell!" He laughed at his own joke. "Just kidding!"

Jarad knew that Genis would be safe. As they talked the three of them noticed that the squatters had continued on, not even noticing that the rest of their party was being left behind. Genis shook his head. "Just as well. I'd prefer if they were out of harms way when I set this stuff off. Come on Cameron, let's go make some memories." With that, he and Cameron turned away as Jarad watched them for a moment as they continued down the tracks. His son turned and gave him a wave.

Jarad stepped off the shoulder of the rail bed and down and across the ditch. He would follow the spine of the ridge that capped that side of the river gorge. The going was easy as there was little underbrush because of the solid rock substrate covered by only a thin layer of soil made living difficult for plant life. The only thing growing were tufts of grass and a few, widely-spaced and stunted shrubs. He followed an interconnected series of game trails that would lead him down to the river.

The river was quieter than he thought it would be, especially this time of the year when the water flow was near its highest, though most of the sound was coming from up further in the gorge. He did not know how he was going to get across the river, but there was supposed to be a wide, shallow ford near where he was at.

He partly walked and partly slid down the hillside, grabbing at branches and sturdy shrubs as handholds to control his descent. He made it quicker to the river than he thought it would take, so time was on his side. He figured he'd need it to scale the other side, as he looked across the river. He followed the bank downstream, waiting for the river to quiet down, indicating that he had reached the ford. It took him about fifteen minutes before he reached where he needed to be. The river side would have been a great summer camping site if he were so inclined. The water swept smoothly between the two banks; the ground was level and there were many trees. He scanned the murky flow before him. It seemed to him that the flow was pretty high, but he should only have to cross it once.

He looked for and found a suitable walking stick to help him cross the river. He cinched his backpack tighter and rechecked his holster. Then he made a final scan of the far bank.

He stepped into the river and immediately fell in! He had lost his footing. Fortunately the water was not deep and he was able to immediately stand up. He shouted out a curse. Ah, he did not want to be completely wet, but that worry was too late now! He was too angry to feel cold. Oh well, he mused to himself, now he did not have to worry about falling in.

He poked the piece of wood into the water ahead of him to check its depth. The water was thick with a light color because of the snow melt, so it was difficult to know where to step. But the bottom of the river was solid and he understood why this part of the river was used as a ford, though it came up past his knees and pushed against him with quite a bit of lateral mass. He could manage.

He found a rhythm. He would poke with the wood, take a step with his left foot, lean on the wood and follow with a step with his right, then repeat the motion. He focused only on this, as he wanted to get across the river as quickly as possible. Now that he had reached the middle of the river, the last thing he wanted to do was fall again and possibly get swept downstream.

He made it across. He threw the stick down and scrambled away from the river. He checked out his gun to see how it fared. He pulled it from its protective plastic cover and inspected it carefully. The pistol was dry, so he it stuffed back into the wet holster, strapping it securely. He looked up at the barrier before him. This might be tough, he thought, as he could not see any game trails in the immediate area. The going was evidently too steep, even for deer. He moved downstream as the ridge appeared less imposing. After a while, he found a game trail and started to climb.

Just as he started up the hillside a tremendous explosion reverberated around him, causing him to jump before realizing it was Genis's handiwork. Now it was a race back to the bridge. He wanted to get there first, though he had the disadvantage of not really knowing where he was going. Genis had it easy.

The climb up was a slog. He fell down twice, sliding on loose stone and once jamming his elbow hard against the sharp stones. He sighed, got up, and continued trying to traverse the granite shards. At least it was not raining, he thought to himself. He did not want to get wet. He laughed dryly at his own joke.

He came to the top of a ridge and thought that he had made it to the top, but it proved to be a false summit. But he was near. He moved across a broad field of scree. He disliked traversing loose rock like this, but it was his only path. All at once, he felt himself pitching as if on a boat and he fell hard on his chest. He began to slide downward. Instinctively he flailed about, trying to grab anything that might arrest his fall. But there was only rock and it was sliding with him. Downward he continued to slide until he came to an abrupt halt. With a thump he landed on a hard surface, finding himself straddling a tree that jutted out almost horizontally from the rocks, pain shooting up his abdomen. He had made with the tree at his groin, thus the pain. He endured the temporary moment of nausea that also accompanied such blows; he was just glad to have stopped his downward slide.

Once the pain had abated, he looked at his situation. Someone was watching over him! If his slide had not been arrested by the tree, he would have fallen over the blunt cliff and upon a bed of sharp rocks. If that drop didn't kill him, it would have left him grievously wounded. He lifted up a quick prayer of thanks and then surveyed his surroundings for options. He only had one route: straight up.

He rested for a few moments more and then carefully edged forward off of the tree and back onto the scree. Moving at a snail's pace, he slowly climbed up and out of the scree and onto something that was more *terra firma*. In a few moments he crested the ridge top and was greeted by a cool breeze. He sat down and again rested, surveying the view before him. He could hardly believe that he had just crawled up from the river below, but he was truly at the top of the ridge. After scanning his surroundings, he stood up again and immediately turned left and headed back up river. There would be no paths, roads, or railways on this side of the river – only what the good Lord and the animals he created had provided.

It took him two hours to get to the bridge. He pulled out the little radio he brought with in order to communicate with Genis. It had survived the river. Genis was waiting for his call.

"Have any troubles?" he asked after hearing Jarad's voice.

"Oh, none at all," Jarad lied. "Can you see me?"

"Yes, I've been watching you for a good thirty minutes. Can you see me?"

Jarad looked across the span. He saw Genis waving at him. He waved back. "I'm ready when you are. Let's get this show on the road. I'm going to go check the tank. I'll let you know what I find. Out."

When Jarad approached the homemade tank, he was impressed by how much damage it had incurred. The explosion easily tossed the huge metal vehicle twenty yards or more. It was now lying on its side. He scrambled up on top of it, looking for the fuel cap. It was forward of the cab, now lying parallel to the ground. He popped the cap off and fuel began to dump out. He immediately refastened the cap. "Good!" he said aloud to himself.

His nose caught scent of a terrible odor, Jarad immediately knowing what it was. He peered into the front slit cut into the thick metal plate welded to the front of the cab. The slit served as the only forward vantage point for the driver. Inside he saw the bloated corpse of a man, thrown to the side of the wide cab, stacked on his head. He stepped away from the machine to catch his breath. Not that long ago the sight of a putrid corpse would have made him retch. But not now. He had seen too much for that to bother him now. He would have liked to investigate the other dead bodies, if only to ascertain their identities. After all, these were his former neighbors in Purcell. Instead, he simply left them to the flies. He called Genis again on the little walkie-talkie.

"We got fuel," he said, "a lot." Genis gave a holler and then told him to get ready to receive the arrow.

Jarad could see Genis standing in the distance. Though he could make out Genis's broader movement, he could not really see the finer actions of he was doing. He could tell by Genis's stance that he was pulling on the bow, but he could not see the arrow from that distance. Nonetheless, the string became more apparent as it approached him. He watched the line being pulled down into the gorge, following a near-invisible weight. Genis had missed. The walkie-talkie beeped. Genis was paging Jarad.

"String was too tight. I'm gonna try again. This might take a minute or so," he said.

A few moments later Jarad watched Genis again launch the arrow. This time it soared in a silent arc over his head, the string practically landing on him. He gathered it up and began tugging the line, looping it around the palm of his left hand and elbow. It was easy to gather up.

Soon the string changed into a rope. The rope filled up his hand quickly and he tossed the pile to the ground. Now he was simply weighing in the rope as if hauling up a boat anchor. When the rope had finally given way to the wire cable, the work got heavier. He was sweating and sore in the shoulders before he had the wire braid in his hand. He did not realize that it would be that heavy and he had to sit down to rest. He signaled Genis from his sitting position that he had the cable.

After a bit he stood and dragged the cable toward a likely anchor point. He kept in mind Genis's instructions and found a suitable pine tree on a small rise behind him. He wrapped the cable around the tree twice before pulling it up fairly taut and taking up the excess cable.

He pulled a pair of cable clamps and a wrench from his

backpack and tightened the cable up securely. It should now be ready. The single strand of silver-gray spider's web now connected the two sides of the gorge, tracing a gentle arc high above and parallel to the missing span. As it was now Jarad knew that the metal rope could support the weight of a small automobile.

He signaled Genis on the radio. They spoke briefly and then Genis told him to get ready. Pretty soon a plastic jerry can slowly swayed down the cable and across the open space and into Jarad's awaiting hands. That was easy. He removed the empty fuel can from the trolley and waved his hands toward Genis. Soon, seven empty containers had been shuttled across, some large, some small, some metal, some plastic. They were ready.

Then Genis signaled Jarad and he pushed off from his perch, allowing gravity to shoot him across the gorge. He whooped in excitement. Jarad admired Genis's bravery and aplomb, which often bordered on reckless. But he sure knew how to get the job done. As he approached Jarad at speed, he motioned for him to move out of the way. He had a lot more mass than an empty gasoline container. He sped past Jarad and up toward the tree that anchored the cable before rolling backwards and finally coming to a stop. Genis was wearing a pair of heavy leather gloves and he used these to brake himself. He then pulled himself back toward Jarad, bouncing to give himself movement. Jarad helped him step out of his harness.

"Piece of cake," he said. "I told ya, a piece of cake," he repeated.

The two men quickly gathered up the cans and Jarad retrieved the siphon from the backpack, which he had laid on the ground near the cable anchor. Within twenty minutes the men had drained all of the fuel out of the raider's tank, filling all of the seven containers. "Not bad, though," Genis consoled Jarad. "We now got, say, thirty-some gallons more than we had yesterday. This stuff is worth its weight in gold."

Genis then helped Jarad to move the cable anchor point to a higher elevation. This also necessitated using the upturned bulldozer as a launch point. When the cable was secure, Genis used Jarad's walkie-talkie to signal James, who had taken up Genis's former position across the bridge. "Here comes the first fuel can," he said.

They latched the plastic container to the trolley and gave it a push. It jetted smoothly down the cable and into a small group of men. One of them waved back when they had it secured. They repeated the action until they had returned all of the fuel containers.

"Alright," Genis announced, "your turn." Jarad blanched. He had been dreading this moment from the very minute that Genis had outlined his plan days ago. Genis helped Jarad get into the harness, which resembled a bosun's chair. He had also brought along a second one for his own use.

He had Jarad remove his holster, as it interfered with the harness. Genis stuffed the gun and holder into Jarad's backpack. As he fitted the harness to Jarad, the two men began to hear voices in the distance. Looking across the bridge, they saw a small crowd of people gathering. "Looks like we got an audience," Genis joked.

This was almost too much for Jarad. He was already tempted to retrace his steps back to the river ford and risk drowning rather than hurl himself down the zip line. One part of his brain knew that the cable was perfectly safe, but it barely held the advantage over the other the less-rational part that viewed it as suicide: certain death, a plunge down the chasm, being dashed on the rocks below...

"You all right?" Genis asked, noting Jarad's distress. Jarad could only manage a nod and before he could gather his wits Genis gave him a push. Jarad was too petrified to scream, though he tried, as he had a sensation of falling into space. But just as quickly the whir of the trolley wheels near his face reminded him that he was gliding along the zip line. Before he could bring himself to actually enjoy the sensation, there were hands grabbing at him and pulling him to a rest. Someone was patting him on the back; others were laughing, but in a kind way.

"Hurry up Jarad," another voice said. "Genis is already on his way across." As if coming out of a daydream, Jarad was jerked back to consciousness. He unstrapped the harness and stepped out of the way. Seconds later he heard Genis hollering as he too sped across the void.

That was it. It was over. Jarad was struck how anti-climatic the moment felt. He had been so fearful of the zip line and now it was all behind him – over as quickly as it had begun.

"Good job, Jarad," a woman's voice said to him. It was Myla. She gave him a peck on the lips. "How was the ride?" she asked. "Was it scary?"

He crinkled his nose and shook his head negative. "Not at all," he boasted, and then he whispered in his wife's ear. "I was terrified. I almost filled my shorts." Myla let out with a burst of guffaws, laying her hand on her husband's shoulder for support. "You're braver than I," she said.

***

Chapter 10

Jarad could not believe that he was making yet another trip to Blue River. As he walked along the old road – no rail bed this time! – he considered how surreal his life had been since the grid failed. Strange how quickly life changed. Blue River was at first a sanctuary when they had to flee Purcell, and then became a trap when the raiders passed through, and now it had been abandoned completely, making it effectively a ghost town. Amazing. His life was like a cheesy B-flick. He now understood fully the old adage that fact is stranger than fiction. And here he was now planning a trip to Alberta by driving a car on the rails. He began to laugh, startling his son.

"You okay, dad," Cameron asked. "You've been mumbling to yourself."

He did not immediately respond to his son. Cameron was growing up, at times quicker than he should. He looked at his son from the corner of his eyes…the boy seemed pretty well adjusted…

"What?" Cameron asked, noticing his father's glance. "What?" he asked again. "Tell me…"

"Nothing," Jarad said, honestly. Then he laughed again. He looked again at his son. "Don't you think it is weird that here is the two of us, each carrying a gallon of diesel on our backs, hiking up to a ghost town to – hopefully – retrieve a car that we are going to drive on the rails?"

Cameron considered his father's words in the measured fashion he did most things. Then he, too, began to giggle a little.

"Yah, I guess it is a little weird. And we're gonna drive to another country so mom can have a baby!" That last comment sobered Jarad up. Yes, he thought to himself, to have a baby in a hospital so that she did not die...

Life for Jarad was a roller coaster. When things were desperate and then they chanced upon a little bit more to eat, or a place with more security, or help from friends, then life suddenly became good. But after this onset of peace, when there was a little extra in the larder and no one shooting at you, a person had time to consider how life *was not* so good. That life was not good at all. The reality was that they were living the existence of opportunists and scavengers – often risking their lives over scraps. What kind of life was this for his children, with no future?

And he knew that was the key: no future. He wanted his kids to have a future. Really, he would have wanted to go to Alberta even if Myla was not pregnant, because there Cameron and Annie would have a future. That was all the incentive he needed.

A pair of cow elk stopped and stared at them from the middle of the road ahead. By habit Cameron and Jarad froze in their tracks. They knew that if they did not move, the elk would not be able to see them. What the elk needed was to get their scent. Both of the animals knew something was before them in the near distance, but they could not be sure what. They swung their muzzles in the air before them, searching the void for some sort of odor, any sort, to let them know if they should run or simply continuing their meandering about looking for grazing. They must have gotten a whiff of human scent because both bolted off the road with surprising grace and raced up into the trees to lose themselves in the forest.

"Too bad you didn't have your rifle, dad," Cameron said. He then thought about carving up an elk carcass and packing the meat on his back. "Maybe not, that would have been too much work to haul back to Junction."

"I agree. I wouldn't have shot one even if I had my rifle. I'm not starving…yet."

They walked on and on, neither of them talking. Cameron especially found the walk a bit boring, but for Jarad there were many memories along the road. In time they came upon the metal stub of pole where a solar cell was once located. Otty had gone to retrieve it, but someone had beaten him to it. They had since learned that it was Benson, but at the time this was very mysterious. Then the burned out remains of a yellow ranch-style house, the first house he raided soon after his arrival in Blue River. He remembered how difficult it was to haul all of their "loot" back to the church that served as the community pantry, and then dashing out of bed late at night, watching it burn. No one ever did find out who torched it. They passed Howard's little cabin, which had once been scouted out by people from Junction before they knew how many were living up in Blue River. He chuckled, remembering how Howard referred to them as vandals. He wished Howard had not died. He really liked the old codger.

And then their old place. As they approached the old cabin, the neglect and abuse were obvious. Windows had been busted out and everywhere there was leaf litter and branches. Nature was making her slow claim against it. Jarad did not even bother to enter it. Neither did Cameron.

"Well, here we are," he said as they approached their car. It was an older Chevrolet station wagon. It was a great vehicle in its day, but now it looked like the abandoned artifact of the past that it was. He and Cameron were going to change that.

"First, let's pour some fuel into the tank," he told his son.

"And then we'll see if it'll start." He did not think it would, but he was not above making his job as easy as possible. If he could get the engine started, then he could begin recharging the capacitors. If not, then he would have to find a jumper battery. But he knew where to look for that.

The car was covered in a patina of dirt and pine needles. He might even have to wash it before they headed for Alberta. Dumb idea, he thought. Maybe the windows, he conceded, but nothing else.

The keys were still in the ignition. The door opened and he was even met with a chime! "Fingers crossed," he said to Cameron as he seated himself in the driver's seat. He turned the key to 'on' and then pushed the start button. Nothing happened. He twisted the key back and forth and repeatedly applied the start button, but still nothing.

"Well, let's go find ourselves a battery, Cameron. James told me where a good one might be."

The two of them moved slowly toward James's old place. They passed by Otty and Ellie's house and the old double-wide trailer where Breann had lived before she killed herself. Jarad was not sad to see her go. Their path took them by the charred remains of the combination church-community center. He would forever remember the circumstances that caused that important structure to burn down – a show of power by the coup leaders in Washington that they controlled the grid. Damn them, was the only thought Jarad could muster in his mind.

They headed for the yellow house with the attached garage. Jarad tried to pull up the garage door, but it was either jammed or locked. Jarad found a way through the house and then opened the swinging door from the inside. He needed the light to see inside.

He looked around until he found what he wanted: a portable welder. It was a large unit with an attached gasoline engine. Jarad wasn't interested in the gasoline, doubting there was any remaining anyways, but he was interested in the battery. It was just where James said. He looked for tools to remove it from its carrier.

Within a few minutes they were heading back to their car. Cameron had found a hand truck, so they didn't have to carry the heavy old-fashion lead battery. They just pushed and pulled it along on the two-wheeled dolly.

Jarad parked the battery toward the front of the car and reached in the cabin to release the hood. Cameron was a step ahead of him and raised the hood and perched it on its prop. Jarad then dug out his jumper cables from the back of car, reaching right in through the shot out rear window. He attached them to the car battery. The under-hood light came on.

"Looks like we got juice," he said excitedly, seating himself behind the steering wheel. He pushed the start button and the engine turned over, but didn't start. He tried it again, but it still refused to fire.

"What's wrong, dad?" Cameron asked a bit discouraged. He also had a large emotional investment in the car.

"I suspect that the fuel lines are empty. We ran the engine dry when we came here, remember?"

"Dad, we got another problem!" Cameron said, in a voice that combined excitement with worry.

"What?" Jarad asked, poking his head out the door.

"Come here, quick. It's bad!"

Jarad moved quickly to stand by his son. He was pointing to the ground. There was a trickle of diesel fuel running away from the car and through the leaf litter.

He swore. "If it's not one thing, it's another," he sighed. He quickly disconnected the jumper cable. No use draining the battery, he reminded himself.

He crawled under the car, tracing the wet streak of fuel. He found the reason for the leak and then crawled out again, recalling how it got there. "Remember when we first left Purcell and we ran into that barricade on the road," he asked his son. Cameron nodded. He would never forget that as long as he lived. "And remember the men shooting at our car?"

"Yah and you shooting back!"

"Well, one of those shots punctured our fuel tank. Remember? I'd forgotten that." After they had escaped from the road block, Jarad had Myla park the car on the pass leading away from Purcell in order to charge the capacitors.

"I remember that they shot out a tire! That was scary," Cameron whistled. He had some dramatic memories, too, Jarad knew. He wondered if Annie and Cameron were going to grow up traumatized somehow…oh, the worries of parenthood.

Jarad crawled back under the car. He couldn't see where the bullet hole had entered the fuel tank; he could barely locate the tank itself. But they had only put a single gallon into the tank which suggested that the puncture was pretty low. He should be able to access it.

He went toward the rear of the car to locate the original entry point of the bullet. There were multiple bullet holes, all of which made Jarad sick in his stomach – it made him angry to think that men were taking shots at his family. Refocusing on the situation at hand, he realized that most of the shots were grouped low in the left rear of the car, which explained why he had gotten a flat tire that day. Most of the bullets had passed through the rear sheet metal of the car and out the left rear quarter panel. Except one.

He peered in the hole. It was teeny-tiny. But he had an idea. He returned to James's house and found a long dowel in James's stash of building material. James enjoyed working with wood. He was the one that made the caskets for the dead while Blue River was still a community. He then searched for another crucial item: duct tape. He could not find any at James's place so he went over to Genis's. There he found a couple of rolls.

Returning to the car he checked the penetration of the dowel into the bullet hole. It would work fine. Removing it, he carefully wrapped a length of it with duct tape. Not too little, not too much. With experimentation he found the right amount. Taking the axe from his wood stack, he turned it over to use it as a hammer. Very carefully he tapped the tape-covered dowel into the hole, jamming it into the fuel tank. "That should do it, he told his son."

Adding more fuel and shimming again under the car he could tell that the flow had stopped. He doubted that his plug would hold long, but it was holding at the moment. He reattached the jumper cable and with a few more attempts the engine rattled to life. It rocked a bit until all the air was purged from the fuel rail, but soon it was running as smoothly as ever. Jarad had Cameron dump in the second gallon of fuel and he set the capacitors to charge.

They tossed what they needed into the back of the car and Jarad drove slowly back to Junction – it was another surreal moment.

*

The car was silent as Jarad entered Junction on electricity. He didn't want to draw attention to himself. He had learned through the grapevine that a large percentage of the people in Junction shared Benson's thought and also wanted to leave the community. He now realized that there might be some resentment directed toward him and his family since they were proactively working toward getting out of town. But that couldn't be helped, he knew. Each would have to find his or her own way. Part of him felt selfish for leaving others behind; the other part was grateful for the opportunity. If some people in Junction could not see how much personal risk he had taken on their behalf and then resented his leaving, so be it. He was a cop; he was accustomed to being simultaneously loved and loathed.

Myla came out of the house to greet them when they returned. She had complete confidence in her husband, so much so that she had already begun packing and making other preparations. She knew that he would show up with the car. But she was also unsettled by strange emotions that were triggered by the sight of their Chevy. Nonetheless, she began cleaning it out and making preparations.

"Don't get in too much of a hurry, babe," he said to her with a smile. "I still got the hardest part to do."

She pulled her head out of the car, her hands full of items drawn from the back seat. "What's that? I thought getting it here was the big deal?" she asked.

"I still got to get the tires off the wheels and then, somehow, get it onto the track." Her arms drooped and she sighed heavily. "Two steps forward, one step back," she grumbled. "Always something. But I know that you'll figure out something."

Jarad actually was not too worried. Just getting the car down to Junction was a victory and a huge step toward their goal. He was jazzed.

He squatted down on his haunches to take a look at one of the tires. He had no idea how tires were actually attached to wheels. Then a light bulb went off in his head: the spare tire! He had mounted the spare tire on the left rear of the car when the original was shot out by those men when they busted through the barricade. He would examine it – after all, most of the tire was already shred from the wheel.

He opened the rear hatch of the car and dug down to the spare tire well. He pulled out the wheel which still had attached to it the remains of a tire. He carefully examined the mechanism by which the tire adhered to the wheel. He discovered that it was quite simple: the sidewall of the tire was bonded to a wire cable, which was forced over a lip molded into the wheel. Clever! He always wondered how that worked. He figured that he should be able to cut the cable with a hacksaw.

He went house to house until someone lent him a hacksaw and then he sat down on his front porch and went to work. It was difficult to get the blade down into groove where the cable sat. He experimented until he found a solution. He simply made a perpendicular cut into the plastic wheel, parallel to the hub and through the retaining lip, continuing down through the cable. It was hard work, but the cable did cut and with it half the tire was removed. He then cut through the other side. The wheel was now free.

He glanced at the car. He could imagine jacking up each corner of the car and removing the tires as needed, but how was he going to get it onto the tracks? He sat back and thought about this problem. He considered his options, knowing that there were not any mobile cranes or boom trucks around to physically pick up the vehicle. No, he would have to be more subtle than that. If he could get the car parallel to the tracks he might be able to lift an axle at a time, but the rails were quite high. How could he overcome the rails? He got it! It would be simple. Indeed, it was now so patently obvious that they could practically leave at any time. The thought stirred him. He would be leaving; they would be leaving. Junction would soon fill his rear view mirror and disappear behind them, perhaps forever. This was meant to be a one-way trip. Hell, they could leave tomorrow! Ah, another surreal moment!

He went into the house to talk with Myla. They had some things to discuss.

*

It appeared that most of the town had come down to watch Jarad mount his car onto the rails. It was interesting to watch the faces of the people as they observed what was taking place. The general impression was one of curiosity, but marked with a distinct tinge of sadness. Jarad had come to realize that while many were happy for Jarad personally and his opportunity to escape Junction with his family, the sight of him leaving was a reminder of their own predicament – of their own sense of being trapped. Otty's presence helped to mitigate the dour mood of the crowd, but even he was moved by the sight.

Jarad had brought the little Chevrolet down to where the highway crossed the tracks. Here the rails were level with the road surface, as supports had been built into the road surface to make the rail bed traversable by vehicles traveling over the highway. He had carefully maneuvered the car to where each wheel was now sitting on top of a rail, the car parallel to the tracks. Genis helped him as he first lifted the left real wheel with a small hydraulic bottle jack. They then replaced that tire and wheel, which was actually the spare, with the wheel alone that Jarad had cut the tire from. When it was bolted on and then lowered down, the wheel straddled the rail perfectly. So far, so good.

They then began to lift up the left front corner. Once the wheel and tire assembly was removed, Genis pulled a heavy knife from a sheath attached to his belt and stabbed the sidewall with it. The tire deflated almost instantly with a *poff*, and then he quickly and easily cut around the thin sidewall on both sides, removing the heavy tread. He handed the wheel to Jarad who quickly cut both cables with the hacksaw and the wheel was soon separated from the tire. They refastened the wheel on the hub and again lower the wheel onto the rail. He then did the same on the two remaining tires and wheels. Within one hour the car was ready to do.

A few folks had come up to ask Jarad if he thought that they might attempt the same thing with their own vehicles. He encouraged them to do so, but cautioned them that the vehicle's tracks had to match the rails fairly closely. But there was no reason why it should not work, especially now that they had enough fuel for a few more people to try.

They were set. The car was packed, nothing was stopping them. Even Jarad's repair job on the fuel tank was holding. Plus they were packing an extra five gallons if needed. Jarad had filled the fuel tank and that in itself should get them there, not even counting the now fully-charged capacitors. It should be a simple matter.

Send off was going to be sunrise that next morning. An impromptu farewell dinner was going to be given at the community center: potluck, everyone to bring a dish. Elaine was organizing it so they did not end up with nothing but potato salad.

The dinner was nice. There were no formal speeches, though Peter did address everyone. He explained to those assembled why they were going and that this was not to be the end. Otty would be monitoring the radio for their message. Once they got to their destination, they would attempt to arrange a transmission of a signal on the radio – at a specific time and frequency – to let everyone know that they had arrived safely. While they hoped to be in Alberta within a few days, the first schedule effort on the shortwave was not to be for a week. And that was assuming that they could rustle up a ham radio operator to forward their messages. Cameron had discovered that the radio did not work properly – most of the channels were not functioning, explaining why Howard was limited to his Spanish-speaking contact in Central America. But regardless, somehow, someway, they would make contact and let everyone in Junction know how their trip went.

Towards the end of the dinner Benson walked in carrying a large metal bar and a canvas bag holding something heavy. All eyes turned toward him as he approached Jarad. Everyone knew about the falling out that they had, and most were surprised by Benson's absence down at the railway tracks while Jarad was getting the car on the rails. Simple curiosity would have been reason enough.

Benson had a sour look as he stopped before Jarad and dropped the heavy bag on the table in front of him. Jarad didn't know what to think, so he just watched. Benson lifted the long metal bar from his shoulder, wielding it like a baseball bat. He looked at it in Benson's hands as if questioning what he was about to do with it. He then handed it to Jarad. "Here," he said straightforwardly, "it's my best one." He then reached in the bag and removed a medium-sized sledge hammer, a large pair of bolt cutters, and an expensive hacksaw, setting each of them on the table. "You'll need these," he said.

"I don't understand," Jarad responded, now standing and holding the pry bar. Benson pursed his lips. Everyone could tell that he was still a little upset though none knew why – Jarad did – but he was obviously trying to make amends.

"If you were to look closely at the map that you're using to get to Alberta, you'll notice that you're gonna have to change tracks. The one that goes through town only goes east and west. At one point, you're gonna have to go north. That's what these tools are for. There'll be switches."

He explained that a switch allowed a train to move from one track to another. Normally the switch was locked up with a pad lock. He could remove it with either the bolt cutter or the saw. The pry bar was to serve as the lever to work the mechanism and the sledge was for if the mechanism was sticky or refused to cooperate. "Just pop it a few times," he said, "you ain't gonna break anything."

Jarad just stared at the tools and then at Benson. He reached his hand over as a gesture of reconciliation. Benson paused and then took it in his own hand. The men shook hands firmly. No one said a word. Benson looked around himself and asked if there was any potato salad. Everyone laughed and Benson went and got in the chow line for a plate. Myla got up and went over and gave him a hug. Benson was always awkward around women, but he took her hug and blushed, never saying a word, reaching around her with a plate in hand.

***

Chapter 11

Again, Jarad estimated that everyone was out to see them off. He felt very conspicuous, but also loved. He was unsure how to respond, so he busied himself with preparations. He even checked the engine oil twice and the integrity of his dowel-and-tape plug at least three times. They were ready.

Myla was elected to drive. It was thought that once they had reached a safe operating speed, say twenty-five miles per hour, she could set the cruise control. But she would have to stay planted in the seat in case of any emergency.

"What sort of emergency," she asked Jarad.

He shrugged, partly out of irritation. "How can I know? If I knew, then it wouldn't be an emergency." He went back to packing.

Both Peter and Jarad would remain armed and sitting on top. Cameron wanted to sit up front in the passenger seat so he could keep a look ahead with his binoculars. His father seconded that idea, though Annie made it known that she would want to take her turn as well. But now she was crying softly in the back seat, forlorn that she was leaving the love of her life, Jimmy. The dog was put in the back seat, his tail wagging crazily, as he knew he was about to be off on another adventure. Oh, to be like the dog, Jarad thought to himself.

Everyone was in place, except Jarad. He was looking under the car one last time, making sure that the fuel wasn't leaking. This was his big fear, but Myla reminded him that they had plenty of tape should he need to reset it. That did not help his anxiety because they might not realize the leak had returned until it was too late. She promised to watch the fuel gauge. That satisfied him and he returned to the top of the car, his feet resting on the front hood.

She started the car and slowly sped forward. Everyone turned to wave at the crowd. If only out of excitement Myla began honking the horn, which startled Jarad. He was so uptight and nervous that the horn caused him to jump, but he did not say a word. It was not right to yell at Myla. She was probably as anxious as he was.

As predicted by Peter the car tracked nicely, though the whine from the wheels was odd. The plastic wheels made a strange hollow, almost moaning, sound as they rolled over the rails. Once the car reached their cruising speed of twenty-five miles per hour, Jarad was surprised at how fast that was, but he knew any slower would simply draw out the trip. After a couple miles he got more comfortable and he began to loosen his grip on the roof rack.

The terrain before them was completely predictable: ridge lines, trees, rock walls, and the occasional flash of river. Under different circumstances they would have enjoyed the view, but this was not normal. This was serious business. And Jarad did not know if and when they would run into trouble, be it a barricade, a tree across the tracks, or even an oncoming train. He was not at ease.

He tried to converse with his wife, but it required too much shouting. She was saying something about stopping later on. Two hours he said. He asked Peter if he needed a break. He nodded no. Jarad could tell that Peter was both excited and relieved. He really wanted out of Junction. Jarad wanted to ask him about that.

He moved to where he was a bit closer to Peter, indicating to him that he wanted to talk. Peter swung his legs over the hood to sit next to him, but then Myla complained that he was blocking her view. So he pulled them up. Both men laughed.

"Why hadn't you left Junction before now?" Jarad asked him, reaching over to speak more clearly in the rushing breeze. Peter nodded his head that he understood Jarad and he thought a few moments before answering.

"That's a good question," he responded, having to shout a little over the ambient noise. "I've asked myself that many times." He told Jarad that he could have left at any time, but problems kept cropping up and he felt a duty to address them. He did not want to become the default leader of Junction after the grid failed, but that was simply how things played out.

"I think that Elaine would have been a better choice, but she didn't like being in the hot seat," he continued. "When Otty moved down from Blue River, I felt a burden being lifted from my shoulders. Otty just kinda naturally moved into the position of community leader. Fine by me."

Jarad nodded that he understood. Otty was that type of person: a natural leader whom people instinctively rallied around. Otty did not need power, he did not seek power, but neither did he shirk from it and he seemed to handle it well. That was the perfect kind of leader, Jarad mused to himself, assuming the person was competent. Otty was definitely competent.

The sun had become smothered by a cloud cover. It looked like they might get some rainy weather if they could not keep ahead of the westerly winds. Jarad did not care. They were moving and he was happy. Uptight, anxious, concerned? Yes, but happy. He knew he would sleep well that night.

And that thought presented a new problem. Where and how were they going to spend their nights? Should they wait till they came to a side rail? There had not been any rail traffic for months and Jarad knew that they would not be meeting anything from behind them as Genis had blocked the rails with a rock slide. But they were bound to meet up with railway switches which meant that they could expect anything. He would talk it over with Peter and Myla later.

Time was moving more quickly than he thought because Myla began to signal to them that she was going to stop the car. Peter and Jarad could hear the motor begin to wind down and the car began to slow. Myla had chosen a straight section of the rail so they could keep an eye on the tracks ahead. After the car came to a halt, she stepped out. "Potty break," she said as she headed toward the trees. "And no one follow us," she shouted over her shoulder with her daughter in tow, a roll of toilet paper in the other hand.

They had gone approximately fifty miles. Fifty miles! That would have been three days hard hiking if they had gone on foot. Peter and Jarad looked at the map. In a couple more hours they would encounter their first few communities, although they were very small. Still, that meant people and people meant danger.

The three adults agreed to take another break in two more hours, unless indicated otherwise. They did not want to roll into a town unprepared, no matter how small it was.

The terrain was gorgeous, especially now that the clouds had given way to a bit of sun. The constant twenty-five mile an hour breeze necessitated keeping a jacket on, but both Jarad and Peter appreciated the sun against their faces. The kids were quiet; at least Jarad could not hear them.

It was not long before they had to stop again. Myla and Jarad saw the danger at the same time: a small landslide had tossed a tree across the rails. Peter and Jarad jumped down, and Jarad then wrestled a chainsaw out of the back. He hated to fire it up and attract attention to their presence, but he hoped that nobody would be nearby. Just in case Peter kept an eye out, his rifle in hand.

Cameron, Annie, and Jarad made short work of the little tamarack. Champ helped by barking the short piece into submission as the three of them rolled it out of the way. They were soon back down the rails.

Unexpectedly, they crossed a road. This would not normally be an issue, but Peter and Jarad thought that they had them all mapped out. What they realized was that the detail on their map was too coarse for their needs and only showed the major roads. Even more, judging by the copyright, it was also very outdated. Peter could only shrug. There was nothing he could do about it, now or earlier. It was the only map he had – that anyone had. Maps were obsolete. People navigated by GPS, not maps. This artifact belonged in the hands of an archivist, not a traveler.

This was all obvious now, but it was not when they had planned this adventure a week or so ago. Jarad chuckled. He was being dumb again. He had a solution, right in front of his face. He knocked on the sunroof. "Honey," he shouted to Myla when the panel opened. "Turn on the GPS. Is it working?"

A few seconds later she shouted "yes." Of course it would be, he thought to himself, the power grid had nothing to do with the GPS satellites. He leaned his head down into the cabin of the car. "Can you give me a heads up whenever we are near a road or about to cross one? I want to be ready. Our map isn't all that good." She said that she would. He turned around to tell Peter what he had discovered. Peter laughed. "Duh!" he shouted in the wind.

The rail bed primarily followed the river, which was to be expected. Rivers were always the low ground in any mountain range. That was why explorers like Lewis and Clark followed rivers through this area. The river was on the right side of the car as they traveled east, but soon they found themselves over a trestle crossing the river to the other side. It was a strange feeling to be so high in the air without any reference to the ground below. Rail bridges were also so narrow that its edges were barely visible to Jarad or Peter from a side view. This did not help Jarad's fear of heights and he clasped the roof rack especially tight.

When the trestle met land again on the other side of the river, a road appeared on their right. It ran parallel to the train. Myla indicated after the fact that there was a road and that it would follow the tracks for about fifteen miles or so before intersecting it. Jarad nodded his head in acknowledgement and thanks. Peter and Jarad both monitored the road carefully.

They came upon some horses walking along the road. No riders, just horses. Seven of them. They barely acknowledged the car as it overtook and passed them. They must have escaped from their pens, Jarad surmised. But then he saw an odd sight – in fact Peter saw it the same time and pointed it out. He asked Myla to slow the car down and directed Cameron to give him the binoculars.

Pulling the binoculars through the sun roof and up to his eyes, he glassed the object on the road. It was a body, lying in the road. A kid's body – a boy – Jarad thought, maybe ten or eleven years old. Dead, but not long. He swept the vicinity with the binoculars, but did not notice any houses. What was this boy doing out here? Horses and then a corpse…strange, Jarad thought.

Myla was motioning Jarad. "What's up?" she asked. Jarad again ducked his head into the cabin and told her what he had seen. She agreed that this was odd. She just shrugged; she had no answers.

As they moved along a house appeared in the distance. It was an aging double-wide trailer with a detached garage and with a collection of out buildings, one of which appeared to be a chicken coop. Jarad glassed the residence. The front door was open, but there was no evidence of movement. He did not want to stop so he did not say anything to Myla, but he shared what he saw with Peter. Peter borrowed the binoculars and viewed it himself. He handed the glasses back to Jarad, shaking his head negative.

Then they came upon two more bodies on the road past the house. One was large the other small. With the binoculars Jarad could see that the large body was that of a woman and the small one that of a little girl. But something was strange about them. They were dead and had not been dead for long, but something was unusual, but he could not place what it was. He told Myla to stop the car and to stand up through the sun roof. He wanted her to see this too.

She scanned the bodies with the binoculars, trying to manipulate the adjuster to zoom in on them, but it was already at maximum setting. "I know what you're saying," she agreed with her husband, "but I don't know what's wrong with them. They had only been there a couple days at most, but something isn't right about them. And why are they in the street? Were they shot?" she asked.

He had no answers and it did not matter anyway. They could not help the people now. Myla restarted the car and they continued down the tracks. A few minutes later Myla stood up, though the car was still driving along. "Wow that is quite a breeze. I'd need a coat. By the way, I think that we're approaching a town. A little one. The GPS is not really working all that great. It won't track the roads unless we're near them." She disappeared again into the cabin of the car. It was warmer there.

More and more homes appeared along the road as they neared the little town. And an increasing number of bodies were found, some in the road itself, some in yards or adjacent fields. And the doors to the homes were often open, as if the people had left the houses so suddenly they had neglected to shut them. It made Jarad feel uncomfortable and he wanted to be out of the area.

They slowly passed through the little community. It was about the size of Junction, but built up on both sides of the tracks. The road crossed over the rails and then continued on in perpendicularly toward the horizon. One person had collapsed on the road very near the rail bed. Myla stopped to look at it, but from a distance. She did not want to leave the comparative safety of the car. She told her kids to not look because it was gross.

She examined the body with the binoculars. It was a young woman, maybe in her late teens or early twenties. She lay on her chest; her arms sprawled out forward and to the side. What attracted Myla's attention were the dark smudges, some of them appearing to be raised and rounded, on her neck. And all of her fingernails and many of the finger tips appeared to be black, as if dipped in thin ink. She had never seen these symptoms in person or in her studies.

"I have no idea, but this place gives me the willies. Let's move on," she said, retreating back into the cabin of the car. The engine came to life and soon they were speeding down the rails. Jarad just held on. He agreed with his wife, these sights of dead people were unsettling. Whatever was striking down these people was best avoided.

They stopped an hour later for another bathroom break. But no one wanted to be gone from the car for long. During the stop, Jarad manipulated the GPS to get a view on what lay ahead. Unfortunately, he discovered what his wife was talking about. The GPS was not working correctly. The navigation software was programmed to track the roads, not the railway. It did not have data for the tracks, only the roads near the tracks. If the rail bed strayed from a road, the data became worthless. What they did know is that another community was still ahead and it was fair sized.

*

This time they did not slow down as they approached the town. It was bigger than the last one – houses appeared sooner and there were more of them. Thankfully the streets were also not littered with dead bodies. These folks had evidently gotten the word about whatever it was that was spreading and left town. Or maybe they were all dead, that this disease was spreading from east to west and they were heading directly into it. Or maybe it was something local. He had no way to know, but suspected that this disease outbreak explained why Junction had not received any visitors from the east. They were too busy dying.

The terrain began to change. They were moving out of the mountains and toward a wide, flat valley. They could see it in the distance. They knew from the map that they were entering a more highly populated area and consequently were sure to encounter more people. But Jarad hoped that things would continue to go as well as they had so far. Why not, he asked himself. Why would they not?

They were not near any roads, so the GPS was currently offline. But the weather was holding and the day was agreeable. It was good traveling weather. They also all began thinking about lunch. Jarad wondered if they should just snack and keep going, or stop and eat. Peter said he was fine either way. Myla wanted to stop and let the kids and the dog out for a while. They were all feeling cooped up, even in spite of the plague scare. So they stopped, just like that.

"So what are we going to do for tonight?" he asked Peter and Myla. "Do you want to stop and get a motel, or keep on driving?" They all moaned at the thought of a motel, even the cheapest dive would be a luxury.

"Really, a motel!" Cameron asked, delighted.

Annie rolled her eyes. "Of course not, Cameron. Think about it…dad's joking."

Cameron smiled sheepishly. He continued eating his sandwich. In fact, everyone was eating heartily. Amazing. An hour or so back they had just past a place strewn with dead people, witnessed up close a corpse malformed by some disease, and everyone retained their appetite. People adapted. Life went on. Another surreal moment, Jarad thought again. He was counting them up.

During lunch the three adults returned to discussing their plans for that evening. Where were they going to spend the night? Should they have a fire and possibly attract attention? What if it rained? How could they maintain security? What if there is traffic on the rails?

They poured over the map, but it was not really that much help. It lacked details. And, of course, the GPS would not cooperate, so they decided to play it safe. If the tracks were clear, they could easily get halfway to their destination by the end of the day, but they knew absolutely nothing about what lay ahead of them. They decided to cross over the valley they were about to enter and then dash across to what they could see far ahead to be more mountainous country. There they would hope to find a railroad siding to pull over and spend the night, out of the way of any passing train.

Everyone returned to the car when Jarad light-heartedly called out "all aboard." Everyone resumed their places, except now Annie wanted to be up front. She was tired of sitting with the dog, which kept shifting from one side window to the next, always needing to sample by smell the ever-changing environ. Annie was still moody since her separation from Jimmy, but at least she was now being somewhat sociable.

The rails never really descended nor climbed, at least not very steeply. Instead it was as if the rail bed was the constant and the terrain it cut through was the variable. They just sped along at a constant speed, the countryside giving them the impression of altitudinal change, though there really was none. But it was fascinating that they were tracing a route that had been established easily a hundred years earlier. They were seeing the world through the eyes of railroad engineers, not of those that traveled the roads and highways. This way was much more interesting. If anything, the most notable feature of the tracks was their directness. They went straight, everything else weaved around them.

The ridge lines gave way to flat lands. The land became increasingly dry and was soon practically treeless. The landscape was of desolate farmland, but still steeped in the verdant colors of spring. By summer the greens would be replaced with browns and yellows, but for now the land was attractive, though in an austere way. Farmland meant farm towns, and farm towns were always connected to the rails. They kept their eyes peeled ahead.

Peter pointed out to Jarad that none of the fields had been plowed. For that matter, where were the cattle? This was cattle country and most of the crops raised in the area were converted into hay for the long winters. There was no activity, no life, in the fields. They did see the occasional deer and Cameron even spotted a cluster of horses near some trees, but no cattle.

They saw farm houses, barns, silos, and other buildings in the distance, each far from the other and once they came upon a series of grain elevators alongside the tracks. But no people. No cars in the distance traveling silently along the highways and service roads, no children playing outside the dusty and disheveled hovels used by farm hands and their families – nobody, anywhere. Not even a corpse.

"Mass displacement," Peter shouted out to Jarad. Jarad shrugged. He did not understand what Peter meant. "No people…everyone's gone. I suspect they're internally displaced and are encamped somewhere." Jarad trusted Peter's assessments. He had seen so much in his prior life. It was sad to think that those primitive conditions Peter witnessed overseas – in any one of the many small wars that the United States was continuously fighting – should be visited upon this country. But it had. Jarad could see that around him.

The land itself became even more level and the reflection of light off of metal-roofed buildings in the distance told them they were within a few miles of the town. As if on cue, homes began to appear with increased regularity, as they always did when nearing a settlement. People tended to live near people, as simple as that.

An old white two-story farm house was coming up quickly along side the tracks, with the requisite twisted cottonwood and cheap, overused swing set. Jarad wanted to stop and investigate it.

He passed his idea by Peter, but Peter was unsure. Why take a chance? What could they hope to gain? Myla felt the same way. Both of them wanted to play it safe. Jarad would have to go without satisfying his curiosity.

"Mom!…stop, stop, stop!" Annie yelled.

"What?" Myla asked, alarmed.

"Stop the car!" she yelled. Myla stepped on the brakes, bringing the car to a sudden, but smooth, rolling halt. Jarad stepped onto the hood, creasing the sheet metal with his weight, as he braced himself against the forward momentum.

"What the hell!" he mumbled. Peter also swore, seconding

Jarad.

Annie and Myla stepped out of the car and moved down the tracks to see what had gotten Annie so upset. It was some sort of trap. A heavy piece of angle iron had been fastened between the rails with a pair of large c-clamps. Jarad, Peter, and Cameron also came forward to see what had gotten Annie's attention.

"Good job, honey," Myla said, putting her arm around her daughter. "I wasn't watching the road."

Instinctively, the adults looked suspiciously around them, searching the immediate area for highway men or similar bad guys. Who knew that they were coming? Were they spotted and this is an ambush? Jarad pulled his rifle up to the ready. He did not like the feel of this.

Peter spoke up. "This has been here for quite a while…it wasn't intended for us." He showed everyone the weathering the metal had endured. "I suspect that this was put here months ago."

That news made everyone feel less vulnerable. Jarad put his rifle down again, letting it hang across his back again from its sling. He gave his daughter a hug and told her that she was doing a great job and then he returned to the car and looked at the damage he did to the hood. "You know, we're still making payments on this thing…" He said, smiling at Myla.

They took a break. As their tool kit did not include any pliers to back off the clamps, Peter was attacking them with the sledge. Jarad turned back toward the old farmhouse. His curiosity was getting the best of him, but he did not want to risk a trip for no valid reason. The dog gave him one.

Suddenly Champ took off down the tracks and toward the old house, barking furiously. Everyone looked up to see a cat dash through the vetch that entwined the fencing. Annie and Cameron were calling for the dog, but the dog ignored them. They both turned to their mother for help. She looked over at Jarad. He knew what her look meant.

"I'll be right back," Jarad told them as he took off after the dog. "I'll get 'em."

He crossed the ditch and ambled over the remains of an old, disused barbed-wire fence. The house in the near distance appeared deserted. Jarad saw no ghosts peering at him through the dusty, sometimes broken, window panes. Nor were there any dogs barking or whining to announce his presence. No sign of life, not even birds in the trees or shrubs, only that one cat.

Champ was a purebred American water spaniel and he was an outstanding pet. Brilliant, devoted, and brave – the perfect dog for the family except for his predilection to chase small furry animals: cats, squirrels, and worst of all skunks.

Jarad loved the dog, but he was not going to waste too much effort getting him back. He was willing to sacrifice the dog for his family's safety, but Myla wanted the dog back for the kids' sake. The dog is a comfort for them. Also, what would it teach the kids if he was quick to abandon what they considered to be an integral member of their family?

He approached the house as if it was a potential trap. His gun was raised and a round was chambered. The safety was off. He moved from cover to cover; not like a trained soldier, but with the practical movements of experience. He had no military training, but he had gained survival skills. He knew what he was doing.

Using as cover the shrubby overgrowth that marked the fence line, he moved toward a small structure that he figured to be a chicken house. There were no birds inside. Good, he thought to himself. He peered around the corner of the coop and toward the debris-strewn yard that marked the terminus of the driveway. There was a sedan parked out front, covered in dust and caked dirt, making it seem ancient and long abandoned, though Jarad knew this was not so. It was simply one more artifact of the great change that swept the area.

He stood and stared for a bit, checking for movement – movement of any kind. Everything was dead, except for the bare stirring of lilac boughs, tipped with blossoms. The light breeze brought a lovely aroma that contrasted starkly with the lifelessness around him. Even Champ seemed to have disappeared.

He approached the large picture window that now served only as a mirror to reflect his approach. Curtains prevented him from peeking into the interior. He moved toward the front entrance. It was recessed. The door was half open and crust of sediment driven by the wind indicated that it had been open for quite some time. He figured that the house was surely abandoned.

He gently pushed the compliant door with this shoulder, pausing for a moment to listen. It was completely still inside, though his nose began to give him a clue as to what await him: death. Something dead was inside the house. Entering he could see into the front room. Two corpses lay relaxed on the couch, one leaning against the other. It was a man and a woman, and the gun held languidly by the man's hand resting on the cushion explained the scene. Another murder-suicide. Or more probably, a double-suicide. The man was simply the one who pulled the trigger.

He looked at the corpses briefly. Both retained dark shadows around their necks that resembled bruising, not unlike the corpses littering the streets miles back. Their eye sockets were pronounced and the skin seemed exceptionally drawn and tight, framing the skeletal structure of their bodies. They had been greatly dehydrated before their deaths.

There was nothing else of interest to Jarad as he briefly scanned the immediate area around him. An old flat-screen television that had been converted to a televisor remained hung on the wall in the front room, a pair of bullet holes betraying someone's frustration with the devise. Strange, Jarad thought to himself. Perhaps the man was angry with being cut off from the outside world, the televisor his only portal to escape the isolation of this lonely country setting. Sometimes not knowing what was going on in the world was as fearful as knowing.

A dog pranced through the open door, following Jarad's scent. It was Champ. Jarad shook his head. With the dog now around his feet, he headed to the kitchen to see what he might find. It was surprisingly well stocked. The pantry had an ample supply of canned goods, suggesting to Jarad that the couple did not end their lives due to hunger. He found a small cloth bag and filled it up with tinned meat and canned peaches. He knew his priorities.

He returned to the outside. "Come on," he told Champ and turned back toward the tracks. He thought of his family and friend waiting back at the car. They had places to go. Where? He was not exactly sure, but he knew how to get there.

***

Chapter 12

Jarad did not share with Myla what he had seen in the white farmhouse. She would not find it particularly notable or interesting. She did appreciate the bag of food though, especially the peaches. These would be dessert tonight after dinner.

As the car began to gain speed and return its eastward path down the tracks Jarad and Peter resumed their conversation. They discussed the significance of the angle iron braced to the track. "I don't think that it would've derailed a train, but it shows the desperation of the people," Peter said.

"Or maybe not," Jarad countered. "Maybe they were just looking for loot. Who knows?" He told Peter what he saw in the farmhouse, but it did not even so much as cause Peter to raise an eyebrow. They had both encountered dozens of suicides since the grid fell.

An approaching grain elevator reminded them to pay attention to what lay ahead of them – they were nearing another small farming community. The aged and deserted elevators were monuments to times past. Many of these huge structures were long obsolete and stood as memorials of a more prosperous generation. The enduring economic malaise combined with an equally persistent drought in this region stripped the surrounding communities of the wherewithal to continue. They died, many of them slowly and agonizingly.

The houses in the small community were small but arranged in an orderly pattern as dictated by the truncated city blocks that flanked the railway. The downtown area was pathetic in its decades-long impoverishment as plywood coverings out-competed store windows as the most common fronting for the old commercial buildings. There were no customers out today, indeed few vehicles of any sort. Jarad supposed that those who could have escaped had already done so, while those that remained – the elderly or disabled, their cars parked neatly in their driveways – found solace in a different form of escape and lie now dormant in their beds and sofas. There was life, but only in the fluttering of the pigeons disturbed by the passing of the strange car and in the new leafs springing from the cottonwoods and lilacs. No human life was evident.

"No threats here," Peter shouted to Jarad. Peter was now wearing sunglasses, which caused Jarad to smile. Peter looked like a tourist, making the rifle he was holding seem out of place.

The whole image of the now passing town was one of forlornness. One more ghost town, but, thankfully, again devoid of the littering of corpses visited only miles back. Nothing made sense to Jarad. But the sadness of the world around him now only caused him to be further thankful for the bright future ahead of him. Life was good! At that moment, it was good.

He reached down to scratch his leg, just above the sock line. He felt grubby and knew that he reeked of body odor. He would have welcomed a chance to bathe, but he would still have to redress himself in his dirty clothes. They rarely washed their outer garments anymore; it was too much work, too impractical. He scratched himself again. Such is life in the Wild West, he mused.

Myla too was in good spirits. As they left behind the little town and moved onward toward the mountains ahead, she knew that soon they would be halfway to their destination. Alberta was calling! And the trip had gone so well. They had decided earlier that once they reached the mountains they would stop at the first track siding they came to in order to avoid any possible oncoming rail traffic, even though this was quite unlikely. Still, they wanted to rest as securely as they could.

A couple hours later they stopped for a leisurely dinner, giving Jarad an opportunity to recheck his fuel tank repair. He did not even want to touch the dowel, only making a visual check for leakage. There was just the barest evidence of fresh dampness. The constant vibration was sure to encourage at least some of the fuel to escape. But it was fine now. He mentally crossed his fingers. After everyone had finished eating, they remounted the car and sped off.

As if following a script, they came upon a siding near the base of the first grade leading toward the top of the pass into the mountains. They were tempted to stop – as they had earlier agree to – but the afternoon was still early and they could still get some miles in before evening. Plus, Jarad was getting so itchy that he wanted to settle for the night where there might be some water to bathe in. Peter reasoned that there should be many railroad sidings in the mountains, so there was no reason why they could not find one with water. And, he agreed, there was still some sun left to burn. So they decided to continue on until the stars aligned and they encountered both a siding and water.

Two more hours passed and it began to get cooler as they climbed up toward the pass. Jarad discussed with his wife about the approaching night, wondering if it might get really cold, but Myla assured him that she had brought a lot of blankets and old quilts in addition to sleeping bags. They would be fine.

Finally, they reached a siding that was near a roaring mountain stream. Jarad was not sure that he could bear the cold, but he was not going to back down now. After they made camp and were sure that both switches were in the right position, he stripped naked and waded into the stream. The slick rocks helped to make it little work for the current to sweep him off his feet and he fell into the shallow water with a splash. Fortunately the snow-melt water was so cold that it numbed the pain. He made quick use of the soap before scrambling out. None of his kids would join him once they felt the chill in the water. He shivered back into his smelly clothes, refreshed but wondering if it was worth the effort.

As he joined everyone around the fire that Peter and the kids had made, a strange noise began to fill the space around them. A syncopation that was both felt and heard bounced between the rock walls from which the rail bed was cut, the sound growing quickly in intensity. Everyone looked up to see two large helicopters in the distance, both high in the sky and moving south.

Peter ran and grabbed the binoculars from the car and quickly scanned the aircraft. "Sikorskys," he shouted. "Military…strange colors though…I don't recognize the roundels." The helicopters were soon too distant to make out even with the binoculars and he dropped them from his face. He was clearly in thought as he continued to stare at the planes in the distance. "They're not US military," he said with surety and firmness. "I wonder where those birds came from, where they're going, and what they're up to."

"And," Jarad proposed, "whose are they?"

The adults discussed possibilities as to the origin of the noisy interlopers. After some thought Peter became convinced that they were Albertan. "Why they're transiting American airspace, I don't know," he added.

Myla returned to her task. Annie was helping her position a tarp over the top of the car and out toward the side away from the tracks. "You boys get the tent," she said. She pulled it tight and trapped the far end with rocks, making a slope that tapered away from the little station wagon and providing a shelter out of the rain underneath.

Jarad peered under the tarp and at the rocky floor it had created. "Looks comfortable," he said.

Myla laughed. "I got a couple big heavy quilts to lay down as padding. Hopefully that'll make it just like home."

"Yah and we can use these wooden ties as pillows," he chided her, kicking one with his boot.

"Jarad, come on," she said, anger rising in her voice. "What else am I supposed to do? There's not enough room in the car…"

He knew that he had gone too far. He reached over and gave her a hug, reassuring her that it was fine. "And, heck, it's only for one night," he reminded her.

The kids were out gathering additional firewood. It would be an hour or two before sunset, but now was the time to prepare. They seemed to be in the middle of the proverbial nowhere and that suited Jarad just fine.

Peter was using the hood of the car as a table as he reviewed the map, which he had unfolded completely. "We're going through the Indian reservation tomorrow," he said, pointing it out.

"Is that a concern?" Myla asked, looking up from her work.

Peter shrugged. "I don't think so, but it's a weird world right now. I don't know anything for sure, but it might be something to lose sleep over." He smiled at her. "Don't worry about it; I'll be the one losing sleep, okay?"

"Deal," she said. She was not worried so much as surprised by Peter's words.

"Myself, I'm feeling good," Jarad interjected, partly to

soothe Myla's worries. "Here we are, halfway home and everything has gone well. Like they say, if the past is the best predictor for the future, then our future is bright." That note of enthusiasm recast the moment and things became more positive.

Evening settled without drama. No stars were visible as a cloud cover had settled in, being pushed by light winds that made the flames lean and dance. It cooled off quickly, causing everyone to bundle up a bit and to hug the fire to keep warm. Cameron was unable to raise any radio stations on his little windup radio. "Must be the hole we're in," he muttered, looking up into the darkness.

Finally, all settled in for the night. Myla and Annie to a makeshift bed in the back of the station wagon and the "males," as Myla called them, into sleeping bags spread over a spread of quilts. They found it surprisingly comfortable and soon all were asleep, except Jarad. "Damn fleas," he swore softly. "Thanks Champ." But even the fleas could not disturb his peace of mind. They were halfway there.

*

It had sprinkled lightly during the night, but the winds had died away. The day opened with the optimism of "smooth sailing" as Jarad noted during their post-breakfast packing. His enthusiasm was contagious and all were in good spirits. They were a day and a half away from Alberta.

Jarad made sure to reset the track switch after they returned to the main line. They continued to climb before leveling off and the landscape became one of rugged mountains and dramatic skies. The rail bed seemed to weave around the mountains in long looping arcs that wound back and forth continuously out of sight before them. Though the scenery was stunning, so was the cold. It was not particularly comfortable sitting on top of the car and both Jarad and

Peter had wrapped themselves in Myla's quilts.

Three hours later they finally traversed the final pass and began the descent down to the high plains to the east. The weather had not improved, but neither had it gotten any worse. The kids were getting bored and both lamented being stuck in the car. Myla wished she had some reading tablets for them to use, but she did not. Paper books would have been nice, too, but people did not keep them much anymore. They were more relics and heirlooms than practical entertainment. Novels were nowadays found on electronic reading devices, not paper.

The GPS unit began to function again as a road came up alongside the railway. At least now they could use it now in overview mode and it contained better detail than Peter's paper map. But if the road strayed too far from the tracks it would continuously try to recalibrate itself. Very annoying.

To have something to do, Cameron would continuously scan the terrain ahead of them with his binoculars for hours at a time. Consequently he was the first to see the car speeding down the highway, far in the distance. It was moving in the opposite direction of their car and toward the southwest. After he pointed it out, everyone watched the small red speck disappear into the indefinite horizon. The fact of the automobile created excitement and everyone waited with anticipation for what lie ahead.

Soon the highway drew near into view, though no more vehicles appeared. As the GPS indicated they would briefly intersect the road before it moved away again tangentially. They all stared ahead as the tracks and the highway quickly angled toward the other.

Twenty minutes later Cameron again made a discovery and began to get excited. "There's people ahead….and they're on horses!" He started to count out loud. "Seven, eight, nine…nine horses," he reported. "Three or four with people on them!"

Myla passed this information on to Jarad, who in turn relayed it to Peter. Neither of them could make sense of it, but it would not be long before they discovered what it all meant.

They were Indians. As they neared the highway they could make out the cluster of horses, but only a couple were mounted with men. They did not understand the significance of the horses until the road block came into view. A collection of abandoned cars and trucks were parked perpendicular to the highway lanes, cutting off the flow of traffic. Incredibly, razor wire had been strewed across and in front of the automobile barricade. Men sat on the ground or portable chairs, armed with rifles and monitoring the roadway before them, talking in small groups or resting. One fellow was reading.

As they moved upon them, Jarad saw a man pointing excitedly in their direction and soon more men stood, their faces all pointed in their direction. The men's faces were incredulous as the car sped past them. Jarad did not know how to respond so he simply waved. The car quickly passed and the men were soon out of sight.

"What was that all about?" Myla shouted from the sunroof portal.

"I don't know, honey. Give me a second and I'll talk with Peter."

He signaled and Peter shimmied toward him along the roof top. The men discussed what they had just seen and they came to the same conclusion. They had just circumvented a serious road block. Whoever it was keeping guard over that barricaded highway back there had neglected to include the railway tracks. And it appeared that the men were Native Americans.

"This could get interesting," Peter half-shouted into Jarad's ear. "Did you see the look on their faces?" He was not being facetious, he was not smiling. He suspected that something was going to happen. "I don't know who they're trying to keep out or why, but I think that we just turned over their apple cart."

Jarad shared their thoughts with Myla. She only nodded that she understood, without offering up any opinion of her own. She knew that they had no control over what happened next. They could only go forward.

Nothing happened for an hour or so, but then the unexpected occurred: they were buzzed by a light airplane. Jarad was so startled by the sudden appearance of the plane that he just about jumped off of the car. He glanced over at Peter, who only gave him a nod of the head, acknowledging Jarad's surprise and apprehension. The plane returned, slowly circling in the air above them at a surprisingly far distance. They were being monitored.

They saw the horses near the tracks before they saw the pine logs that had been dragged astraddle the rails. There were four men ahead, each on a horse and each armed with a rifle. As Myla brought the car to a stop in front of the impromptu barricade, more mounted men appeared on both sides of the rail bed, with another pair coming up behind them. The mounted horsemen remained silent as Jarad and Peter watched from atop the car. Jarad and Peter made a display of laying down their rifles, but both kept them within reach. They also noted that all of the men sported red kerchiefs around their necks and some even wore feathers in their hair. "Yup," Peter muttered to Jarad barely moving his lips, "Indian country." Jarad simply nodded.

Finally, one of the fellows from near the barricade steered his horse around the logs and toward the car. He was an older man, with a stern though not unkind visage. At first he did not say a word, but stared unblinkingly at Peter and Jarad. Finally he spoke.

"You're trespassing on sovereign land," he said slowly in clipped syllables. Neither Jarad nor Peter responded to his words; they simply waited. There was nothing they could do anyway. Myla and the kids were also silent. The man then stared intently into the interior of the car, seeming to examine its occupants.

A vehicle was heard arriving in the background. A moment later a truck pulled up atop the right bank. The old man backed up his horse and spoke briefly into a walkie-talkie which he had pulled from his belt. Some of his words were obviously English, but many of them were not. He then pointed at the truck with his rifle. Jarad did not move. "All you people," he said, "into the truck."

Jarad looked over at Peter and then down at Myla. He nodded his head toward the truck and jumped down from the car onto the gravel. He was the first up the bank. He extended his hand down to pull up one at a time Myla and his kids. He then joined them and Peter in the box of the old pickup. The driver was hidden behind dark window tint. The driver took off as soon as Jarad was seated.

The truck bounced over the rough ground as it raced to some destination in the distance, a couple of men on horses sprinting after them for a short distance before trailing off. A large plume of dust formed behind the truck, curling up into the box and making it difficult to breath. Myla attempted to speak to her husband, but because of the combination of being rattled about and the stifling dust, she changed her mind. Instead she conveyed her concern through her eyes. Annie was scared and clung to her mother's arm. Cameron sat stoically, but keeping a grip on his binoculars to prevent them from bouncing against his chest.

Jarad's thoughts were going everywhere. He felt defenseless, but knew full well that his destiny and that of his family was not immediately within his own hands. He just hoped and prayed that whoever he had to deal with would be reasonable. All he knew to this point was that he was a trespasser.

The ride in the back of the truck mercifully leveled out after the driver found a road, and the ride smoothed out and the dust disappeared. They were on pavement. After another twenty minutes or so the truck stopped in front of a large ornate building. It was a casino! A man wearing a surgical face mask appeared as soon as the truck had parked. "Don't move," he said softly in a muffled voice. He quickly scanned the dust-covered detainees in the back of the truck. "Okay, come on out," he ordered them. Four armed men were waiting to escort them and after everyone had jumped from the pickup they were directed into the dark interior of the cavernous structure. There were no bright lights to welcome them.

They were led down a deeply shadowed hallway, illuminated only by swaths of rectangular light angling in from an occasional exterior window. But it was comfortable inside.

The small party of captors and captives continued in a circuitous route around the interior of the building of one hallway after another until they found themselves marched alone into an apparent conference room. A collection of sun lights in the ceiling provided illumination. As directed by one of the guards they each took a chair around the table. The door closed quietly behind them. There was a second door on the opposite side of the narrow, carpeted room. Jarad knew it too would be guarded.

This was evidently their holding cell, but it was as nice of a pen as any prisoner could want. Myla commented how she felt out of place, herself being so smelly, dusty, and disheveled. "I think that the *de rigueur* attire is a bit more formal than what we are wearing," she chided, betraying her ease. She was feeling less stressed as much of her apprehension had surprisingly melted away. "I think that we are out of costume."

"What's gonna happen dad," Annie asked him. "Who are those people?"

Jarad looked at his daughter. She was in many ways a mirror of her father, though she took her cues from Myla. If Myla was worried, Annie was worried; if Myla was at ease, so too was her daughter. Annie was also less stressed. Jarad gave her a little grin.

"Native Americans," he said quietly. "I guess that they feel we are on their land without permission. This is strange. We're Americans, they're Americans – we shouldn't need permission to be here. That's assuming this is still part of America."

Peter had been silent since their "arrest," but he been trying to make sense of their situation. Jarad's words prompted him to share his thoughts. "It seems to me that conditions have gotten to the point politically that our native friends here had to assume more overt control of their reservation. This is understandable. We've done this too, I mean, we did blowup a county bridge." He chuckled. "That was audacious, don't ya think? My question is: what are these folks afraid of? Why are they blockading the main highway and why did they feel that they had to take us captive? I mean, we aren't a threat? Something's up…I just don't know what it is."

A couple minutes later there was a light tapping on the door and a man walked in. He paused in the entrance as he talked quietly with someone else in the hallway. "I'll be fine, I'll be fine," he whispered repeatedly. He closed the door behind himself. The man was short and slim, nattily dressed in dark trousers and a pressed, multicolored print shirt, his narrow face framed by two long neat braids. He was middle-aged and had dark chiseled features. He also wore that same red kerchief around his neck. He smiled and nodded his head.

"Forgive me if I do not shake your hands," he said kindly as he looked around the table, taking one of the empty chairs. "I'll explain that momentarily. My name is Elton Fast Runner and I am a tribal elder. I've been asked to attend to you folks. I'd say welcome, but I am not sure that would be appropriate considering the circumstances."

Jarad introduced himself and everyone else in the room. Fast Runner smiled and repeated his nodding with the mention of each name. It was apparent to all that the man was trying to make the best of an awkward situation. "So, what are the circumstances?" Jarad asked forthrightly. "Why are we here? We're trespassers?"

Fast Runner pushed himself away from the table on the wheeled chair in order to cross his legs. He was making himself comfortable for what might be a long interview. "Before I answer that, why don't you folks give me some information about yourselves? That might help me to better explain what is going here. Fair enough?" he asked.

Jarad, Myla, and Peter looked at each other before Jarad started to talk. He began his story in Purcell and shared their background stories, how they ended up in Junction, and their motives for traveling to Alberta. Myla added information that Jarad missed, whereas Peter remained silent. He was content with being described as a retiree.

"Well, that is quite an interesting tale, I must say," Fast Runner said. "And I can understand your wanting to get to Alberta. We do quite a bit of business with them ourselves. In fact, we're negotiating purchasing power from them. But it is apparent to me that you folks are missing a lot of background information. Let me fill in those blank spots before I tell you why you are sitting in this room with me." He looked again around the room. "Can I offer you something to drink, water?" he asked, playing the host. When it was agreed that everyone was thirsty, Fast Runner moved to an adjacent alcove and returned with an armful of bottled water. "I apologize that they are not chilled," he said. "You understand."

After he reseated himself in his chair he began to share with them the impact that the collapse of the grid had on his people. "You know, we value our traditions and our culture, but we are as dependent upon modern amenities as you are. The loss of power was very difficult, especially for many of our elderly." He shook his head. "Very difficult," he repeated.

After the collapse of the grid people on the reservation also were hurting for resources. Fortunately the tribal structure helped to mitigate the problems caused by this and an orderly distribution network was established. Also, the tribal government was able to get some food and others necessary items from their native brethren across the border in Alberta, "but they got issues too," he added. Though times had been difficult, they were faring better than most of the non-native people in the region. "It's been tough, we've tried to help, but then things got very difficult and we had to quarantine our borders." He raised his hands to stop questions. "Let me explain further," he said.

In the past couple weeks plague had broken out. "Just like the Middle Ages in Europe…you know the stories, right?" Unknown to most Americans, he continued, is the fact that the plague bacterium is endemic to the Western United States. "You'd hear about people contracting plague occasionally in the news – even around here – but it is easily treatable. Nobody dies from it anymore. But that is assuming people can get treatment. That's the problem right now. For whatever reasons," he continued, "a huge breakout had occurred in the past month and is spreading like a wildfire. That is why we had to close the border and keep people out. We can't help them…we don't have the medical resources…" he paused as he explained, canting his head from side to side as he tried to find the right words. "We had to protect ourselves," he said unapologetic.

Jarad expressed understanding. He shared their experiences with the raiders from Purcell and how they were forced to blow up the bridge to protect themselves. "And bury the railroad tracks," Cameron added. Fast Runner was impressed, if not a bit astonished. But Jarad could read some doubt in the man's eyes.

"So, that brings us to right now. We are concerned that you folks might be carriers. I trust you understand," he said.

"We're obviously fine, so what do we do? Can we get back to our car to continue on our way?" Jarad asked.

Faster Runner made a face, as one does when they are the bearer of bad news. "I wish it were that simple," he said. "Things are never what they appear, especially during these times. Here's the catch. We are not a united people. There are some of us…who, for lack of a better term are rebelling against the tribal government. And so our resources are stretched even further. To put down the rebellion we need weapons and to purchase weapons we need money. So, it was thought that you folks might be willing to help out. We let you go, you pay a fine. After all, you said it yourself: you *are* trespassing." He opened his hands and gave a half smile, hoping he was making himself clear. His words were greeted with laugh from Peter.

"Oh, I see it all," he said with disgust. "Let's shake down the refugees! Money's no good, but maybe some bullion…grandpa's old silver coins…the family jewels. How about illicit drugs? I'm sure that you can trade heroin for some AK-47s."

Fast Runner blushed and stood up. "I'm sorry you see it that way," he stammered. "We've extended courtesy to you people, explained our situation, and you have the…balls…to compare us to jihadists! You white people are all the same…" He was interrupted by someone pounding on the door. The man did not wait to be ushered in and immediately addressed Fast Runner. "What! Here, now?" Fast Runner responded to the man with disbelief. He rushed out the door without a word to the others, shutting the door sharply behind himself.

The three adults again looked into each others' faces, unsure how to proceed. "The man's a cull," Peter said softly. He shook his head in disgust. "He has us here by the…," he paused and looked at the kids, "…vulnerable," he continued. "And has the audacity to ask us for money."

"If all they wanted was our money or anything else, why didn't they just take it when we were still back at the car?" Jarad asked. "Why bring us here? Doesn't make any sense."

"He's lying to us…or at least hiding something from us," Myla added. "There's something squirrely about him. I don't trust him."

Peter got up and went toward the same door Fast Runner exited from. He put his ear to the door and listened. He looked back at Jarad and Myla and shook his head. He couldn't hear anything. He stepped to the side, putting a finger up to his pursed lips, indicating to everyone to remain silent. He then gently opened the door and peeked into the hallway. Nobody! He moved the door further open and looked both ways, up and down the hallway. They were alone.

Closing the door quickly and quietly he moved with broad

steps across the room and tested the other door. Opening it, he found the same results: they had been left unguarded. Again closing the door, he made a quizzical face to everyone else in the room. "What the hell is going on?" he asked.

Jarad got up and moved to the first door, repeating Peter's actions. He too looked both ways in the darkened hallway. Their guards were gone. Why, he wondered, this did not make any sense. "Something's up," he said to the rest. "This may not be good."

He started to feel hot and removed his jacket, tossing it over the nearest chair. "I'll be right back," he said to the others. "Peter, check out that side," he told him, pointing toward the other door. The two men disappeared.

Cameron and Annie turned toward their mother, bombarding her with questions. What was going to happen? Could they go back to their car? Was there anything to eat? Myla had to smile with that last one. But then, it had been awhile since they had last eaten. "Check out those cupboards," she directed her children, pointing to the same ones from where Fast Runner had retrieved the bottled water.

The kids returned with more water, a jar of instant coffee, and a bar of dark chocolate. "Can we eat it, mom?" Annie asked.

Myla was about to answer when Peter and Jarad both returned. There appeared to be nobody around. Worse, Peter had thought that he had heard automatic gunfire in the distance. "It must be fairly close to hear it through a closed window," he said evenly. He looked at Jarad and Myla, a hint of concern in his eyes.

"Myla, stay here with the kids. Peter and I are going to try to get a handle on where we are and how to get outta here." Jarad looked at his wife. She was worried now, not for her own safety but for his. He gave her a wink and then both men disappeared down the first hallway.

Annie looked at her mother, worried. "What should we do?" she asked.

Myla put on a brave face. "Let's do some praying," she said. "And then eat the chocolate."

She led her children in prayer, which was a good thing to do. Not only did it give her and the children peace of mind, they truly believed it was effective. They had long felt God's hand on their lives, long before the collapse of the grid and throughout their life in Purcell, but they did tend to lean more on him now than they did then.

Afterward all attention was on the chocolate bar before them. "Is it still good," Annie asked as Cameron carefully divided the thin dark-brown slab into three equal portions.

"Yes, of course," Myla said with a smile, trying to evoke a sense of ease to her children. "I betcha that chocolate can last a thousand years and still be good."

Annie rolled her eyes. "Whatever mom," she said doubtfully.

Cameron and Annie both quickly wolfed their portions down, making all sorts of sounds of satisfaction. Myla was in a quandary. She really, really preferred chocolate with coffee, but there was obviously no way to brew a pot. For that matter, even to heat up some water for making instant coffee from the little jar the kids had found.

Then she got a great idea. She opened up a water bottle and took a swallow of the warm contents. She then made a funnel out of a piece of paper she found in a drawer. Carefully she measured into to funnel what she hoped was the correct amount of coffee crystals, tapping the paper to direct the dark brown crumbles down into the bottle. She then recapped the bottle and shook it vigorously.

"What are you doing, mom," Annie asked, again with that tone of voice that is the hallmark of teenagers across the world.

"I'm making coffee!" she said triumphantly. She removed the bottle and took a swig of her concoction. "Hmm!" she said, surprised. "Not half bad." She then further broke her chocolate square down into quarters, consuming one. She rolled her eyes in pleasure, chasing the chocolate down with a mouthful of her room-temperature coffee.

They were startled by the sound of people running down the corridor behind them and the muffled voices of men. All three looked toward the door toward the rear of the room, which suddenly burst open. A man wielding a gun stepped into the room and swept the area with his eyes, quickly fixating them on Myla and the children.

"Who are you?" both the man and Myla said simultaneously.

*

"What 'ya think?" Jarad asked Peter as they moved quietly down the dark corridor.

"I think we need to know where the bad guys are," he said. Both men paused as their path opened up into the foyer area where they had entered the building only an hour earlier. The room was small and was evidently a hub to more hallways as there were doors that led off in different directions. The men were attracted to the large window from which sunlight was pouring in. They stood on its opposite sides and peered simultaneously through the pane and toward the outside.

Their only view was of an empty parking lot. There was no obvious movement of people or vehicles. But the muffled sound of automatic gunfire betrayed the scene. There was a firefight going on somewhere outside.

"Come on," Peter directed Jarad. "Let's go up on top if we can and see what's going on."

The men pulled open doors until they found a path to the roof. There was a stairwell that led upward. The men moved quickly up the steps. Jarad was sweating by the time they had reached the top level. He was not feeling well. He also felt more tired than he should and he wondered if he had not been eating enough. But he would worry about this later as Peter led him out onto the roof through a large metal access door.

The two men headed toward the main entrance area, but stopped and instinctively kneeled down when the sounds of automatic gunfire rattled around them.

"Over there," Jarad pointed with a nod and the two men turned toward the crackling of small arms fire piercing the air. They stood behind a wooden facade and craned their necks to see below. Jarad could see a few men squatting behind a concrete barrier. He pointed them out to Peter. He nodded; he had seen them too. Suddenly, one of the men stooped up and let go with a barrage from his assault rife. Jarad and Peter tried to see who his target was. Peter pointed.

"Over there," he said, pointing with his index fire and sighting down it as if it were a rifle. "Look at the mound earth at the far end of the lot – just right of the exit. See it?"

Jarad peered into the sun, shading his eyes with his hand, and down toward the end of the asphalt lot. On the remains of a small hill, most of which had been cutaway to make room for the parking area, a couple men were trading shots with the fellows immediately below them. It was an oddly conspicuous place to be exchanging gun fire from.

"See, they're just drawing fire," Peter explained. "They're keeping those two guys below us busy. Look over there, to the left."

Jarad shifted his gaze. Three other men with rifles were approaching from the far side of the landscaping that separated the rear parking area from the one below them. The two men behind the concrete barrier did not realize the predicament they were in. Jarad and Peter watched the drama unfold before them.

As the three men neared their quarry their compatriots on the small hill quit firing. Jarad noticed that the two groups were communicating by radio. He also noticed that the three men were wearing colored scarves; not the red of their captors. It was difficult to see from their vantage point, but it appeared to be a blue or gray.

The three men paused just yards from the two unsuspecting red-scarfed men. A final burst of gunfire from the mound rattled over the heads of the two men, causing them to duck again behind their barrier. No sooner had the volley ended than the three other men pounced on the two red-scarfed men. The red-scarfed men both swung their rifles around to face this new threat, but were gunned down before they could get off a shot, their bodies slumping hard against the pavement.

"Looks like they're playing for keeps," Peter said, turning away. He sat back and leaned against the facade. "I think that we are in the middle of a tribal civil war. I wonder which side is the good guys." He looked over at Jarad.

Jarad wanted to get a quick scan of the surrounding area, to not only see where the fighting was occurring, but also to find a way out of their prison. He wanted to get back to the car. The two men then got up and shuffled – crouched over – along the edge of the roof to the other side of the building, stopping and taking quick looks before moving on again. It did not take them long to get a measure of their situation. It seemed that the blue scarves, as they now called them, were winning. At least there were more of them than the red scarves. And they had reached the casino. Jarad was now worried about his family.

"I need to get back to Myla and kids," he told Peter with urgency. Peter agreed and the two men headed back to the metal door and back down the stairs. Peeking carefully into the corridor, the men quickly retraced their path back to the conference room where Jarad's family remained. They found the room packed with men, his wife and children in the center. They were all wearing blue scarves of various hues and they were all staring at Jarad.

***

Chapter 13

"Hi Jarad," Myla said cheerfully, "come on in."

Jarad and Peter entered the room. He returned the nods of the men as they greeted him. Some smiled, but most were serious and did not pay him much attention. They appeared to be checking in with the older man sitting next to Myla, after which they left quickly.

"Jarad, Peter, this is Thomas Charley. He's a tribal elder." The older man stood and exchanged handshakes with Jarad and Peter. Charley was the polar opposite of Fast Runner: he was fairly tall, strongly built, and had long salt-and-pepper hair tied into twin plaits tied with thin leather wraps. Except for the braids, the man looked ex-military to Jarad, and his dark, wind-chapped skin suggested that he spent a lot time outside, like a rancher or a farmer. His grip was strong. And he wore a blue scarf.

"Your wife here was telling me about your adventure," he said, taking his seat again. "And it seems that Fast Runner was trying to shake you down." He looked to his side and toward the floor like he wanted to spit the man's name from his mouth, but he refrained. The motion was understood.

"Red against blue, eh?" Peter ventured.

Charley grunted. "You noticed, huh? Yup." He sighed heavily. "Sad days…sad, sad days."

Charley sat with both arms pushed against the edge of the table as he spoke. He recounted the events that followed the collapse of the grid. Echoing Fast Runner's words, Charley gave accounts of the hardship that was generated among his people and how this led to a division in the tribal government. A few leaders, such as Fast Runner, were part of a faction that tried to take control of the entire reservation and were willing to take up arms to do so. But Fast Runner was not the leader; he was only a lackey, as Charley described him.

"Oh, he's slick that's for sure. And I'd like to get my hands around his scrawny neck," he said, making a wringing motion with his thick, muscular hands. "He's done a lot of damage, hurt a lot of people. People have died."

"What's motivating these people, Fast Runner and the…rebels, the red-scarves?" Peter asked. "He said that he was getting some help for some Native groups across the border in Alberta."

"Like hell," Charley growled, giving the table a slap with his palm. "That son of a…the man's a friggin' drug runner! Or guns…whatever. His friends across the border are all black-market types. No, these people only want to set up a cartel to control the illegal trade that funnels through here. Because of where we are, geographically speaking, my people have always been traders. Traders before the white men came, traders with the white men…you know the story. Hell, we're still traders. Fast Runner and his compadres just want to trade in the wrong things…where the money is. Big money…you know what I mean. Hell, there ain't no United States no more – at least not around here. But people are still trading. You think the drug trade ended when the power died? Nah! Still a big problem here…"

"So, what about us? Can we leave?" Jarad asked.

"Oh, you're more than welcome to leave, but I wouldn't recommend it…not quite yet. From what your wife here tells me, it sounds like you'd be heading right into the trouble if you returned to your car. We're pushing these boys west and off the reservation. This might take a day or two." He looked around room, as if trying to remember where he was at. "Let's see if we can't rustle you folks up a couple rooms. How about if you spend at least one night – I'll pick up the tab, I got connections – and then we'll rethink this in the morning? Sound good?" He smiled broadly at his own joke, but Jarad knew he was serious. He liked the man.

"Sounds good," he agreed, looking toward Myla and Peter for their affirmation. They each nodded. He turned to his son. "Cameron, looks like we're gonna spend a night in a motel after all!"

*

They still could not shower! There was no running water in the casino. And the toilets did not work, though Myla found a solution. The casino used to sell a lot of bottled water to the tourists that would flock in to try their luck against the slot machines. She found cases upon cases of bottled water in the storage area of the foyer concession stand. They used this to both flush the toilets and fill the tubs. It was a lot of work, but it was well worth it. But they still couldn't wash their clothes – not if they wanted to leave the next day. They considered waiting an extra day or two more, but then decided that getting to Alberta should be their priority. Anyway, they had all become accustomed to living in dirty clothes. It was the norm.

Dinner was snack foods: chips, candy, and warm sodas. The kids were in heaven! The televisors did not work and there were no diversions for entertainment, but the beds more than made up for this. None of them realized how exhausted they were until they laid down on the mattresses. Under different circumstances they might have complained that the sheets were musty and the rooms a bit dusty, but not now. Instead the rooms, especially the beds, were unadulterated luxury and indulgence.

After quick baths in tepid and shallow water and plenty of soap, all turned in early. Jarad especially appreciated the bath, as he was increasingly feeling ill. Myla suspected that he had a fever, but only a slight one. He also complained of a sore throat and achy joints, but these were nothing that a good night's rest would not cure. She also found some pain relievers in some little envelopes on a display rack. She grabbed them all, along with other useful items, and gave her husband a couple tablets. They both fell immediately asleep.

The next morning only Peter was up early. He was out and about long before the others. It was not that he was anxious to leave and to be back on the road, he was just by nature a curious person and this was a new environment to be explored. At least within limits. He walked around the perimeter of the parking lot and used Cameron's binoculars to reach even further out. There were practically no people about. Either they were still sleeping, or even this native community has suffered from an exodus of residents. By the time he returned to the casino, Jarad, Myla, and the kids were up. He found Jarad chewing on a piece of beef jerky and slouched on a divan in the foyer. He was looking a little rough.

"You okay," he asked him, concerned. Jarad was flush and his eyes were slightly bloodshot. His voice was raspy and he moved a little listlessly.

"I'm fine," he said. "I think that I picked up a bug. About time. You'd think we'd all have been sick by now, many times over. I guess all of this hustle and bustle is catching up with me." He took a long draft from his bottle.

"What is that?" Peter blanched, indicating the brown liquid

that filled his water bottle.

"Coffee," he said. "Home made coffee. Wanna try some?" he asked, offering Peter the bottle. Jarad explained how it was made – Myla's special recipe.

"Gosh, thanks, that's very generous," he said with a snicker. "But I'm watching my caffeine intake…" He winked, sarcasm painting his face. Jarad laughed softly in a hoarse chuckle.

They waited most of the morning for someone to come by the casino, but no one did. Jarad could understand it; they were not really a priority. Thomas Charley had bigger concerns than five vagrants looking for a ride.

Around noon Charley entered the foyer, followed by a kid just a couple years older than Cameron. He introduced Jarad to the boy.

"Jarad," he said, greeting him with a handshake, "this here is Lester. He's gonna be your chauffeur and run you folks back out to your rig on the tracks." He looked more closely at Jarad, suspicion in his eyes. "Are you okay?" he asked.

Jarad nodded. "I'm fine," he rasped.

Charley again looked carefully at Jarad, especially after hearing his raspy voice. "Well you don't look okay," he asked, "you look like hell. What, you stayed up too late partying?" He smiled, his eyes twinkling.

"Listen," he continued, the change in his inflection to something more serious grabbed everyone's attention. "You people got guns? You might face some trouble as you approach the border – highwaymen. You know, you're not the only ones heading north." He explained that highwaymen were menacing refugees as they made their way to Alberta. "There's nothing we can do about it, at least not right now. You'll be on your own. But you're probably the only people on the rails. I doubt that they're watching the tracks. Still..." he shrugged. "The rails pretty much parallel the highway, so unless you're really lucky they'll probably see you coming."

Jarad nodded. He was not surprised. Highwaymen had been a problem around Purcell almost immediately after the grid collapsed, so why would this area be any different? There was always someone ready to take advantage of another's misfortune.

"We're a day away," Jarad said. "Just a day away. I suppose there has to be something..."

"Yup, if you run through the night, you should make it. Maybe that's the key. I doubt they'll be too active at night," he agreed. "And I wouldn't worry about any other rail traffic. There hasn't been a train through here since forever."

He again jutted out his big hand and Jarad took it, shaking it firmly. "I...we appreciate your kindness. We couldn't have made it without your help."

Charley just nodded and then shook Peter and Myla's hands, too. "Take 'em Lester, they're all yours," he said. With that Charley waved at Annie and Cameron and headed back out into the sunlight. He was a busy man.

Lester led them to a big SUV and they all climbed in. He headed down a paved street before turning onto a gravel road that led them away from the town and into the scrubby countryside that was trying very much to be green and to awaken from its winter slumber.

Jarad mostly rested as his throat was too sore to talk, but Peter quietly and smoothly "interrogated" the young Indian man. He wanted to learn about the current plight of the native people. What he found was that their situation was not much different than that of non-natives. The collapse of the grid was an equal opportunity disaster. Lester did mention that hundreds of people were stranded at the casino when the power went out. Most left after a day or two, not wanting to pay for a room when there was no more gambling to be had, let alone restaurants to eat in. Most of these were Albertans who would come by the bus load on long weekends. A surprisingly large number of people loitered about a bit longer – the incorrigible gamblers whose optimism transcended reason. But soon the place became the dark cavern that it was today.

But Lester was not interested in that sort of thing. He only lived near the casino because his mother worked there. What bothered Lester more than the loss of the grid was that he could not finish out football season. And this coming year was supposed to be his senior year and it did not look like it was going to happen. But what he really wanted to do was to go to Maryland. "Maryland?" Peter exclaimed. "Why would you want to go to Maryland?"

"Cause my sister lives there. She said it was really nice. Really green," he said in the slow cadence of many native speakers. And she lived on the ocean. Lester had never seen the ocean. He also talked about how he constantly worried about her – he had not heard from her since the power went down. Peter made sympathetic sounds.

Finally the tracks came into view and Lester followed the metal lines until they brought them to the car, sitting incongruously on the rails. Lester parked the big car next to the little Chevy.

Jarad and the others inspected their vehicle. The rifles had been taken, but everything else seemed to be intact. Evidently the men had more pressing concerns than to bother rifling through the meager possessions of a bunch of stinky vagrants. Jarad reached through the missing rear hatch window and pushed through the sleeping bags and other things before finding his pistol still safely stowed in its holster. Damn, he thought to himself, he was going to miss that rifle, but at least they were not totally defenseless.

Lester helped them roll the telephone poles off of the rails. Soon both logs rested in the ditch at the base of the bank. As they turned from this work, the *wup wup wup* of distant helicopters echoed softly around them, quickly increasing in intensity as the machines flew overhead. "There they are again," Peter said. He watched them pass, holding his hand as a visor over his eyes. "Do you see these very often," he asked Lester, who stood along side him and who was also watching the aircraft fly by.

"Yah, they pass over about every two or three days, almost always two at a time, sometimes three." He shrugged lightly, not particularly interested in them. "They never come here."

He turned and sprinted up the bank, pausing only to give a broad wave to everyone and then he was gone, the truck moving quickly out of view.

The travelers retook their usual positions in and on the car, except Cameron and Jarad. Cameron moved up on top to sit by Peter, Jarad moved into the car. He had obviously contracted something and his fever was getting worse. Myla kept him dosed up with ibuprofen and this made him a bit more comfortable, but he still was getting chills and his throat was getting worse. He could talk clear enough, but the effort was painful so he chose not to. He also did not want to face the constant breeze on top of the car. Instead, he tried to sleep in the "bed" that Myla made up for him in the back of the little station wage. She had dropped one of the rear seats, which allowed Jarad to lie down more or less, though he had to share space with a couple boxes of bottle water and much of their other supplies. He was uncomfortable, but he kept his mouth shut. If all went well he'd wake up tomorrow morning in Alberta – that was what he was counting on

They were off! Myla and Peter earlier agreed that they should make up as much time as possible and minimize their stops. They had reviewed the map and realized that they should be meeting up with the branch line heading north in about five hours. From there they could take a short break before heading north and finally into Alberta. There were connecting rails that would allow them to switch from the eastbound tracks to the northbound ones. Then it would be another four hours or so to the border. "Fingers-crossed," Myla said.

The drive to their break point was uneventful. They passed steadily and relentlessly over the steel lines that mirrored the bright overhead sun. The rails seemed to project forever ahead of them, ever reaching toward the horizon. Myla slumbered in the front, her retinue broken only by regular assessments of her husband's condition. His fever worried her and if she did not know better, she thought that he had contracted mumps, which as with many of the childhood diseases from two generations back – measles, chicken pox, and rubella – had seen resurgence in spite of vaccinations. But it seemed worse than the countless cases of mumps that she had seen as a nurse. His fever was higher and his coloring seemed odd. Perhaps this was how an adult responded to the mumps' virus. She did not know. She wondered what else it could be. It was apparent that Peter was concerned, too. She decided to discuss Jarad's condition with Peter when they took their supper break.

Cameron had initially tried to keep an eye on the horizon with his binoculars, but the constant wind generated by the moving car proved too much of an obstacle. Bored, he positioned himself on the roof rack so that he could recline and take a nap. Peter made the boy loop his belt around the railing, so he did not inadvertently roll off the car while sleeping. 'Your mother would never forgive me," he told him. Cameron complied, and then pulled his coat up over his face. It was not long before he was asleep.

Once they reached their probable destination, Peter directed Myla to go both forward and reverse on the tracks to make sure that the switch in the rails was the one that they wanted. Neither the paper map nor the GPS was useful in this regard – both ignored the railway. Once they were sure, Myla got out the food supplies – a choice of snack foods, canned vegetables, or combinations thereof – while Peter wrestled with the switch. This one was sticky and Peter had to make liberal use of both the lever and the sledge hammer before he got it to cooperate. Jarad slept through both the loud banging and the meal.

Myla sat with Peter as he slowly ate the contents of a can of beans. She shared her concerns about Jarad's sickness and expressed a fear that it might be serious. "I've never seen him so hot," she said. "He's sweating profusely, though he complains of the chills."

"You weren't with me when Thomas Charley approached me about your husband, but he thinks…and I agree with him…that Jarad has plague," he said quietly, whispering the last words so as to not alarm the kids. "They've been seeing a lot of it and they all start out the same, fever and sore throat."

Myla jumped a little when he said that and her eyes moistened, but she did not respond immediately. She pursed her lips as she considered what Peter has said. Then she nodded her head, saying she agreed with him.

"But I didn't want to believe it to be true. I've never seen someone who had contracted plague, at least not someone alive…" she paused, choking back her tears. Her mind's eye revisited the dead bodies they had seen lying along the roads. "What'll we do?"

"Alberta," he said firmly. "We gotta get to Alberta. As

Charley said, we are not the first people trying to get to Alberta. You know that this plague problem has to have spread up there or at least the fear of it. I would be surprised if there weren't refugee camps at the border. The Albertan government is gonna want to keep this outbreak contained, and there is no way in hell they're gonna let a bunch of plague-ridden refugees enter their country in an uncontrolled fashion. We gotta get him to the border. There should be medical services there."

These words encouraged Myla and she again nodded that she agreed with him. "But what about the highwaymen?" she asked. "I'm afraid…I'm afraid what might happen."

"We run in the dark and we run silent. Unfortunately, even in electric mode, the car makes quite a bit of noise with those plastic wheels. I guess you better pray. We should be there a couple hours after sunset or so." He got up from his seat, tossing the empty bean can along side the tracks. They were not stowing their garbage.

"Ready?" he asked her. She sniffed, nodded, and got up. She checked on her husband again and then returned to the driver's seat and started the car. She was ready to go. Peter and the kids returned to their places and the little car quickly gained speed on the northbound track, the distinctive hum from the wheels increasing in volume. They were almost there!

The rails passed over the most forlorn landscape that they had yet encountered. The land was a modulated flat plain that was formerly farmed, but had now been released to Mother Nature who quickly covered the fallow fields in weeds. But many of the weeds had already blossomed and great swaths of muted colors greeted the travelers in the late-day sun. The fields would have been beautiful, if they had been noticed, but they were not. Thoughts were elsewhere.

While Myla worried about Jarad, Peter worried about

highwaymen. He did not share his fears with Myla as it would not have been constructive. Hopefully they would simply roll into Alberta, encountering no one, friendly or otherwise. But he felt vulnerable without his rifle. Yes, he was aware of Jarad's service pistol, but a pistol was no match for a rifle. And he was sure that the highwaymen would all be well armed. He wondered how closely the tracks paralleled the highway – the map gave no detail. He realized that he would know soon enough.

    The setting sun also brought with it a decrease in ambient air temperature and it got increasingly cold on top of the car. Unfortunately, there was no room to be had in the cabin of the car, as Jarad took up both the rear seat and the space behind it. Peter had anticipated this and gathered up any spare quilts for him and Cameron to bundle up with. As he wrapped himself in the heavy layers, he wondered if they harbored fleas. He sighed heavily. The first bite would tell him.

    They had never traveled on the rails at night and the deepening shadows played games with Myla's mind. She began to see the movement of men and horses in the folds of lands that the rail bed cut through. Because of the growing dimness, she did not initially see the highway that came up parallel to them on the right. For her it was a foreboding sign. You can not have highwaymen without a highway she thought to herself.

    Cameron was looking forward to the setting of the sun, because it was then that he could get his little radio to work. When the sun finally hid itself behind the western horizon he began to energize the capacitors in the radio with a rapid twirl of its little crank. After an initial burst of squeaks and static, the sound of music with a definitively tinny quality filled the one little speaker. Tonight's selection was Country-Western and the twang in the voice of the singers and distinctive sounds of the steel guitars in the background delighted Cameron. Indeed, he found everything associated with the radio to be gratifying. In some ways, since this radio was Cameron's primary association with Alberta it had become an enchanted box that transformed his evenings into stirring journeys of imagination. As Alberta had become such a singular focus for his mother – a place where all of their problems would be solved – that Cameron had internalized this, giving Alberta an almost mystical quality. His radio – magical as it was in his nonelectric world – reinforced the awe and wonder. Alberta had become a Utopia. And he was almost there!

Peter's mind was whirling. He stared north into the blackness. It had become too dark to make out the specific features of the land before them, except for the dark horizon against the twilight sky. He was trying to think like a bad guy. Where would he post an ambush if he were a highwayman?

Peter had a long history of experience with bad guys: jihadists in the Middle East; mujahedeen in Afghanistan; radical secessionists in the United States. But each of these was driven by higher motives than simple thievery. Highwaymen were thugs, opportunists, parasites who simply took that which was not theirs. This was a different beast and Peter tried to put himself into their shoes. Yet as much as he tried, intellectually and emotionally, he could not get them to fit. But he had to come up with something. For all of his experiences in counter-terrorism and for all of his military training, one would think it should be a simple thing to analyze a situation from the perspective of a bandit. So he reframed the question: If I were to ambush a patrol of Taliban irregulars to gather intelligence information, how would I do it? He smiled. He had actually done this. Now it was a simple equation.

He would find a stretch of road, not too long or short and preferably with a twist in it and that was boxed in by two high banks or similar earthen barriers. No trees or grassy areas, as people expect ambushes from such places. From high ground people can be trapped front and rear. Indeed if it is done right, a few well-placed and well-armed men can tackle a fairly large group of hostiles. And that was one of the keys: being well-armed. Peter did not know about the bad guys, but he knew what piece was missing in his equation: a lack of a decent firearm. Speaking of which, he decided to ask Myla to hand him Jarad's pistol. Any gun was better than no gun.

But before he could, he noted a light ahead of them, dancing, as if from a fire. He tried to focus on the source with his old tired eyes to make sense of it, but it was quickly lost from view when the tracks made a slight jog to the left, sweeping the car with it. He called to Myla to ask her if she had seen the same flash of light, but she had closed the sunroof and she did not hear him through the open window. He pounded on the roof to attract her attention. The sunroof opened up in response.

"Did you see the light?" he asked her, shouting over the wind and wheel noise.

"Light?" she shouted back. "What light?"

"Ahead. I need Jarad's pistol."

"Okay." There was a long pause.

As the car rounded the bend in the tracks a huge light suddenly appeared before them. It was a bonfire, burning next to the rails. They had come upon a campsite. Suddenly Myla screamed and the car came to a rapid stop, almost throwing Peter and Cameron from the roof. The dark outline of a man stood in front them, straddling the center of the tracks. Behind him was the fire and quickly he was joined by two other men. They were all armed. "Damn it, Myla…you should've run him over!" Peter said, only loud enough for her to hear. Facing the men, he put his hands in the air. He told Cameron to do likewise.

One of them shouted a loud hoot and the three men quickly approached the car, their rifles drawn and pointed at the vehicle. It was difficult to see their faces as the fire was to their backs. Peter could hear Jarad making sounds. The excitement must have woken him up.

"What have we here?" the center man spoke. He seemed genuinely surprised. Peter realized that they had stumbled upon the thing they were trying to avoid: the highwaymen's camp. Damn, he mused to himself.

A second man wielded a small flashlight and swept the interior of the car with its bright white LED light. He peered through the glass at Myla and Annie and then looked through the rear passenger window, which was open, flashing the beam across Jarad's prone body. He spoke. "Everybody, out of the car," he ordered, in a voice that was younger than the man in the center. Myla opened her door and stood behind it. She directed her daughter to crawl across and exit through the same door, indicating with her hands for Annie to stand behind her. But the men noticed them right away.

"Women!" the third man said, off to the right. The flashlight brushed across Myla's and Annie's faces and then their bodies. Both shielded their faces from the bright, probing beam. "Hot damn," the third man continued, "A pretty daughter and a pretty mama." He whistled coarsely, causing the younger man to give up a wicked laugh. They were both getting excited.

"The man in back, he needs to get out too!" the younger man said, pointing with his flashlight. "What's wrong with him? Is he sick or something?"

"He's got the plague," Myla said firmly. "And you'll get it too if you don't leave us alone."

The mention of the plague stirred up gasps from the men and they whispered among themselves. "Plague or no plague, nothing that a bullet can't fix," the man in the center warned.

Peter spoke, louder than he needed. "We're unarmed and we got nothing of value. Let us leave," he said. The light turned toward him, across to Cameron where it paused for a moment, and then back to Peter. Peter turned his face away from the beam to avoid its harsh whiteness, but kept his hands in the air.

The center man responded to Peter. "I'll decide that!" he warned him. "I'll decide that, ya hear? You gotta have something." He paused, looking at the car. "Ain't that clever," he said. "Ain't that clever, boys." He looked again at Peter though Peter could not see any of their faces, only their distinct outlines against the light from the yellow flames. "I think you're lying. I bet you got all sorts of money…or coins…or something. Hell, you got women, that's good enough, right boys." His two accomplices gave up another round of unpleasant sounds.

"Gold!" a harsh voice called out from the car. "I got gold!" it repeated. The left rear door opened and Jarad slowly struggled to pull himself upright out of the back. Myla moved quickly to help him. He was covered in sweat. "No," he told Myla, "stay with Annie."

It was obviously very difficult for him to speak and his harsh voice was barely louder than a whisper. "I will give you gold," he told them. "In my boot. In my BOOT!" he shouted, wanting to make himself heard.

He slowly and deliberately reached down with one hand and

unlaced his right boot. With difficulty, he managed to pull it off his foot. He tossed it onto the hood. "Myla," he said, breathing hard. "In the insole…in the insole." Myla reached into her husband's boot and pulled out the insole, tossing it aside. The flashlight kept track of her actions. Reaching in again, she felt something pushed into the ribbing of the sole of the boot, but had trouble removing it. She pounded the heel against the hood of the car until she was able to dislodge it. She shook the boot upside down and a piece of metal fell with a heavy *clang* onto the sheet metal of the car. It was a gold piece. The man in the center grabbed it.

"Look at what we got here," he said, amazement rising in his voice. "A genuine gold piece! We've struck it rich, boys…struck it rich."

"One more," Jarad said. He again laboriously unlaced his other boot, reaching down with both hands to remove it. But as he lifted it up in the darkness with his left hand, his right had smoothly and simultaneously grabbed his pistol. When he tossed the boot onto the hood of the car, he deftly slid the pistol up against Peter's knee. Peter glanced down and noted it, quickly returning his gaze to the three men, all of which were fixated on the boot. This time, though, the center man did not wait for Myla. He grabbed the boot and quickly retrieved the second gold piece himself.

"There's gotta be a third," the younger man complained. "You gotta have more" he shouted at Jarad. Jarad swung his head back and forth. He did not have any more. "Then I get the girl," he said, reaching for Annie.

Annie screamed and clawed her mother with both of her hands as the man wrenched her away from her Myla's side. Myla cursed and flailed at the man's face with her nails. He kicked her savagely in the stomach, causing her to collapse onto the gravel with a moan. Cameron hollered and jumped down from the car whereas Annie tore herself free from the man, both of them reaching for their mother who lay gasping on the rail bed.

Peter, seeing his opportunity, picked up the pistol and pointed it at the outline of the younger man and squeezed the trigger. The man collapsed simultaneously with the explosion which rented the night air. A second blast dropped the man in the center and a third was directed at the man on the right, who also fell in a heap upon the hard ground. Just as Peter was able to direct a shot into the middle of the third man's chest, the man reflexively squeezed off a round from his rifle, but too late to save himself. Though he would never know it, he scored a hit and Peter fell backward onto the roof of the wagon, a bullet piercing his right shoulder.

Jarad stood still, too exhausted to move toward his wife, who lay gasping on the ground. She was finally able to get to her knees, but she was sobbing heavily, her one hand holding her stomach. "My baby," she cried out between her sobs. She struggled to her feet, grabbing for the door to help support herself, pain causing her to heave breaths.

"Myla," a hoarse voice called out.

"I'm fine," she responded. "Lay down, Jarad...please. I'm okay," she lied, knowing there was nothing that he could do to help her. Her stomach was cramping and she, too, needed to sit and rest. "Annie, Cameron, one of you needs to drive. Momma can't right now." She pulled herself across the front of the car's cabin and collapsed onto the passenger seat.

Peter sat up, the others unaware of his plight. He felt his shoulder with his left hand and could only feel the slickness of blood. He cursed, gritting his teeth to the pain. He knew he was on his own, but he was not secure for travel.

"Wait," he shouted. "I've been shot."

"Oh, no!" he heard Myla's muffled voice call out from the cabin.

"I'm okay," he consoled her, though he was not sure if he was really fine or not. He rolled back onto his left side and tried to secure himself between the railings of the roof rack. He pulled the quilt over himself, though it was damp with blood. He hoped he was not bleeding to death. He could do little to staunch the flow of blood, except hold his shirt and jacket against the entry wound. "Okay, I'm set," he called out weakly.

"Annie, you drive," Cameron told her. "I'll help you from the roof." He climbed on the hood of the car and posted his face over the sunroof portal, his back facing the front of the car. He helped his sister to get the car started and into gear. The car began to move down the rails, past the fire, and into the darkness, dragging for a short distance the corpse of the middle man. As the car gained speed, Cameron helped his sister to activate the cruise control. They were perhaps an hour to the border, but Alberta was not on anyone's mind as the little Chevrolet traveled north through the black inkiness, under a breathtaking riot of stars.

***

Chapter 14

Jarad had dreams, the most vivid that he had ever experienced or could ever imagine. He dreamed that he had been brought into the presence of the source of all light, being reborn in a second birth, except that instead of being drawn out of a womb he was being lifted high, upward by light rays, white lights…white everywhere. People spoke to him in muffled voices, but he could not understand and he could not answer. But it was only a dream, for when he did awake – when he did return to a world that he knew – he could barely open his eyes. For when he did, a light above him seemed to pierce his brain and caused pain to pulse in his head. Oh did he have a headache! He wanted to go back to dreamland! There he floated among the angels, here his head pounded.

"Hi dad," Cameron's voice called from the distance. "You awake?" he asked softly.

Hearing his son helped him to clear his mind, and he used his son's voice as an anchor point to pull himself fully to the present. He mumbled a response, though it was incoherent, coming across as only a sound. His eyelids fluttered as he tried to gain control over them. Opening them, the first thing he saw was a white bed cover. He was in a bed, his head and torso inclined upward. He again batted his eyes to gain control of his vision. Looking around he realized that he was in some sort of a medical facility. Cameron called to him again.

"You okay, dad?" he asked, concern in his voice.

He turned his head toward the direction of his son's voice,

looking for him. Seeing his eyes he gave the boy a smile. "Hi Cameron," he said weakly, his voice still hoarse. "Is everyone okay?"

"Yah, everyone's fine. You're all in the hospital, 'cept me and Annie. And Champ's in jail. They put him in a kennel with some other dogs until a vet could check him out."

He nodded that he understood and then looked down at his arm. There was an IV taped to it. His headache began to abate and his mind got clearer. He looked around the room again. It was as if he was waking up a second time. He tried to sit all the way up, but could not. He was too weak.

He looked again at his son, who was watching him intently. Jarad noticed the concern for him in his eyes. Jarad suspected that he had had a rough night. "What happened?" he asked him. "How'd I…we...end up here? Where's your mother?"

Mom was in a different tent, he explained. This was a tent, too, he indicated by circling his hand in the air. A military hospital tent, he said. They were in a camp for refugees and there were a lot of large tents where the doctors and nurses worked. But he had not been able to go anywhere. They told him he could sit with his father or sit back in their own tent, but he could not wander around. "And I didn't wanta wander 'round, I just wanted to see things before I came and sat with you," he explained.

"Tell me what happened last night. The last thing I remember is Peter shooting the gun and mom getting hurt – I remember her talking – and…" He shook his head, trying to recall the memories. "And we got back into the Chevy…and I wake up here."

Cameron recounted the events from last night. After everyone loaded back up into the car, he helped Annie get the car going again. They drove about forty-five minutes or so and they came upon big bright lights that illuminated both the tracks and the highway. There were buildings and they could see a couple of blue flags, and he knew that they were at the border crossing. He helped Annie stop the car as near as they could within sight of the building that had people in it. Pretty soon some men came running toward them, two of them armed with rifles. All three were soldiers. Cameron told them what had happened and the one man without the gun radioed for help. Two ambulances came and took his parents and Peter away.

Annie and he were put into a bright room where another military man came and talked with them. Then a woman came and she was in a uniform too, but she was not military. She was with the Salvation Army. This woman took them to what she called a "family tent" and got them situated. They had access to some food, toilets, and showers. Annie and he agreed to shower, though they still had to redress in their same clothes. They thought about sleeping in the cots, but they did not want to be separated from their parents, so Annie went and stayed with her mom and he came to sit with his dad. He had slept in the chair that night, for what little sleeping he could do. He was still a bit wound up from all the excitement.

"What happened to mom? Why is she in the hospital?" Jarad asked. He knew that she was hurt, but that she was also safe. His memories were foggy; everything was foggy. And it was only vaguely that he knew Peter had been hurt, but was also somehow not hurt…he could not remember.

"The man kicked mom in the stomach when she tried to keep him from taking Annie. I wanted to kill him!" his voice growled. Jarad was surprised by his fierceness. Cameron was quiet for a moment. "She lost the baby," he said softly. This news took a moment to register with Jarad and he was silent for a bit as he contemplated it.

"How is she doing? Where is she?" he asked, unsure if he was repeating himself. His head was slowly clearing and he was becoming increasingly aware. He paid careful attention to his son's words.

"She's in the other tent," he said again, pointing with his thumb over his shoulder. "She should be up and about later this morning. She's okay, just really sad about the baby. Really sad. Makes me hate that man."

Jarad reached for his son's hand and held it. He understood his feelings. The fact that the man was now dead did little to lessen the anger. He also hurt for his wife. For himself he did not feel a sense of personal loss so much as being confronted with a future that was not to be. When his wife told him months back that she was pregnant, he went instantly into father mode, thinking of how he was going to provide for this new child. But pregnancy is less tangible for men than it is for women. Women carry their babies, they feel their babies, and in a fashion they already know the child even before it is born. Not so for men. They do not really feel the full import of being a father until the squalling infant is put into their hands. That is when men bond with their child. But women bond much earlier. Jarad lost a potential child; Myla lost a child.

"Where's Peter?" he asked Cameron. "How is he?"

The question surprised Cameron for a moment and he was unsure how to respond. "I don't know," he said honestly. "Maybe he's in here somewhere." He stood to look at the rows of beds, most of which were empty. "I haven't seen him since last night, when he entered the ambulance with you."

The lights near him seemed to shift for a moment and a

shadow was cast upon his bed. A man in medical scrubs had approached. "Good morning, how are you feeling?" he asked. He was a tall thin fellow, young and sporting a military-style hair cut. He took Jarad's arm and examined the IV. He then scanned the IV bag and a small electronic monitoring device. "Everything looks good," he said.

"Good," Jarad said. "Say, can you help me to sit up?" The man smiled and began working levers underneath the bed. "This is not a fancy hospital model, that's for sure" he told Jarad. He had Jarad lean forward so he could adjust the bed into a more upward position.

"Perfect," Jarad responded. "Now, can you tell me where I am and what's wrong with me?" He smiled. "Honestly, I am not sure where I am, except that this is Alberta."

The man chuckled at Jarad's request. "I am not sure what your whole story is – I mean, I wasn't on shift last night, but according to the chart you have a mild case of plague."

"Mild!" Jarad exclaimed. "I'd hate to have a full-blown case."

"Oh, you would have pretty quickly. If you hadn't made it here when you did, you probably would've died from it in the next couple days. It's quite nasty and we've seen our share of it lately." He went on to say how the plague and a host of other "rare" diseases had been exploding in the regions south of Alberta. "That's why we've had to set up these camps, to keep people from flooding into the country. But the numbers are dropping. If this continues, we'll be done here in a couple months. There'll be few left to help."

"Are you my doctor," Jarad asked.

"No, I'm a medic…a nurse. I just try to keep patients alive until the doctors can kill 'em." He smiled. That was evidently a medic joke. "Are you two ready for some breakfast?"

The idea of food reminded Jarad how hungry he was and how much better he was feeling. But he was not sure how hungry he was, as if his body was still waking up. He was willing to try to eat so he gave the man a yes, and he immediately left to go fetch two trays of food. He returned about fifteen minutes later.

"I warn you about the food," he said, handing Jarad and Cameron each a tray. It was scrambled eggs, toast, and something that resembled hash browns. "Pretty typical refugee camp fare. It might not taste too good, but there's a lot of it. If you want seconds, just let me know."

Jarad extended his thanks, but then quickly asked about Peter before the medic disappeared. "There were three of us last night that needed medical attention. My wife is in another tent, my son tells me. But I don't know where our friend Peter is. Peter Rafferty…I'm not sure what is wrong with him, but …" he turned to Cameron to help him.

"He was shot in the shoulder. This one," Cameron said, tapping his own right shoulder with his fingers.

"I don't have any patients this morning with bullet wounds…at least not today," he said, thinking. "But I'll check the inpatient bed charts and see what I can find. Peter Rafferty, right?" Jarad nodded and the man walked off, moving to another patient a couple of empty beds away.

He wanted to stand up, but then he realized he had a catheter. He grunted in frustration. He would ask the medic to remove it on his return so he could use the restroom the usual way. And then he hoped to be able to walk around a bit.

Jarad asked Cameron what it looked like outside. He said it was kind of boring, not what he pictured Alberta to be. In fact, it was not any different from the Indian reservation they just came from. This caused Jarad to laugh, which disheartened his son. Jarad told him that Alberta was a big place and it had all sorts of different terrains, from the high plains to the Rocky Mountains. He told his son to not get discouraged. "You know what they say, don't judge a book by its cover." He laughed softly again. Cameron laughed with him.

The medic came by after a while and said that there was no record of a Peter Rafferty. There had been a gunshot wound treated late that night, but the man had left. He did not leave his name. "Maybe he was the secret agent type," the medic joked. Though Jarad chuckled at the man's joke, he wondered how close that was to the truth. Peter was an enigma. He wanted to talk to Peter about last night. Cameron told him that Peter was able to quickly kill the three men with only three shots. Jarad shuddered. That wisp of a man was more than met the eye. But it was strange that he did not leave his name. Or did he? Perhaps there was more to the story.

The medic removed Jarad's catheter and pointed to the restrooms. He called it the washroom. He asked Jarad if he needed any assistance to use the facilities. "I don't want you to fall down. It makes me look bad as a nurse and then I don't get dessert after dinner." Jarad laughed so hard at the joke that his side hurt.

"You keep that up and I'll fall for sure," he warned the nurse. Even Cameron laughed. Cameron thought that was the funniest thing he had ever heard.

"I'll be fine," he told the man. "My son here will be my sturdy shoulder to lean on." First Cameron helped his father put on a robe, though he could only drape it over one of his shoulders. He then walked with his father as they headed toward an exterior door. He wanted to be outside. Jarad pushed along the IV holder which was on a wheeled stand. He intentionally put some of his weight on his son, partly to let him know that he appreciated him being by his side and partly to simply touch him. He loved his boy.

The morning was windswept, but the sun was attempting to wrest the coolness away with its bright rays. The two of them found a sheltered spot on the lee side of the tent and allowed the sun to warm their faces. He wanted to go see his wife, but he was not exactly dressed for the occasion. But Jarad was very happy at that moment as he sat with his son. Not only was he alive, but he seemed to be feeling better by the minute. He did not know what medicine they were giving him, but as far as he was concerned it was a gift from God.

He agreed with his son that the surrounding landscape did little to inspire great thoughts in one's mind, but he reminded him that the tent did have electric lights. *That* was a good thing he told Cameron and one of the reasons why they made the trip that they did. And, best of all, they were in Alberta! He wanted to shout, but he decided not too because he was still very tired and his throat was still very sore. He carefully manipulated with his finger tips the swollen lymph nodes in his neck. They were tender. Oh, how he was glad that he was not still in the back of that car. He had never been sicker in all of his life.

He had to go to the bathroom and he reminded Cameron that this was their original mission when he got out of bed. Cameron helped him negotiate his way to the portable toilets and waited dutifully for his father outside the door. When they returned to Jarad's hospital bed his wife and daughter were waiting for him.

"What a sight for sore eyes," Myla told him as he shuffled up to his bed. They hugged tightly and kissed each other on the lips. There were tears in both of their eyes though neither of them overtly cried. Myla knew that Jarad was aware of the loss of the baby – she could tell in his look – so it was not mentioned. They would talk about it another time. Annie also gave him a hug. She was beaming and so happy to see her dad.

He sat in his bed, swinging his legs back up and covering himself with the thin blanket. Though he felt much improved over the previous night, he was still exhausted. As the medicines worked their wonders in his veins, he rested knowing that he was not only going to live, but his family was united and all were well – in spite of the circumstances.

"Peter's gone," he told his wife. She wrinkled up her face as she did when someone had told her a story and she did not believe them.

"What?" she asked. "Gone? Gone where? Where could he go," she laughed, doubtfully. He explained to her what the medic had told him.

"That man is mysterious, for sure," she said. "I like him – he's smart in a practical, experienced way. But he is not all that he appears, I think."

She also shared her recollections from the previous night. It startled her when the gun went off, but she admitted that she was so glad to see those men drop to the ground. She feared for her daughter's safety. She shuddered thinking about what could have happened.

"And where the hell did you get that gold?" she scolded her husband. "And putting those pieces in your boot and then having me dig them out. Ooh, gross!" She smiled and giggled lightly. She put her palms out, shaking her head at her husband in disbelief. "Are you keeping secrets from me, husband?" she challenged him, only partly in jest.

"Busted!" he told her. He explained how he had "inherited" the gold pieces and where he had hidden them.

"You mean there's more?" she asked again amazed. "Do you realize what a fortune that gold is? We could buy our old house in Purcell two times over. And to think those dead highwaymen got a pair of them." She signed in disgust, as only women could.

"No, they didn't," Cameron said laconically. He made a funny face and slowly pulled the two gold pieces out of his pocket and showed them to his mother. He smiled and wagged his tongue at her.

"You little…" she said in amazement. "You little sneak!" He laughed lustily. He was enjoying this.

"When did you do that?" Annie asked him. "I didn't see you."

"When the men were shot, they both just dropped the gold on the ground. It glowed. I just picked them up and put them into my pocket. As simple as that." He shrugged his shoulders. "I didn't mean to get the gold; it was just sitting on the ground."

"So what's next?" Myla asked. "Here we are in Alberta. This is the very place we wanted to be and by God's grace, here we are. Now what?" She looked at Jarad. His face expressed uncertainty.

"You know, I was so focused on getting here I didn't even think about what we'd do once we got here," he said. "I don't know, honey. Something will happen. But I'm sure that they won't let us spend the rest of our lives here in this field hospital."

"Well, I'm going to get a jump on things. Annie said that the Salvation Army is running the camp. I'll go talk to one of their officers. Maybe he or she can give us some direction. They're competent folks; they're very well organized." She looked over at her daughter. "Show me the way, babe," she said to her daughter. "You know the way to our tent."

She got up and gave her husband a kiss. Annie gave him a kiss, too. "Get some rest," Myla said. "I'll check things out and let you know what I find." She turned to her son. "You coming or staying?" she asked. He got up to join his mother.

"This place is boring," he said. "Maybe I can find something to do."

Myla laughed. "Sweetheart, we're in Alberta. That's enough," she said.

Jarad lay back on his bed, pulling the sheet and blanket up to his neck. His thoughts began to wander as he considered his wife's words. He languidly watched them pass down the little aisle between the beds, Myla in the middle and her arms around her kids, one on each side. But even before they had drifted from his sight his eyes had closed and he was fast asleep.

*

Jarad was antsy. The antibiotics he was taking intravenously were working their wonders on his body. He was recuperating quickly, which the doctor said was to be expected as the disease had only begun to get a hold of him – Jarad was lucky his case was not more severe. Nonetheless, he still had to spend at least one more night in the infirmary. He argued with the doctor that he felt he was fine, at least good enough to sleep with his family in their tent, but the doctor disagreed. "We need to watch you for another twenty-four hours." That was that, the man was an officer and he was used to being obeyed. Jarad muttered something under his breath, but fortunate for him the doctor was not listening.

He had slept for four straight hours and was now enjoying his lunch: a pathetic looking sandwich and something that the medic had identified as canned pears, though Jarad was not convinced. The best part was the chocolate pudding for dessert. "At least it smells like chocolate," he said, making a face at his wife.

Myla was giving Jarad an update on their domestic situation. "We got a nice little tent to ourselves. It has four cots and there are showers!" Myla explained to her husband.

"The tents have showers?" he asked.

"No, silly, they're not in the tents. They're in these special trailers. And…" she drew the word out for suspense, "there's unlimited hot water. How wonderful is that?"

"Great, except I would still have to dress in my flea-infested clothes. Might they have a means to wash clothes, too?" he asked.

"They do," she assured him. "And if you'd noticed, we've taken your clothes. The kids are washing them as I speak." Jarad could see that Myla was very happy.

"And…" she said again, in a way to suggest that she had additional special news, "Peter does not exist! The Salvation Army major said that she had not heard the name nor seen the face. Peter is not in any of the hospital tents and he's not in the refugee camp. He's disappeared."

"That is bizarre!" Jarad agreed. "I wonder where he is at. I mean, Cameron said that the man had a bullet wound in the shoulder. A person simply doesn't start hitchhiking down the highway with that kind of wound. Maybe he went nuts…"

"No, Peter would not go nuts…that man was in tune with reality," Myla countered. "No, something else is up and nobody's talking. So I guess we just get on with our lives and maybe someday we'll get a letter in our vidmail inbox. But I would like to thank him for saving our lives."

"Oh, dammit, that reminds me of something," Jarad said.

"We need to get our message out to Junction that we're okay. That we made it."

"I already talked to the Salvation Army major. She's checking with 'her people.' Evidently the Salvation Army runs a volunteer radio network with their church members – for emergencies and that sort of thing. We'll know soon enough," Myla assured him.

When he told Myla that the doctor was going to keep him for at least another day, she was not surprised. "I figured as much," Myla said, pulling out a computer tablet from a bag and handing it to her husband. "There's no internet access here – I'm told because of security issues, but maybe you can find something to read. I'll come back later." She walked away from his bed, but then stopped and turned around. "Oh, and by the way. We're all on antibiotics as a precaution. Thanks a lot." She smiled. He knew that she was delighted to be on a prescribed medicine, any medicine. It indicated civilization, not the Stone Age.

*

The next day finally came though the doctor did not arrive until well after breakfast. He gave Jarad a once over, asked a few routine questions and then signed him off on the computer tablet he was carrying, discharging Jarad from the facilities. He reminded Jarad to pick up his antibiotics at the dispensary. When he had finished he looked over at Myla and commented that he had seen her name come up.

"You're a nurse, right," he asked her. She nodded. "Too bad you weren't here two or three months ago. We could've really used you then. But things are staring to unwind now."

"So what's been going on?" she asked him. He stared at her, like someone who is surprised when a person does not know the obvious.

"Well, I guess you two have been out of circulation for awhile." He explained that after the Albertan government had secured their southern border and as the number of refugees declined, the government of Alberta was extending humanitarian aid services to outlying areas in Montana.

"That explains the helicopters," Jarad said. "We've been seeing them regularly flying in pairs. We were wondering where they'd been coming from and where'd they been going, but mostly what they've been doing. Makes sense, now."

The doctor indicated that he had to move on, but told Jarad that he would send the medic over to review his post-infirmary care. He shook both Jarad's and Myla's hands. And then he left.

It did not take Jarad long to get dressed. And the clean clothes Myla brought him felt glorious. He was clean, having taken a shower that morning, and now he had fresh clothes on and his health was rapidly on the mend. He was happy; happier than he had felt in years. He grabbed his wife's hand and headed for the dispensary. She knew the way.

Afterward Myla led him to their tent. It was vacant. The kids were visiting Champ who was still under quarantine. There really was not much else going on. The Salvation Army was operating programs for the children in the camps, plus their usual religious services on Sunday, but nothing right now. Besides, Champ appreciated the kids' company and hated being separated from them.

Jarad lay down on "his" cot, eating some pretzels out of bag. The kids had been allowed to take some supplies from their car, which was just in sight of the camp if a person looked in the right direction. The camp authorities were not concerned about rail traffic, but had nonetheless lifted the car off of the rails with a large wheeled forklift, setting it well out of the way of any possible train. Jarad did not care if he ever saw the car again. It had served its purpose. He was already looking toward the future.

"So, what's next?" he asked his wife this time, between bites of his snack.

"What, today?" she asked. "Oh, I don't know, maybe games with the kids. What did you have in mind?"

"No, not today, I mean with our lives. What's next? Where do we go from here? Do we leave the camp and get moved and resettled in some town or what? I've never been a refugee before. It is a new experience." He was being feisty, but was still serious. The future – both immediate and longer term – had been filling his thoughts.

"I don't know, honey," she said. She was reclining on her own cot, which was next to Jarad's. "I've been too busy with the here and now to spend much time thinking about the next day, let alone the next year. But, you're right; we can't live in this tent forever. We've been here all of two days and the kids are already bored."

"Who can blame them?" Jarad replied. "They've had a lot of…um, how do I say it… 'emotional' investment in coming to Alberta. I think that it's been sort of anti-climatic for them."

"Maybe," Myla agreed, "but they're fine. Jarad, I'm so happy being here! I regret losing the baby…" she paused and sighed, trying not to cry. She reached over to touch her husband, holding his hand. "But," she sniffed, "this is our future. I'm very glad to be here. You think the kids have invested emotionally in Alberta, look at me. I'm your poster child for emotional investment." She rolled her lips inward, her eyes showing thoughtful reflection.

The two of them continued holding their hands, both of them staring upward, each looking at nothing more than their own thoughts. Within moments, Jarad began snoring softly. He had barely made it "home" from the infirmary and he was already done for the day. Myla was glad, though. He needed his rest. She got up and went looking for the kids. They were right; there really was not a whole lot to do.

***

Chapter 15

Myla was directed by the Salvation Army staff to the office – a converted travel trailer – of a representative of the Albertan government. The lady who worked in the office was the government agent assigned to help refugees get out of the camp and resettled. She indicated to Myla that it was a formidable task.

"Where are we supposed to send people? Most are from Montana, but there are few opportunities for them back home to support themselves, so here they remain. Still, some get tired of camp life and return back across the border."

"What about allowing people to stay in Alberta? Alberta seems like a pretty nice place to be right now. I mean, you have a functioning economy, electricity, normal life. Is it possible for people to immigrate to Alberta?" Myla asked.

"Yes, of course it is," she responded. "But we prefer getting people back into their own homes and communities. That is one reason why the government had begun a series of humanitarian missions to the state of Montana: to alleviate the suffering, establish some order, and give people hope." The woman spoke like the bureaucrat that she was. She did not want to sound discouraging, but then she did not want refugees to get any ideas about staying in Alberta. She seemed to be saying that the nation of Alberta was glad to help, but eventually everybody needed to go home.

"What about immigrants with skills, like my husband and I? He is a police officer and I am a registered nurse. Surely we could find positions within the country and carry our own weight. I mean, these are both useful skills and we are both educated..." Myla realized she was beginning to sound desperate – the very image she did not want to convey to this woman. She sighed before continuing. "My point is that we bring skills that would be useful to Alberta. I mean, is there a demand for nurses?"

The lady smiled, but it was a "professional" smile, given by those who are paid to be caring and sympathetic, but are no longer able to conjure up either emotion. The realities of working with needy people, many of whom were generationally dysfunctional and purposely needy beyond measure, drove long-term caregivers to the inevitable courteous numbness. She had heard it all.

"My, those are indeed nice skills to have and you are both quite fortunate, but the reality is that Alberta is not hiring, so to speak. You must keep in mind that while it is true that we do have a functioning economy, it has fallen into a serious depression. Like most countries, Alberta does not function in a vacuum. It is important to carry on trade with other nations. Well, that has come to halt. We're just limping along. So until times get better, it would behoove you to make plans on returning to Montana.

"I'm from Idaho, but I get your message," Myla said, a bit gruffly. "In other words, we're out of luck."

She did not respond to Myla. She only smiled thinly.

Myla got up and shook the woman's hand and quickly left the office. She returned directly to her tent, intentionally not making eye contact with the few people she encountered. Reaching her tent, she secured the zipper flap before throwing herself on her cot and burying her face in the thin pillow. There she cried and cried and cried, her husband sleeping soundly and completely obliviously on the cot next to her.

*

"Mom...mom, you okay?" Annie was whispering, gently rocking her mother's shoulder. Myla was still prone on the bed and her face still concealed in the pillow, but her crying had ceased. Her emotions had swung from self-pity to a smoldering anger. Annie's touch had brought her out of her prayers – she had been arguing with God how her feelings were justified: what right did the Albertan government have in expecting her and her family to return to Idaho? To return to the Stone Age? Did they not recognize the risks that her family had taken in order to come here? Did that not validate their desire to live and work in Alberta? Did she not *earn* her right to be here? In her own mind she had. She rolled over and peered up at her daughter.

"You okay, mom?" Annie repeated. "What's wrong? Why've you been crying?"

"Don't worry, honey. I'm just more frustrated than anything. It just pisses me off that some woman, who doesn't even know me or us...or our situation... can with a wave of her hand boot us out of the country!" She began to rant.

Annie listened patiently. She did not really understand what her mother was talking about, except the part that they would have to leave. That upset her a little bit. Though she still missed Jimmy and would do almost anything to be back with him again, she did not want to make the return trip. It was too scary to consider.

Finally Myla began to wind down her oration. "I'm not a refugee, I'm a professional! They can't treat me like this! Who do they think they are?"

"You're an illegal alien," Jarad said softly, opening his eyes and propping himself up on his elbows. He looked around the tent, at Annie and then at his wife. "I don't remember getting a visa from the Albertan government giving us permission to be here," he said to her. He sat up and roughly scratched his scalp with his fingers and then yawned broadly. Myla was glaring at him. "Well, it's the truth," he said.

"Whose side are you on?" She yelled at him. Her rant took off again, now with a fresh wind. She mostly repeated what she had just said to Annie, assuming Jarad must not have heard her clearly. Jarad cut her off.

"Stop, Myla. Just stop," he said sharply, patting the air in front of him with outstretched palms. "Flip this around. Put yourself in their shoes. How far are we into Alberta? Huh? Two-hundred yards. Two-hundred stinking yards! That's it! And we are boxed in by a high fence topped with razor wire and patrolled by armed troops. We are intruders, Myla. They did not ask us to be here. And they surely did not have to welcome us into this camp, let alone give us the medical care that they did. And feed us…"

"And give us showers," Annie added.

"Yes and showers," he said, nodding at his daughter, "and clean clothes if we want them, and three meals a day. I don't know what more you want them to do for us, honey. Give us jobs? Find us a house? I think that they've done quite a bit already."

Myla got so frustrated that she broke into tears again and sat on her cot, holding her hands to her face. Jarad knelt down by her and wrapped his arms around her. Annie stood to her side and caressed her on her back. Both tried making soothing sounds to calm her down.

"This isn't the way it was supposed to work out!" she said between sniffs. "This isn't the way it is supposed to be. We're supposed to be happy here…we're supposed…to live better lives here." She felt that she had approached a very important milestone in her life; that what happened next to them would be the defining moment of the rest of their lives.

Jarad did not respond to her. He knew that she understood the situation they were in. And he recognized that her rant was more about vocalizing her discouragement than a denial of the reality of their circumstances. He could do nothing more to help than hold her, so he did.

Finally Myla collected herself and glanced around the tent. She had finished venting, as she called it, and was ready to deal with the conditions as they existed. "Come on," she said to both of them, "let's go for a walk."

Jarad took her hand as they strolled down the gravel lane that separated the tents. Most were now unoccupied and they had no immediate neighbors. They headed past a row of plastic latrines and toward an open expanse that provided the best view of the terrain beyond the fence. Their viewpoint offered an uninspiring view of flat dry land, treeless and barren to the horizon, and with little sign of life save for a few veins of green grass in the rugged, brown-hewn earth. They knew it was farming country, but it hardly appeared to be worth the effort. Jarad wondered aloud what kind of pioneer would have chosen to settle in this area.

"Maybe they were like us, Jarad," Myla said flatly. "Maybe they had run out of options. You can only go so far before you gotta stop. You gotta stop sometime…" She stared at the clouds, which provided the only relief from the dreary landscape. The clouds were beautiful. "I suppose this land has its attractions, but from this vista it's hard to see 'em."

Cameron showed up. He was panting and he hung his tongue out for emphasis. "I've been looking for you guys," he said. "The Salvation Army lady told me to tell you that they are going to radio out our message, starting tonight. She told me that you'd want to know that. Whew," he wheezed. He looked out across the fence in the same direction as his parents. "What're you guys looking at," he asked. "There's nothing out there…"

Jarad laughed. "Yup, we just found that out. Didn't we honey?"

Myla did not respond, only giving her husband's hand a squeeze. Emotionally she was against the wall – or the fence in this case. Suddenly she laughed at her own joke, which released a lot of tension. "Oh, Jarad," she said, taking in a deep breath of fresh air, "it is what it is, isn't it?"

She took her husband's hand and led her family to the recreation tent, or rec tent as it was called. She wanted to play a family game and the kids had told her that there was a collection of games for people to play. Most of the tables were empty, so they chose a smaller one that would just fit their family and Myla asked Annie to find a game to play. She returned with a puzzle. "A thousand pieces! I love puzzles," she said excitedly. She dumped it out on the table and everyone began flipping the pieces over so that they were all color-side up and then they set to work reassembling the image that matched the one on the box.

It was fun! The kids were able to share their feelings and their parents listened. Soon jokes were being made and everyone's spirits rose. Myla was trying to simply enjoy the moment and not worry about the future, not even the next day. But her revelry was broken by the appearance of a tall man in uniform, directly approaching their table. He stood before them and all faces turned toward his direction. He wore the uniform of an Albertan Army officer.

"Hello," he said kindly. "Sorry to interrupt your game, but I'm looking for Jarad and Myla Traverson. Am I in the right place?"

Jarad glanced at Myla before addressing the man. He nodded that they were the people he was looking for. He offered his hand to Jarad. "My name is Captain Weiss. You were referred to me by an acquaintance of yours, Peter Rafferty."

The mention of Peter's name quickly roused both Myla's and Jarad's curiosity. Jarad stood and took the man's hand and then introduced his wife and children. The military man shook hands all around.

"Could I take you away for a few minutes?" he asked. "It looks like you're having fun, but I shouldn't take too much of your time. Some place a bit more private, perhaps?"

Jarad mentioned their tent and apologized to the kids. They were having fun and said that they would be just fine. The three adults headed for the exit.

"Peter Rafferty, huh?" Jarad said. "We've been very curious as to what happened to our friend. He sort of disappeared!"

The Army captain nodded. "Yes, I can understand the mystery. He is a very interesting fellow. I'll tell you more once we get to your billet."

When they entered the tent, Jarad offered the man one of the kids' cots to sit on. Jarad and Myla moved their cots to bring them closer to the man so that the three of them could converse comfortably.

"So how did you come to know Peter," Myla asked.

The man smiled. "When Mr. Rafferty arrived at the camp, he sent word to the camp commander and he was promptly brought to our attention. Mr. Rafferty is a person of record with the Albertan government." He noticed Jarad and Myla wince when they heard this. "In a positive way," the captain affirmed. He smiled again. "Peter is a great guy! So don't worry, I'm not here to question you folks about gun-running or something!"

Jarad and Myla relaxed and although they were full of questions they allowed the man to speak. "Actually, I'm here to recruit you, Jarad – if I can use your first name – for a job." This caused Myla's eyebrows to rise. She looked at her husband, who returned her glance.

"Wow, a job!" he said amused. "I'm ready for a paycheck."

The captain looked around the tent. "Yah, I understand." The three of them laughed. "But let me share some background information first. I am sure that you'll find it interesting."

He explained how the United States had imploded and reconfigured itself along sectional lines. "I suppose you know this, right?" he asked. Myla and Jarad shared what details they knew, but they were obviously unaware of recent developments.

"Well, let me see..." he said, thinking about where to start. "Idaho and Montana as territories are of interest to the Albertan government. As you could imagine, border security is of utmost importance to any nation, including Alberta. The current unrest in the regions around us has been of great concern to our government."

"So what does that have to do with Idaho and Montana," Jarad asked.

The man paused; he was searching for words. He did not want to accidentally disclose more information that he was allowed. He brought his hand up and touched his chin contemplatively. "The respective governments of these two states have solicited the assistance of the Republic of Alberta. That is where you come in. We would like you to help us in our first mission to Idaho. We have already committed ourselves to an extensive outreach in Montana. We are now in the preliminary stages of expanding that to Idaho. But let me fill in the blanks."

He explained that there had been rapid political developments in the past few months, even weeks. Utah had formed the Beehive Republic, "or something like that," the captain said. "Maybe it is the Republic of Utah." He was unsure. Oregon, Washington, and British Columbia were negotiating to form Cascadia. "BC is a bit out of sorts and there is a high level of social unrest there. So much so, that we've had to close our own border with them." British Columbia's ongoing battle with drug cartels had added to their problems, especially now that Canada had ruled to devolve the province from the union. "They're on their own, that's why they are hustling to form a political union with Washington and Oregon," he explained.

"As you might know," he continued, "Canada has taken physical control of many of the former northeastern states. This was partly to combat social unrest there, which threatened to spill over their own border and to keep undesirable elements from forming a government, or worse. In other words, they did not want a hostile, or for that matter illegal, government to fill that vacuum."

It was making sense to Jarad. "I think I know where you are heading: Alberta fears that a drug cartel or warlord will gain control of some portion of Idaho or Montana and create a lot of grief for Alberta. Sort of what happened down in Mexico and Guatemala?"

"Exactly what has happened in both of those countries," he said. "We don't want to see a repeat on our borders, where some criminal boss creates a safe-haven for organized crime. Neither do the governments of Idaho and Montana. But neither of them have the resources to secure their own territories. I mean, look at the decades-long battles Mexico has fought with the cartels. We don't want that around here."

"So, these missions then," Myla interjected, "aren't simply

humanitarian – they're something more, I assume."

He nodded at her and smiled. "You see it. We not only need to help with the humanitarian relief of these two former American states, but their security as well. And this is a joint concern of both the Albertan government and the two American states, I mean former American states."

"And you want me to help in this, correct? What can I offer?" Jarad asked.

"You know Purcell. You know that area. And you have a background in law enforcement. Purcell has been identified by the Albertan government as the site for our first humanitarian mission in that territory. We would like for you to help us in that effort," he explained. "Mr. Rafferty has convinced us that you are a perfect fit for our work there."

"Forgive me if this is a stupid question, but why doesn't Alberta incorporate Montana and Idaho, or whomever, into their electricity grid?" Myla asked. "I mean, the grid is a big patchwork of smaller grids, right? And when it is up and running, everyone is taking or adding power as they do, why can't Alberta do the same? If the power is restored, this would mean a lot less social unrest."

He nodded at her. He understood where her argument was going. But she did not have all the facts. "Yes, we have electricity," he said, "and, yes, Alberta is connected in a fashion to the energy grid that spans the entire continent. But it's not as simple as it might appear to move electricity about." He grabbed his left index finger with his other hand as he began to enumerate the reasons. "First off, we don't control the switches that regulate the flow of electricity – we only control our own. We can't move power over a network that does not want to receive it. Second, how do we gain access to control over these switches? And remember, it isn't a "switch" like a light switch; it is a bit more complicated than that. Third, we have a limited power generating capacity. We would be over doubling the size of our own national grid. We would have to buy it from Canada or Quebec. Finally, the integrity of the system is not assured. No one in these two states has been maintaining the grid, especially at the local level, from normal wear and tear. We'd have to also go in and repair every line knocked down by a tree branch from this winter, and so on. I mean, how many times during the year did your house suffer a power loss?"

"Sounds pretty formidable," Jarad murmured. "But, assuming that the government of Alberta was able to bring power to Montana and Idaho, how long would this take?"

The Army officer paused again, pursing his lips as he gave Jarad's question some thought. "I can't imagine any sooner than six months, probably more," he said with confidence. "Maybe up to a year and a half, if we're talking about restoring power to every little community and neighborhood."

Neither Jarad nor Myla realized that the solution to this problem was so complex. Over a year, Myla thought to herself. She did not want to live in a place where power might still be even six months away. No thank you, she mused silently. No thank you at all!

"Do you need nurses? After all, I am sure you'll be setting up refugee camps and field hospitals like this one. I could help with that," Myla offered.

"Um, yes and no," the captain equivocated. "We have a different proposal for you." He elaborated on the fact that they had plenty of medical personal, all of whom had gained tremendous experience while serving in Montana. And now, they were now preparing to move those resources, as he called them, to Idaho.

What they did need were nurses to fill in the holes left in the civilian medical system by those who had been recruited out by the Albertan government. "We can offer you a few choices. We have a handful of rural hospitals distributed across the country that are begging for nurses. We'd offer you your pick. And any selection you make will come with a place to stay, probably an apartment, but one big enough for you and your family. As you can see this would entail a temporary separation of you and your husband." He looked at them, testing their reaction.

Myla did not flinch. "I'm game if my husband is," she said eying him. "It looks like a perfect opportunity for both of us. What do you think, Jarad?"

"I'm interested," he said matter-of-fact. "Most of all, I think that this is best for the kids. I mean, they can get back into school and be around people their own age. They might even get back their childhood." He smiled at his wife. "Hells fire, it might be nice getting away from this woman for a few months – years even!"

Myla smiled meanly and hit him on the shoulder. "Hah! The truth comes out," she kidded him. Peace descended over her person. She could not have written the script any better. Thank you Lord, she prayed quietly to herself.

"When do we start?" she asked.

He was startled by the question, but smiled. "Tomorrow," he said.

***

Chapter 16

"Kids, we're moving!" Myla shouted from across the rec tent. The kids looked up from their puzzle.

"Moving?" Cameron asked. "Where?"

"Grand Cache," Myla said. "It is in Alberta." She was smiling so hard her face hurt. She could not remember the last time she was so excited. She felt like a little girl again, as when her parents had just told her that she was going to be spending a week with grandma and grandpa – the best times of her life. She could not leave quick enough.

"Grand Cache?" Annie said, perplexed. "That's a town?"

"Yup, and it's beautiful!" Myla said, jubilantly.

"When do we move?" Annie asked, now animated. Her mother's enthusiasm was contagious.

"Tomorrow! Well, probably tomorrow. Your father leaves tomorrow, anyhow."

"Dad's going first?" Cameron asked. "Can I go with him?"

Oops, Myla thought to herself. She was moving too quickly. She needed to set out the facts with her kids. She sat with them and then began to whisper quietly to them from across the table. She did not want to deal with eavesdroppers and she did not want to broadcast her news. There were many others in this little tent city who were hoping against hope for similar news. She prefaced her news with the fact that it was a secret. She knew that her kids would not say a word to anyone.

"Your dad is not going to Grand Cache at first. He is

returning to Idaho, to Purcell! It's a special mission with the Alberta Army."

The kids looked at each other, excitement and wonder in their eyes.

"And us?" Annie asked. "What about us?"

"We're moving to Grand Cache, which is in the mountains, kind of like Purcell. I am getting a job there as a nurse. Dad will join us later."

"How much later," Annie asked. She did not like the idea of the family being separated. "And why can't we go to Purcell."

Myla explained as much as she felt safe. The kids understood the gist of it. They both agreed that they would rather live in an Albertan town with power than in Purcell without it. Predictably, the crazy lives that they had lived in the past six months had changed their view of life. Though Purcell was "home," thoughts of it did not evoke feelings of homesickness. It was dark and scary and dangerous. At least, those were their last memories of the community. They did not want to relive those times. To encourage them, she told them all about the new town that they were moving to, as much as she had learned herself.

"Will dad be safe?" Cameron asked. He was seeing past her ruse to distract him and kept thinking about his father returning to the very place they had to escape from.

"Perfectly safe," Myla assured him. "He'll be surrounded by the Albertan Army!" The boy nodded. That was good, he thought.

"When can we leave?" Annie asked. She was ready for change. There were few other kids in the camp, and none near her age. She and Cameron had quickly gotten bored with the whole refugee experience. They were ready to move on. Tomorrow was fine, today would have been better!

They wanted to go see their dad, but Myla told them to wait. Their father was still visiting with that army officer. He would meet them here in the rec tent when he was finished. So, the three of them returned to the puzzle, the table buzzing with excited voices.

It was more than an hour before Jarad joined them at the table. They were so intent on their work that they did not hear him approach. He looked down at the half-completed puzzle. "I see you didn't wait for me," he said, pretending to be miffed. He was greeted with three happy, smiling faces.

"Dad, you're going to Purcell?" Annie asked excitedly. Jarad brought a finger to his lips, signaling her to be quiet, looking at the other tables. He winked at her.

"Yes," he whispered. "But only for a little while. Then I'll join you guys in Grand Cache, wherever the heck that is."

"It's in Alberta, dad, in the mountains," Annie said knowingly. "It's beautiful, too."

"That's what I hear," her father said, joining them at the table. "Lucky ducks!"

Myla gave him that look. She wanted to know what more he had learned after she left the meeting. He spoke before she could ask. "I leave as soon as I can, meaning sooner than later. He'd have me leave right now, if I would."

She continued to talk to him with her eyes. "But I'm not willing," he assured her. "Since you three leave the next day or two, I figured that I would leave tomorrow. That would give us time to visit tonight."

She smiled at him, though the look in her eyes said something different. Already he knew that she was beginning to miss him. He understood that. She was beginning a new adventure for both of them, all of them, with her move to Grand Cache. He was going to leave and then return to *them*. She was doing the pioneering work for the family, not him. And she was going to have to do this alone. But he also knew she was excited and he shared that excitement. He smiled back at her.

And so they played. They finished the puzzle and then a second one, followed by a couple board games and countless rounds of pinochle. They played games as if they might never play them again and they wanted to get their fill. But they laughed and laughed and had the best time together as a family that any of them could remember. For the first time in a long time they were making memories that were not centered on deprivation, fear for their lives, or worries about the future. They not only had hope, they were taking the first tentative steps toward acting on it.

Still, they could not control time and late in the evening the only thing each wanted was sleep. So they returned to their tent and got themselves ready for bed.

"Come on, Jarad," Myla coaxed him. "Let's just you and me go for a walk around the camp." He agreed and the two of them left the tent and wandered about with no particular direction, arms around each other and Myla's head upon his shoulder. And they talked. They talked about where they had come, but mostly about where they were going. She expressed fear for his safety, but he countered with his own assurances. He would be fine.

"But you know," he continued, "life is strange. I've always thought that I was the one in the driver's seat. And maybe I am, but I discovered these past few months that being in control of your life doesn't really mean you have ultimate control. I mean, control is often nothing more than making decisions with the choices you're given. Maybe life is simply a series of crossroads, one after another, and our choices are limited to left and right; we go left or we go right. Simple as that."

"I agree," Myla said. "I was thinking similar thoughts. Do I really have a choice about Grand Cache? I mean, what else do I do? Return to Junction? Not on your life! Stay in the camp? Well, no…I already know I can't do that and I most definitely don't want to. Yup, you take what you're given. Those crossroads are always covered in shadows. We can never know where they lead."

Jarad squeezed his wife, drawing her even closer to himself. "I guess that's why we need faith. The good Lord knows we've been relying on him."

Myla looked up at her husband and planted a soft kiss on his cheek. "And I know that he'll bring you back to me…to us," she said softly. They embraced again and then turned arm and arm to watch the dark nothingness through the fence.

*

Jarad was up early that next morning. Indeed, he was out the door before anyone else was awake. He planted kisses on his wife and children, though only Myla woke up long enough to give him one final hug. He grabbed his single bag and hustled out the door, his wife watching him silently in the darkness.

The next three days were a whirlwind. He rode for three hours in the front seat of a nondescript military sedan through the farmlands of southeast Alberta before arriving at a surprisingly large airbase out in the proverbial "nowhere." There he met the leaders of the team he was going to be working with and was orientated into some of the standard practices of the Albertan Armed Forces. He was issued a few sets of uniforms, each with an Albertan flag on one sleeve but without symbols of rank or affiliation, except for a patch on each sleeve and above the right breast pocket which read CA. "What does this mean?" he asked one of the officers he had made friends with.

"CA stands for 'civilian adviser'," he explained. "The uniform means that you are one of us, the CA means that you are not. Does that make sense?"

"Perfectly," Jarad agreed. Both men laughed.

The officer leading the expedition to Purcell, Major Thom Custer, also outlined for Jarad his role in the operation. He was to advise Custer on the people and the situation in the community, which the military had chosen for its first incursion into Idaho.

"If I can ask," Jarad said, "why Purcell? Why not points further south that are a bit more populated and urban? Purcell is a little off the beaten path."

"Many reasons," the officer replied. "First, it is eminently defensible. There are transit choke points that are easy to control with a small force. Second, there is a larger population of refugees than you realize. Washington has not only closed it borders, it is actively pushing out refugees. The situation is deteriorating quickly. Lastly, we got you. Your knowledge of the area and the people will help us immensely. It will save lives. But we'll be moving south as quickly as we can. In fact, we've already sent an advance team to Boise to talk with the authorities there."

Jarad raised his eyebrows in surprise. Things were going quickly in many dimensions. He wished that he was privy to more information, but he knew that he would have to wait until events unfolded. Though he was wearing an Albertan military uniform, he was neither Albertan nor in the military – at least not yet.

The three-hour flight down to Idaho was exhilarating. Jarad had never flown in a helicopter, let alone one so huge. The big Sikorsky was also very noisy, even inside its cabin. He was glad for the ear protection. He watched as the soldiers manning the machine guns on each side of the craft scanned the terrain below. For the moment they were at ease as they were too high for hostiles to harm them. Jarad had learned that the helicopters flew higher than normal as a precaution against gun fire; people on the ground below sometimes took pot shots at the huge whirly birds as they flew overhead.

Word went out that they were approaching their landing zone. The day before Jarad had helped the officers planning the mission to find the best down point for their initial arrival. Jarad looked out the window as the helicopter circled over his old hometown. The burned-out sections were proof of the ill effects of the past seven months. He saw people; tiny little movements on the narrow streets stop and stare up at the noisy machines coming to their town. They reminded Jarad of pictures he had seen of pre-contact Amazon Indians looking up at their first airplanes, fear and wonder on their faces. Suddenly, he felt their angst and tears welled up in his eyes. The sight of his hometown and the devastation it had suffered generated both regret and anger in his heart. He knew their suffering intimately and he was hopeful that he might somehow help them, to somehow mitigate their suffering. His heartbeat began to race and he felt butterflies form in his stomach as he took his position by the flight officer. They were about to land and Jarad fought back the rising anxiety he felt in his chest.

As the big craft settled itself on the ground, soldiers armed with assault rifles jumped out to secure the landing zone. Others followed when given the clear signal. Jarad was the last to leave. For him, this was the strangest homecoming he would have ever imagined. He said a quick prayer and took a deep breath before pulling his goggles down over his eyes and stepping out of the Sikorsky. A deep single step placed him with a jolt onto the hard land. His mind spun as he tried to take in the scene around him, a growing sense of detachment assuming command of his mind. He paused and took a brief look behind himself and back into the belly of the aircraft. He then turned toward the front, his eyes straining to make solid the blurred images cast in swirling dust before him. He knew he was finally back in Purcell, but he wondered where he really was after all.

The End

Made in the USA
Lexington, KY
02 April 2013